FROG IN A WELL

FROG IN A WELL

THE CHRONICLES OF THE PROVERBS
BOOK ONE

INDIA MILLAR

ALSO BY INDIA MILLAR

THE CHRONICLES OF THE PROVERBS

Frog in a Well

Climbing the Dragon Gate

The Tree of Perseverance

SECRETS FROM THE HIDDEN HOUSE

The Geisha with the Green Eyes

The Geisha Who Could Feel No Pain

The Dragon Geisha

THE GEISHA WHO RAN AWAY

The Song of the Wild Geese

The Red Thread of Fate

This World is Ours

WARRIOR WOMAN OF THE SAMURAI

Firefly

Mantis

Chameleon

Spider

Dragonfly

Scorpion

Cricket

Moth

HAIKU COLLECTIONS

Dreams from the Hidden House

Song of the Samurai

PROLOGUE

A few days before my sixteenth birthday, I stole two silver coins from my father's cash box.

If I had asked him for the money, he would have told me to take as much as I wanted without so much as asking why I needed it.

That was why I didn't ask him.

Do not mourn the end
Of summer. Autumn is the
Earth longing for sleep

You may consider me foolish when I say that ever since I can remember, I have dreaded each of my birthdays. It is likely that you will dismiss my apprehension as no more than the sort of silliness that young girls assume to attract attention. But I promise you, this is not so.

My father was a remote, serious man who left for work early and returned late. He never bothered with such trivia as family birthdays, except, I supposed, for Mother's birthday; she would surely remind him about it. It might, I imagined, be expected that in her turn Mother would indulge her only daughter on her birthday, but she was never exactly given to sentiment and often forgot about it entirely—as she did for most things that did not disturb her. She would have been astonished if anybody had questioned her attitude。 She had given Father two fine, strong boy children and only one daughter who would need a dowry in due course. What more could be expected of her?

But I digress. On good years, nothing at all happened on my birthday and the day passed like any other. But on bad birthdays, it seemed to my childish mind that the whole year's accumulation of ill-fortune descended on me on that particular day. On my fifth birthday, my beloved pet cat died for no reason that anybody could see. I knew what had happened. I had cursed it with my bad luck. Another year, my brothers played a dreadful trick on me—they set fire to an outbuilding and told Father that I had done it. They had seen me, they said, take a burning brand from the kitchen and toss it into the wooden hut. When Father asked me—quite gently—why I had done such a thing, I could only hang my head and stay silent. I feared my brothers' retribution far more than Father's punishment. As it was, I was confined to my bedroom for a week and given nothing to eat and drink but plain rice and water.

For some reason, on my fourteenth birthday, I awoke convinced that the day would be different. The sun was bright, the air sweet. My brothers had gone into town to business with Father. Mother was in her apartment; I knew she would not venture out until Father returned for the evening meal, if then.

I wandered around the house and then ventured out into the garden. My brothers must have been training in the dojo; I found one of their wooden practice swords cast aside. Delighted, I picked it up and began to dance on the beaten earth with it in my hand, poking at imaginary enemies and waving it wildly in front of me. Alas, I did not notice the shallow hole in the dojo. I caught my toe in it and landed badly, with the wooden sword beneath me.

When I tried to stand up, I almost fainted with the wall of pain that tore through my shoulder.

I struggled to my feet, using the sword as a makeshift crutch, and ran into the house. I had only one thought in my mind: if I could get to Mother, surely she would take the terrible pain away and make me better. I staggered to her apartment and thrust the shoji open without even calling to announce myself, so great was my agony.

"Mother! I have fallen and hurt myself. My shoulder is… is wrong." I broke off, gasping with pain, my mouth opening and closing like a koi carp anticipating food.

Mother was reclining on a heap of cushions on what she proudly called a "sofa." Father did much business with the gaijin. Even though he laughed at them in private, calling them naïve fools who had no idea how to haggle, he was glad enough to take their money from them. Father had bought the sofa from one such gaijin customer who was returning to his own land and wished to sell his furniture for whatever he could. Very little, if I knew Father.

Mother had fallen in love with the sofa at first sight and had insisted that it be placed in her apartment. I thought Father must have been joking when I overheard him telling one of my brothers that the only time she moved from it was to go to her futon. Even through my pain, I saw that she appeared to be almost submerged in the cushions stacked behind her and in a flash of intuition, I knew exactly what Father meant.

"Mi? Why didn't you call out before you entered, you naughty girl." Mother balanced the namagashi sweetmeat that she had been about to bite into on a cushion and put her hand delicately to her head. "And please do not shout so. I have a dreadful headache and you're making it worse. What is wrong with your shoulder?"

"I don't know." I tried to speak quietly, but my agony was so great the words came out in almost a scream. Mother winced and closed her eyes. "It's my shoulder. It hurts. A lot."

Mother was an ample woman. Not tall, but plump. Her breasts were as full as a puffed-out pigeon's chest, and at that moment I would have given anything to be allowed to throw myself on them. For her to wrap her arms around me and comfort me, no matter how much it increased the pain in my poor shoulder.

"What have you done with it? I suppose you've been doing something silly. Well, what do you expect me to do about it? What do you think your father pays an amah for? Go and find her. She'll know what to do. Oh, my poor head!"

And that was it. Mother sank back into her cushions without dislodging the namagashi and I tracked my amah, Anzu, down in the kitchen, where she was enjoying a cup of matcha tea. She took one look at my crooked shoulder and screamed out loud.

The physician she summoned—I knew it must be serious when she didn't even wait for Father to return home to ask his permission—said I had popped the shoulder clear out of the joint. He popped it back in again and told me I was a brave girl when I didn't make a sound. I couldn't—the pain was so great it was as much as I could do to breathe. He bandaged it firmly into place as well, and when Father saw it, he noticed and asked me what I had done to my shoulder. It was almost worth the pain when he, too, said I had been a brave girl.

From somewhere, I found the courage to mumble that it was my birthday. Father looked surprised and then nodded.

"Of course. Your birthday is exactly a month before Ichiro's." Ichiro was my eldest brother. His name meant, of course, "First Son." Father was not the most imaginative of men when it came to naming his children—I had been called Mi, which means "Beautiful." No doubt a triumph of hope over reality.

"It is, Father," I murmured.

"So, not the best of birthdays for you. Perhaps I can make it up to you with a little treat. I don't think you have ever been to Edo." I shook my head, too excited at the promise in his words to speak. "I thought not. So, would you like to come to my office with me tomorrow? The morning will no doubt be a little boring for you, but the journey will be interesting and I think I will be free around mid-day. Then we could go to a nice teahouse, and you can eat as many sweetmeats as you want."

My happiness was only slightly dimmed by the fact that Father didn't know that I didn't really care for sweet things. I didn't care. If it gave him pleasure, I would eat a whole plateful of sweetmeats to thank him for his consideration.

But mochi, not namagashi.

TWO

The hare trembles in
The grass as he watches dogs
Pass him unnoticed

My brothers—who were both older than I was—spent much of their time with Father at his business premises.

I envied them that they should venture into the world so freely, and I could not understand why—whenever I thought they were in a good mood and dared to ask what they did in Father's office—they seemed deeply bored and shrugged off my questions.

"We do whatever Father tells us to do. What else?" Satoru, my younger brother, replied between sips of tea. I waited hopefully for more, and when nothing came, I turned my inquiring gaze on Ichiro.

"She doesn't understand." Ichiro sounded amused. "Why do you want to know, little sister? If Father's business is boring for us, why would you find it interesting?"

I wet my lips with the tip of my tongue. Whatever they

did, it had to be more interesting than my life, which was the same every day. Nobody took any interest in me, so I could do as I liked. But what was there to like? I had my biwa, which I had taught myself to play, but I had no idea if the music I made was good or—more likely—very bad, indeed.

I had found the lovely, tear-drop-shaped instrument discarded in a storage chest. It seemed to be as sad and unwanted as I was and claimed it for my own at once. After days of polishing with a piece of soft leather, the wooden body had begun to glow and I had dared to pluck the strings, wincing as a sound like a cat in pain emerged. I fiddled with the strings, tightening them one by one, and tried again. And again. Eventually, I found the noises I was making pleasurable and dared to ask my amah if I could play for her.

"Mi-san!" She sounded genuinely astonished and my hopes rose. "Who taught you to play like that? When I was a small girl and lived with my parents in our tiny village, every now and then a storyteller passed through and he would play the biwa at the same time as he told his tales. You are just as good as he was."

I was very pleased.

"I found the biwa in a chest. I taught myself to play it," I said proudly. Anzu gawped at me.

"Will you play some more, Mi-san?" she asked humbly. "It reminds me of my village and family."

I did as she asked, and when I came to a halt—in spite of my brave words, I had little idea of the music that my biwa could make, so it did not take long—I was astounded to see that she was blinking back tears.

I put the knowledge that music—even played by such clumsy hands as mine—could summon deep emotions and thought about it carefully only when my amah went about her duties and I was alone.

Music, I decided, must be a good thing. And surely, one who could make music must have an advantage over those who could not. From that day onward, I practiced every day until I was reasonably satisfied with my performance. Yet, I took no pride in my ability. I had found it quite easy to learn to play the biwa—where was the challenge in something learned with so little effort? And I had only my amah's word for it that my music was pleasing. Increasingly, I longed to hear somebody else play so I could compare myself to them.

It never happened. Mother did not care for music of any sort. She said it put her nerves on edge. Father entertained clients and fellow businessmen at home very often, and their entertainment was provided by geisha, lovely, elegant women who arrived in a whisper of silk kimono, their gaze fixed to their feet until they were spoken to, when they dared to raise an adoring glance at the man they were flattering.

I loved to see these women from the great outside world arriving. I kneeled as silently as I could and pressed my face to the silken shoji of the reception room, hoping that I would not be noticed. I never was, but I was so afraid of being discovered that I dared not linger for more than a moment.

In any event, none of the geisha ever played the biwa. Some of them danced and sang, but the accompaniment was always a samisen. I liked samisen music well enough, but to me it was not nearly as fine as the music my biwa called forth.

Other than my playing on my biwa, I spent my days as free as any wild thing. I had my pony. I only had to ask and a groom would saddle her for me and bring her to the house, and then I could ride for as long as I liked. Our estate was very large—although, as I had nothing to compare it with, this never seemed a privilege to me—and no matter how far I rode, I never came to the end of it. When I was hungry, I turned and went home. There were always good things to eat in the kitchen any time of day.

If the weather was pleasant, I liked to sit on a bench in the garden, simply listening to the birds sing around me.

Other than that? There was nothing. I was a girl, so there was no point in employing a tutor to teach me to read or write. Father's apartment contained many books, and I loved to take them down and look at them, even though the kanji meant nothing to me. I thought their shapes beautiful and I just imagined what they said.

Even though I knew that Father would have no time for such fanciful things, I used to weave tales to myself about what the books actually contained so that the dreariest of accounting ledgers became things of great splendor and joy to my innocent mind.

Although I could not put it into words at the time, I was hungry. I was an empty vessel, waiting to be filled by knowledge. I had everything that money could provide. Yet, at the same time, I felt I had nothing. I longed for something to come into my life without knowing what that something might be. I was truly the proverbial frog in the well, someone who knows nothing of the sea and thinks his own confined space is the whole world.

Until the day Father took me to his place of business— and the real world opened for me.

Listen! Always the
Very first to call, the black
Bird sings from sheer joy

I was so excited, I said not a word on the journey into Edo, to Father's place of business.

I had expected to ride my own pony, but no. Father mounted me on his saddle in front of him. He told me not to be afraid of the horse and instructed me gravely to hang on tightly to the pommel and to tell him if I was afraid I was going to fall off. I was hurt. Not by his concern, which pleased me greatly, but because he did not know that I was an excellent horsewoman and had no fear at all of horses, no matter how big they were.

I held my tongue, of course. I would never have dared contradict Father, but apart from that, I was determined that nothing was going to spoil this day for me.

Father took a road that was familiar to him, but that I had never traveled. I had never dreamed of venturing beyond the great gates of our house. I was used to riding on dusty, rutted tracks. This road was cobbled, and I pulled my head down to my shoulders in shame as I found myself grabbing for the pommel when our mount stumbled and slipped on the paving. Still, I must have acquitted myself reasonably well as Father seemed content.

"I will finish my business this morning as quickly as I can," he said cheerfully, "and then we will go to the teahouse I spoke of. It will be pleasant for me to eat in the company of a lovely girl rather than dry old men."

He laughed, and I thought with great excitement that he meant we would be accompanied by geisha. It was only when he pinched my cheek and smiled at me that I realized he was talking about me.

My breath caught in my throat and instantly I began to worry. What would I talk to him about? I could not remember an occasion when I had been alone with Father, except when I was being chastised for some wrong, and then I never had the courage to speak. And I had no idea how to conduct myself in a teahouse. What if I disgraced myself in some way? And I was to spend the whole day in his place of business—would I get in the way? Worse still, make a fool of myself? All my pleasure vanished as misery smothered my anticipation in a grey cloud.

Fortunately, Father seemed not to notice my discomfort. He was silent himself for some time, and then began to speak quietly. I was alert immediately, concentrating on making the correct response. After a while, I relaxed as I understood he was talking to himself as a way of ordering his thoughts and did not expect an answer from me.

"Who would ever have believed that the gaijin could have become so important?" he said softly. "Had anybody predicted it when I was a young man, they would have been laughed at. But it is so. I should be grateful for it. It is their custom that has made my business flourish. I do not like them, nor do I trust them. But if they bring money into the business, they must be tolerated. More than tolerated, they must be made welcome. Are you comfortable there, Mi-chan?"

I had been so interested in what he was saying that it took me a moment to realize that he was speaking to me rather than himself, and that he was waiting for my answer.

"Yes, Father. Thank you. I am very comfortable," I said quickly.

"Good." The road became uneven, and he was quiet again as he concentrated on guiding his horse along it. I thought fleetingly that he would have been better to allow the horse to find his own way, and I flushed with embarrassment at the unintended criticism.

"Do we have much further to go, Father?" I asked, less because I wanted to know, but more to cover my disloyal thought.

"Oh, a good way yet. Look." Father inclined his head toward the road in front of us. "It will take us a while to get there, but you can see the outskirts of Edo already."

I stared, blinked, and stared again.

What I had thought was mist resolved itself before my amazed gaze as the outlines of buildings, shielded by a dust and heat haze. Many, many buildings. Father kicked his horse into a brisk trot and the buildings seemed to go up and down in time to our rhythm. It was a strange sensation, and I began to feel a little sick, both with the motion —I had no stirrups to allow me to move with the horse, as I would normally have done—and also anticipation.

I said not a word as we approached the great city. I could not. I was so excited, it was all I could do to breathe.

Father seemed not to notice my silence. He reigned his horse to a slow walk as we passed the first houses. I could see why. Suddenly, there was a throng of people, spilling all over the road, their numbers so great that they could not move out of our way and I was afraid that Father's horse would trample them beneath his hooves.

So very many people. I had never seen so many people together. For that matter, I had never imagined that so many people could ever want to exist side by side.

The strange sights and sounds and even the smells enchanted me. I looked from side to side constantly, until my neck ached with the continuous movement. After a while, when the excitement of being in Edo began to lessen slightly, I noticed something very curious. The dense throng of people lessened slightly, and we no longer had to pick our way carefully. But those who were left stepped aside for no one—even very well-dressed men and women on foot, accompanied by servants, had to thrust their way through—yet the crowd seemed to part at once to allow my father's horse to pass by. Fascinated, I glanced up at Father to see if he was issuing some instruction, but he sat serenely, looking neither left nor right.

I found this odd but put the thought aside. Compared to all the new sights and sounds that surrounded me, it was a very small thing, indeed.

"So, Mi-chan, we are here."

Father reined his horse to a halt. I stared at the building he was indicating in awe. It was so very big! Even though it was surrounded by buildings that looked very grand to me, Father's building was bigger and far more splendid than any of them. I stared at it, my head tilted back to take in the height of this wonderful place. It took me a moment to understand why it was so much more impressive than its neighbors, and then it came to me—it was two stories high. I had never seen any building, not even the temple where we worshipped at the major festivals—that had two floors.

Father dismounted briskly and held out his arms to help me down. His horse was so much taller than my usual pony, the ground seemed a very long way down, and I was grateful for his help. I murmured my thanks and watched with my mouth open in shock as a well-dressed man immediately threw back the shoji before us and ran out into the street to grab the horse's bridle. Father nodded his thanks, and the horse was led away.

In his turn, Father led me into the building.

Immediately, the busy noise of the street was muted. The one, large room before me was very light. Despite the fact that men sat side by side over the whole of the floor, they worked in intent silence. It was obvious even to my innocent eyes that each worker had his place—there were no women present, not that I had expected any—and that everything was working smoothly. The thought came to me that the room was like some huge chessboard, with men sitting in each allocated square.

As soon as Father entered, each man stood and bowed deeply. Father bowed once in return and then put his hand on my shoulder and guided me forward. As soon as he moved, all the men sat down again and resumed whatever they had been doing.

"Tanaka-san, this is my daughter, Mi-chan. She will be with us today. I am leaving her in your care." He paused and glanced around, and I thought he looked angry. I must have been mistaken, for when he spoke, he sounded calm enough. "By the way, I do not see my sons here. Have they gone out on some unexpected business?"

The man Father spoke to climbed back to his feet at once and bowed deeply. He was so very old and thin, I immediately felt guilty that I had been the cause of making him stand. I was also troubled by the brusque way Father had spoken to him. Surely a man as venerable as this deserved more respect.

"Kono-san, I am most sorry. Your esteemed sons were here earlier, but they went out some time ago. I am afraid they did not tell me where they were going, nor did they leave a message for you."

The old man kept his head down and shuffled his feet, for all the world as if he was a child who expected punishment. Father's voice was cold when he responded.

"I see. I have an important client to attend to shortly, Tanaka-san. I do not wish to be interrupted until he has gone. If my sons return while I am engaged, then please ask them to come to me as soon as my client leaves. If they are still not returned by then, tell me."

He turned and walked away before Tanaka could answer. I was shocked by Father's rudeness to this old man and decided that I would be as nice as possible to him to make up for it.

"Mi-san, will it please you to sit down? I am afraid I have nothing to amuse you with, unless you would like to play with this abacus?"

Tanaka's voice was as ancient as the rest of him. I bowed deeply, and then immediately wondered if my courtesy was inappropriate—Father had not bowed to him at all. But the old man seemed pleased by my courtesy, so I sat down at once, looking at the abacus curiously.

Father had an abacus at home. When he was not there and I was bored, I had often flicked the colored beads back and forth, making pretty patterns with them. Now, I was curious. Clearly, in this place of business, an abacus was not a toy.

I glanced around me and saw that the workers appeared to be roughly divided into two. In one half, clerks were picking up pieces of paper they plucked from piles at the side of them, and then brushing kanji down urgently, laying the finished papers on a pile at the other side. The other half were flicking at abacus and then jotting kanji down on smaller scraps of paper. Every now and then, these men raised their heads and signaled briskly to one of a number of young boys, who came at a run and took the sheets of paper to the other men.

Suddenly, the urgency of the place gripped me. I wanted to be part of it. I could not write, nor could I read. But the flying beads on the abacus? Surely, it could not be so difficult to make sense of the patterns that were made on it. And if I could unravel the abacus' secrets today, then tomorrow I could practice on the one in Father's office. Surely, he would be delighted that I had taken an interest in his business. The thought filled me with pleasure, and I blurted my request quickly.

"I don't want to play with the abacus, Tanaka-san, but can you show me how it works?"

CHAPTER
FOUR

Dry earth trickles through
My fingers. Yet, with just a
Little rain, it clots

When I think back on that day, I blush at my
innocence.

Although I had no way of knowing it at the
time, Tanaka-san was Father's chief clerk. He was an
important man in the business, with a great deal of work to
do, and I had asked—no, demanded—that he show me
how an abacus worked almost as though he was a lowly
house servant.

Fortunately for me, he was also a kind man who liked
children. He cast a longing glance at his brush and then
cleared his throat before he spoke gently to me.

"But of course, Mi-san. Do you know what the abacus
is used for?"

I had no idea, and said so.

"Very well, we will start with that. The abacus is a

very important tool in any business. It is used for counting. For counting money, that is." He chuckled, obviously pleased with his simple explanation, and I smiled with him, all the time staring at the rows of beads strung on the frame. So, my toy had a purpose. An important purpose.

It counted money.

Suddenly, I was impatient. I glanced around me, amazed at the speed with which the men around me were flicking the beads back and forth. Every few moments, one broke off and made a note on a piece of paper. I found all this activity intriguing.

"Show me how it works, please. Now," I demanded.

Tanaka raised his almost non-existent eyebrows in surprise and then smiled indulgently.

"Not quite so fast, Mi-san. First, I must explain to you what the position of each bead means." He fingered the top two rows of beads that were divided from the rest of the beads in the frame with a wooden strut. "You will observe that all of the top beads are up, and all of the bottom beads are down. Yes?"

I nodded impatiently.

"The beads in the top rows represent the number five. Each bead in the bottom rows represents the number one." He pushed the beads about with a gnarled finger. I nodded. Five and one. I could remember that.

"Now, not only does each bead have a value, the column they are in has a value. This column—" He touched the furthest column to the right, at the bottom. "—stands for the number one. The column next to it stands for ten. The next, one hundred. Do you understand so far, Mi-san?"

He sounded very doubtful, but I nodded my head vigorously. The whole thing sounded right somehow. All Tanaka had said fell into place in my head, just as firmly as the clicking of the many abacus beads all around me.

"Yes, I understand. If I push one bead up from the furthest row, then that is one. Two beads are two. But how does that allow you to add up?"

Tanaka made a small sound in his throat. "Ah." He was staring at me, and I wondered if I had said something foolish.

"Mi-san, I had the honor of teaching both your brothers to use the abacus. It took me several hours to make them understand what you have grasped in a moment."

I was absurdly pleased, and even more eager to learn.

"Will you teach me a little more, Tanaka-san?" I asked hopefully.

"With great pleasure. The abacus is poetry for those who know how to use it, Mi-san. It can add and take away and multiply. If one can use an abacus well, then the door to success in business is opened to you. Watch, and tell me what the sum is I have on the frame."

It seemed to me that he flicked the beads very quickly. When I became more skilled in the use of the abacus myself, I realized that his movements had been almost agonizingly slow. I watched carefully, and after a pause for thought, said uncertainly, "Forty-two?"

"Quite right. Now, I will show you how to add up."

Once again, his fingers flicked the beads, but this time he explained exactly what he was doing. I watched and listened, and when he paused expectantly, I gave him his answer.

"You have added ten to ten, so the answer is twenty. Please, may I try?"

He pushed the abacus toward me wordlessly and I

began to move the beads uncertainly, speaking my movements out loud. After a while, I became more confident and added larger and larger sums quickly.

"That is very good. Very good indeed. But I told you that it is also possible to subtract and multiply on the abacus. Shall we try that?"

"Yes, please," I said instantly. This was not only easy, it was interesting. Far more interesting than riding my pony over well-traveled territory. Even more interesting than playing my biwa.

Alas for my confidence, subtraction and multiplication were far more difficult. I made errors and became angry with myself. Tanaka smiled at my frustration and shook his head.

"Don't worry, Mi-san. I cannot believe how quickly you have learned. I have taught all of your father's clerks to use the abacus, and none of them have learned as quickly as you have. Kono-san will be delighted when I tell him what good use you have made of your time. Tell me, can you play a musical instrument?"

I was confused by the question but nodded.

"I taught myself to play the biwa. But I do not know if I play it well or not."

"I think that you must play very well. It is an odd thing, but people who have an affinity for figures are often gifted musically."

I felt a warm glow at his praise, but my pleasure did not last long. A look of alarm suddenly spread over Tanaka's face. He glanced around and his shoulders hunched defensively, almost as if he was anticipating a blow.

"I think that your father's meeting is about to close. I can see shadows behind the shoji. I must tell Kono-san that your brothers have not yet returned."

I followed his glance and realized I had been wrong when I had thought the floor was one vast, open space. There was one area that was separated by shoji. This must surely be the most important part of this important building, the place where my father spent his time. Instantly, I wanted to see inside it. Even more, I wanted to enter it. To be part of Father's private space. I stood up, amazed to find that my legs were stiff. How long had I sat, practicing with the abacus?

"May I come with you, Tanaka-san?"

His expression was instantly worried. I was not surprised. I was not just a child, but a girl child at that. A creature of no importance at all. Surely, it would be better that I was kept out of the way. But I was determined.

"I think perhaps Father will not be pleased that my brothers have not returned all morning. But perhaps if I am with you, he will forget his anger a little? He did promise to take me to a teahouse as soon as his business was done," I wheedled.

The panic ebbed from Tanaka's eyes and he nodded thoughtfully. "Kono-san is meeting with a very important customer, a gaijin who does much business with him. I have noticed before that gaijin—even the men—seem to like children. Your father would not wish to show anger if you were present. Come, Mi-san, we will catch him as his visitor leaves."

I followed Tanaka as he picked his way amongst the clerks. Even though he was in a hurry, I noticed that he stopped often to ask a question or give instruction. Finding one of the messenger boys standing idle, he gave him brisk instructions to go around the floor to see if he was needed anywhere.

"And if nobody wants me, Tanaka-san?" the boy asked cheekily.

Tanaka sucked in a deep breath as if he was controlling his temper before he replied. "Your mother is a widow, I think?"

"Yes, Tanaka-san." I saw both surprise and pleasure in the boy's face that Tanaka should know this.

"Very well. For your mother's sake, I will forgive your mistake today. In future, do not stand idle. Not for a moment. If nobody needs you, then come to me and see if I have work for you."

The boy bowed, his shoulders hunched around his ears, and scampered off at once. I stared at Tanaka in amazement, wondering how the kind, patient, old man who had been teaching me how to use the abacus could suddenly become such a tyrant. A man who was clearly accustomed to being obeyed instantly.

The answer came to me quickly. It had to be because I had been such a good pupil. I had shown interest and had been keen to learn how to use the all-important abacus. Not only that, but I had succeeded where my brothers had failed. And I guessed shrewdly that there was also another reason, something far more subtle.

I had helped Tanaka out of what I knew would have been an awkward situation for him. Father would be very angry indeed that my brothers had wasted a whole morning when they should have been hard at work here. But my brothers were still absent, so he could not be angry with them. Instead, Tanaka would have felt the lash of his tongue.

But because I was there, and because all gaijin liked children, and this particular gaijin was an important client, if I pleased the client, then all would be well and Tanaka would be saved from Father's anger. He would not comment on it, naturally. It would be deeply embarrassing for a man of his venerable age and importance to be in a situation where he was grateful to a mere girl child. So, the balance would be addressed subtly, with no need for acknowledgment by either of us.

I turned the thought over in my mind. So, business was not all about money. It was also a matter of knowledge, and how that knowledge was used. And also—and I had to think carefully about this—it was a question of who one associated with almost as much as what one knew.

I was delighted with my perception.

Were we friends in a
Different life? Did I know
You well yesterday?

My surge of pleasure lasted no longer than a moment.

The shoji opened, but rather than finding my father standing before me, his gaijin client was there instead. I was of small stature, and this man towered over me to the extent that I had to tip my head back to be able to see his face. I felt that had we been outside, he would have blocked out the sun with his impressive height and bulk. Father was a tall man himself, but next to this gaijin, he seemed to have shrunk.

I couldn't help it. I gasped with shock. I heard Tanaka mumble something beneath his breath, but I couldn't tear my gaze from the gaijin. A moment later, I was literally rigid with amazement.

"Good day to you, Tanaka-san. And who is this lovely little girl?"

He spoke Japanese! To be sure, his accent was odd—had I heard his voice without seeing him, I would have known he was not from Edo. But even his voice fell strangely on my ears. It was very deep, and very, very loud.

I swallowed, searching frantically for a glimpse of Father's face in the hope that his expression would guide me. Should I speak or remain silent? Bow or not? But he was still standing behind the gaijin and I could not see his face at all. When I heard the smile in his voice, I sighed out loud with relief.

"Dickson-san, this unworthy child is my only daughter, Mi-chan."

The gaijin promptly squatted down on his heels so his head was barely higher than mine. He smiled broadly at me, and I managed a timid smile in response. He seemed pleased.

"She is a beautiful girl. And no doubt very clever if she is here to learn the business alongside your sons, Kono-san."

I almost grunted with unseemly laughter. What a strange thing to say! How could a girl ever hope to understand the masculine world of business? Even though he spoke such excellent Japanese, surely this kind gaijin had much to learn about how things were done here. I blinked in surprise when Tanaka-san answered him before my father spoke.

"This is the first time Mi-chan has been here, Dickson-san. It is her birthday, and she is going to a teahouse with Kono-san in a little while." How very humble he sounded, a different man to the one who had scolded the lazy messenger.

"Tanaka-san has kindly taken care of Mi all morning."

Father spoke formally, and I thought he sounded very stiff. "I trust she has behaved herself?"

"Most certainly, Kono-san."

I decided I liked Tanaka very much.

"She has been learning how to use the abacus. I have been very impressed with how much progress she has made. In only one morning, she has learned how to add and subtract and multiply. It often takes me many days to teach the new clerks as much, and then they are not as accurate as Mi-san."

"Ah, beauty and brains as well! You are a most fortunate man, Kono-san. And it is your birthday, Mi-chan?"

I nodded shyly. He laughed—a booming laugh that was so loud it made every one of the clerks on the floor raise their heads—and patted my cheek. With a huge effort, I managed not to jerk away at his rudeness. A furtive glance at Father told me I had done the right thing; he was smiling and nodding.

"Would you care to join us, Dickson-san?" he asked politely.

I almost wailed aloud. This was *my* birthday treat. I could not remember ever spending any time alone with Father—except when he was scolding me for some wrongdoing—and now this gaijin was going to come with us. He was an important man, so naturally, he would claim all Father's attention. My day was ruined.

But I remembered my manners and smiled shyly at Dickson-san as though there was nothing I would like better than to have him accompany us. I worried at once that I had done the wrong thing. I was only a very small girl, how was I to know what the gaijin would find correct? Even though I knew it was not at all polite, I could not resist staring at him.

His hair fascinated me. I had never seen anybody who did not have jet black hair, nearly always perfectly straight. Dickson-san's hair was not dark at all. The sun was shining through the shoji behind him, and it seemed to me that his thick, wavy hair smoldered like fire. Absently, I wondered if this was why the gaijin were called—never to their faces, of course, that would have been dreadfully rude—"red-haired barbarians."

"I would like nothing better than to accompany you and your beautiful daughter, Kono-san." He sounded genuinely regretful. Although he might look very strange, there was certainly nothing wrong with Dickson-san's manners. "But, unfortunately, I have made arrangements to lunch with a colleague. Perhaps I might have the pleasure of seeing Mi-chan in the future when I visit you again."

He smiled at me, and I lowered my head with what I hoped was just the right combination of timidity and pleasure.

"Perhaps so." I could hear the approval in Father's voice, and I was delighted.

I expected Dickson-san to rise and take his leave. I was about to move to one side to allow him to pass when instead, he put his hand out and patted my hair, just behind my ear. This was really too much. I did not know this man, and already he had touched me twice. I expected Father to reprimand him for his rudeness. When he did not, I understood how very important a client he must be.

"Well, what do I have here? A present for the birthday girl?"

I knew my cheeks had flushed bright red—I could feel the heat. I managed to raise my eyes and saw that he had something that shone gold in his fingers. Startled, I put my hand behind my ear, wondering how I had not noticed that it had somehow found its way there without me knowing.

"What's that?" I blurted rudely.

"It's something I found hidden behind your ear. A bit of gold for the birthday girl." The gaijin took my limp hand and tucked the coin into it. "I'm afraid you can't spend it—it's a coin from my country. It's called a sovereign. As you can see, it has our empress's head on it. Her name is Victoria, and this coin is often called a Victoria to honor her. Perhaps one day you might be able to travel to my country and you can spend it then. In the meantime, it's a pretty keepsake of our meeting."

He stood before I could reply. His knees creaked and that made me want to laugh. As did the idea that a woman might ever travel outside Japan. Why, until today, I had never left our estate. Yet, even though it was nonsense, I found the idea very exciting.

Father raised a single finger and I understood he was telling me to stand aside. I moved quickly and stood with my eyes cast down, the coin clasped tightly in my palm. Dickson-san, my father, and Tanaka all walked past me. I stayed exactly where I was, having no idea where I could—or should—go.

It seemed a very long time before Father returned. He said nothing to me, but simply nodded, and I supposed I was to follow him. His footsteps were so much longer than mine that I had to scurry to keep up with him.

The teashop was very elegant, and also full. In spite of that, Father was instantly shown to a secluded, empty table. I had not heard him instruct a messenger to say he would take lunch here, so was a table always reserved for him just in case he might care to eat here? I began to appreciate how important Father was, and I swelled with pride at the knowledge.

"Mochi for my daughter. And I will have rice and sea vegetables. And tea for us both." Father waited until the server had gone before he smiled at me. "Are you still holding on to Dickson-san's coin? If I were you, I would tuck it into your obi to keep it safe. Do you have somewhere you can keep it when we get home? Or would you like me to put it somewhere safe for you?"

Nothing—short of threatening to cut my fingers off— could have persuaded me to part with my precious Victoria. No matter that I could never spend it. It was my birthday present, and I wanted it close, where I could gloat over its beauty and wonder about the strange features of the woman imprinted on it. Dickson-san had called her his empress, and I was intrigued. How could a mere woman become an empress? Especially one who seemed quite young and not venerable at all.

I took a deep breath before I answered. "Please, may I keep it, Father? I will keep it safe. Is it really gold?"

"It is. I believe in Dickson-san's country it is quite valuable."

He sat back to allow the server to place our food and tea before us. My mochi were beautifully arranged and looked both sweet and tempting, but it was the savory steam rising from Father's rice and vegetables that made my mouth water. I saw that he was staring at me with raised eyebrows, and I picked up a mochi quickly and ate it with pretended pleasure, even though I found it over-sweet and sticky.

"Thank you, Father. These are lovely. Please, may I ask something about my coin?"

"Of course." Father took a sip of his tea and raised his

eyebrows. I realized after a moment he was waiting politely for my question, so I spoke quickly.

"Dickson-san said it bore the head of his empress. But he did not mention an emperor. How can that be? How could a woman be the ruler of his country?"

Father blinked in obvious surprise. He took a mouthful of food and I realized with amazement that he wasn't sure how to reply to me. How could this be? Father was a respected businessman. A rich man who had a table reserved for him whether he wanted to visit a particular restaurant or not. Surely, my question should have been simple for him?

"Many things are different in the world of the gaijin," he said finally. "Their ways are strange to us, and I suspect always will be. Dickson-san has taken the trouble to learn to speak Japanese. Most of the gaijin have not. I have noticed that many of them seem to think that if they speak loudly enough in their own language, we will understand them. I do not enjoy trading with them, but I would be a fool to reject them. If I turned them away, then many of my competitors would be happy to take my place."

He paused and I nodded as if he had answered my question fully. It puzzled me that he had not even tried, but I pushed the thought away at once. It was disloyal to my wise and generous father, and that would never do.

"I see," I said politely.

Father smiled. "Do you? Then you are far wiser than I, Mi-chan." His face clouded suddenly. I stiffened, wondering if I had annoyed him in some way. I was relieved when he spoke again. His voice was thoughtful, and I got the impression he was talking to himself rather than me. "Most of the gaijin are absolute fools, of course. But I think

Dickson-san is quite perceptive. We were chatting this morning after our business was done, and he happened to mention that he had not seen your brothers. Naturally, I made an excuse for them. I told him I had sent them in my place to see a colleague on business as I wished to devote my morning to him. I sensed he didn't believe me, but he was too polite to say so. For a gaijin, he is a very subtle man —at times, almost Japanese. I was sure of it when he told me of a proverb from the northern part of his own country.

"'You are surely fortunate to have two such fine sons, Kono-san,' he said. 'Undoubtedly, they will be a credit to you. Alas, I have always been too involved in business to find a wife and start a family. I fear it is too late for a confirmed bachelor such as I am now.'"

"Naturally, I smiled and insisted that he was still a young man and had plenty of years left to find a wife and have sons. But Dickson-san just shrugged and smiled sadly. He told me, 'Many years ago, when I really was a young man just starting out in life, I had a young woman who was very dear to me. Unfortunately, I neglected her in favor of my business and she—not surprisingly—decided to marry a man who was more interested in her than in making money.'

My mouth was a round "O" of amazement. Dickson-san's woman had run off with another man because he was concentrating on building up his business? And he had not only allowed it to happen, but had never taken another wife? Surely, the gaijin's way of life was indeed strange beyond comprehension. All the same, I found it very touching that Dickson-san had loved his woman so very much that nobody had ever taken her place.

Father paused, waiting for me to reply. I was at a loss as

to what he expected, and said cautiously, "That is very sad. Dickson-san seemed to be a very nice man."

"I think he is an honorable man," Father said judiciously. "But that is not the point of what he was telling me. It appeared that the man his woman married was already very rich. Her husband had inherited his wealth from his father, who had worked very hard to build up his business from nothing at all. Dickson-san said her husband turned out to be an idle wastrel, and worst still, a drunk. He thought working in the family business was beneath him, but he was pleased to spend the money it brought in.

"His father died quite young—Dickson-san said of a broken heart when he saw what a fool his only son was. The son cared nothing for that. He continued to spend money without a thought as to where it was coming from.

"In time, he had a son of his own, but, alas, the boy followed in his father's footsteps and—even worse—was a gambler, and a lousy gambler at that.

"That is very bad," I broke in without thinking and spoke humbly to hide my rudeness. "Of course, I am nothing but a girl, but even I can see that a business cannot run itself. What happened to the foolish son, Father?"

"Dickson-san said that the business failed. By that time, the husband of the woman who Dickson-san should have married was dead—mainly through too much drink. His wastrel son tried to gamble his fortune back, and you can guess where that led to."

Oh, but this was high drama! I breathed the important question delicately and was immediately disappointed.

"And Dickson-san's woman, Father? The mother of the lazy son? What happened to her?"

"Oh, I have no idea. He didn't say, and I didn't ask." I was deeply disappointed. To me, that had been the point of the story. Father went on anyway, and I hid my disappointment and listened politely. "The important thing is that Dickson-san told me that there is a proverb in his country that sums such behavior up." He pursed his lips and spoke carefully. "Waraji to waraji in three generations."'

I had been so fascinated by my expectation of what was to come that I had sat forward slightly in my eagerness. I turned Father's words over in my head and frowned my disappointment. I had no idea what he was talking about.

"I didn't know the gaijin wore waraji, Father," I said for want of anything better to say. Father was clearly not fooled. He smiled at me with amusement in his eyes.

"I didn't understand what he meant either. It would have been grossly impolite to have asked him to explain, but I didn't have to. Dickson-san told me anyway.

"'We do not wear waraji in my country, Kono-san. But the lower classes of working people, those who are very poor—rather like your peasants here in Japan—wear a wooden shoe called a "clog." It is, I think, the equivalent of waraji in that they are very sturdy, hard-wearing shoes, except that clogs are made of wood, not straw." I mouthed the word *clog* silently, thinking it very ugly. By the sound of it, the shoe was equally ugly. 'Clogs are worn only by the very, very poor, the sort of people who have to work very hard for very little return. They cannot afford anything better. No one who has any money at all would ever wear them."

"Dickson-san explained to me that the point of the proverb is that in the beginning, the grandfather had to wear clogs until he worked very hard and was fortunate enough to make lots of money. Then, naturally, he never wore clogs again. But because the gods did not smile on him, his son was lazy and foolish. And the grandson took after his father, and also wanted money without earning it. So, the business went bad, and the foolish son had to sell parts of it off, bit by bit, until he had nothing left but the clothes on his back.

"Then he had to take any work he could find just to put food on the table. He became so poor he had to wear the despised clogs, for he could afford nothing else. You see? Clogs to clogs in three generations."

"I see. I think I understand," I said cautiously.

I need not have bothered. Father was staring into space, his expression troubled. I recalled his barely concealed anger that morning when Tanaka-san had told him my brothers were not at work, and I understood that he was not only angry with them, but disappointed as well.

In a flash of insight, I understood that Dickson-san, the despised gaijin, had also perceived Father's anger and sympathized with him, and that he had used the proverb as a polite way to share his understanding of the situation. Or at least, the situation as he perceived it.

He was wrong, of course. *My* brothers would never wear waraji, and nor would their children or their children's children. That would be unthinkable.

Why, then, was I unable to put the thought out of my mind?

CHAPTER
SIX

Can the bird that flies
High above me ever know
The pleasure he gives?

Father did not mention my visit to his office, much to my disappointment. I thought of it constantly, but I did not dare to speak to him about it. My silence was finally rewarded when the following week he sent a servant to call me to him, and he told me—as if it was no great thing at all—that I was to accompany him again, that very day. I was unable to hide my delight, and it seemed to me that Father was pleased with my reaction. It was difficult to tell. He was a grave, silent sort of man who wasted nothing, not even words.

As before, he left me with Tanaka-san, who seemed not at all surprised to see me.

The morning flew, and I only realized it was mid-day when, as if at a silent signal, all of the clerks put down their abacus and brushes and opened bento boxes. Suddenly, I was famished, but I had no food. It had never occurred to me to even think about food for the noontime meal. As Father had left earlier and had not returned, I realized that today there was to be no visit to a teahouse for me. My stomach grumbled rebelliously, and I sucked it in miserably, trying to hide my hunger.

By then, Tanaka-san had opened his own bento box and was poking at the contents with his chopsticks. The box was a lovely thing, sumptuously enameled, and I guessed it was very old. But it was the contents that enticed me. I stared at them, my mouth watering. It took an effort of will to tear my gaze away.

"Goodness me, but my wife must think I am a starving man," Tanaka exclaimed. "Just look at all this food."

I stared at him miserably, sucking in my stomach as it growled loudly.

"I really cannot eat all of this, and it would be a shame to waste it. Perhaps you would like to share it with me?"

He called to one of the messengers—the boy he had scolded on my first visit—to run and bring a pair of chopsticks. The boy glanced longingly at his own bento box but went outside nimbly and returned quickly with a plain pair of wooden chopsticks for me. I assumed he had persuaded one of the many street food vendors to part with them.

Tanaka-san said, "Now, Mi-chan, could you do me the favor of helping me eat some of this?"

I needed no urging, and between us, the bento box was empty very quickly. I thought nothing of it until the homeward journey—as before, Father put me on the saddle in front of him—when it occurred to me abruptly that Tanaka-san's bento box had not been that full at all, and that he had fed me out of the goodness of his heart. I was deeply ashamed that the old man had gone hungry because of me. In the future, when Father decided to take me to his place of business with him, I would make sure to ask the kitchen at home to prepare me a bento box. In fact, I would ask them to prepare one for me every day. If I were at home, I would eat it there so nothing would be wasted. The thought of having a bento box of my own—even if I ate the contents alone in my own room—made me feel delightfully important and very grown-up.

I began to anticipate eagerly the gentle tap of a servant's hand on the frame of my shoji, knowing that if the sound came before the morning meal, Father had sent the servant to tell me I was to accompany him. It was not a regular day. Sometimes it was at the beginning of the week, sometimes the end. Occasionally, a whole week went by that I did not go with him. Father worked every day—there was no day of rest for him—and it seemed natural that I should do the same. It didn't matter to me. The time I did not spend at his place of business was dross and lay heavily upon me. Soon, I cared for nothing except my days in Edo.

I realized quickly that my presence embarrassed my brothers deeply. Although they made a point of ignoring me, occasionally a gaijin visitor would smile at me and I thought would have spoken to me if my brothers had not steered them away instantly. Did they speak to Father about my—to them, unwanted—presence? I did not know, but I rather thought they had. As I continued to be taken to Edo, it bothered me not in the least.

Tanaka-san seemed to enjoy my company. I sat at his side, my abacus ready for any instructions either he or one of the many clerks might call to me. I had quickly become so skilled on the abacus that nobody checked my calculations, something that filled me with great pride.

After a while, I found my fingers worked the beads so

instinctively, I needed to use my brain less and less. So, I used my time to look around me, and to think.

Clearly, Father's business was thriving. With the exception of my brothers, who came and went as it pleased them, all of the clerks and messengers were busy for every moment of the working day. Mealtimes were limited to the time it took to gulp down the contents of bento boxes. I watched, and the more I watched, the more I wondered.

I still had no idea at all what Father's business actually was. Clearly, he was not a merchant. There were no signs of any sort of manufactured goods. Strangers arrived throughout the day. A very few were seen by Tanaka-san before they were passed on to senior clerks, but most of them immediately approached lesser members of staff. Occasionally, a man—generally a gaijin—was taken to see Father, and when that happened, his shoji was often closed for a long time.

I was tempted to ask Tanaka-san about the nature of Father's business, but I was too shy and too lacking in confidence. If he had expressed astonishment that either my father or my brothers had not told me, I would have sunk into the tatami with embarrassment. So instead, I watched and wondered, and with each day I spent in Edo, I became surer of one thing: I wanted to be part of this effi-cient hustle and bustle. I wanted to contribute more than my brothers, who clearly cared little for the business that paid for their gambling debts and kept them in sumptuous clothes—and certainly even more sumptuous oiran.

And just as my love of my biwa had begun to wane as soon as I found it easy to play, so did the allure of my abacus begin to drop away. I had no need to think about the complex calculations I did as a matter of course. I wanted more.

I wanted something that would challenge me. And I knew exactly what that something was.

"Tanaka-san." I took care to make my voice resemble the cooing of a dove, soft and sweet. Tanaka-san held up his finger to silence me until he had finished his calculation and then smiled at me indulgently.

"Yes, Mi-chan, what is it?"

"I have been thinking—"

His lips quirked as he tried—and failed—to hide his amusement at the idea of a young girl thinking. Fond as I had become of the old man, I had to choke down my indignation.

"I am very quick with the abacus. But it seems to me that I have to waste a great deal of the clerks' valuable time when they have to call out to me what is wanted and then write it down for me when I have made the calculation."

I thought I had phrased that very nicely. It was not *my* time that was being wasted, but the clerk's. And the clerk was, of course, a man, and so automatically deserved my respect.

"I suppose that is so. But as you cannot read and write, there is no other option."

Could it possibly be so very easy? I felt quite guilty about seizing my chance with the venerable clerk's innocent words, but I did not let that stop me for a moment. I spoke quickly.

"Of course, that is so, Tanaka-san. But if somebody taught me to read and write, I would have no need to take up a clerk's time, would I?" I went on hurriedly before he could think of an objection. "And that would save Father money. That would surely give him great pleasure."

I was certain I was speaking the truth. I was beginning to learn that money really did matter, and that the absence of it mattered even more. Far more, I thought, than any considerations people like my mother might have about caste. I saw no reason at all to mention to Tanaka-san that I was deeply jealous of my brothers' ability to read and write, and that I was determined to excel them both, just as I knew I was already far speedier and more accurate than they in the use of the abacus.

Tanaka-san's voice broke into my thoughts. "But surely you will be married soon, and then what use would being able to read and write be to you?"

Naturally, he was correct. I had been betrothed when I was a child. It had come as no surprise to me that the event had occurred on my birthday. The match was an excellent one, Mother said. My future husband was the eldest son of a prosperous farmer, and only a year or two older than I was. As a landowner, my future father-in-law was of a much higher caste than my family. In society, merchants and men of business who owned no land—no matter how wealthy they were—counted for very little.

Mother obviously expected me to be delighted by the news, and I did my best to smile and appear pleased. But what does a child know of husbands and marriage? When I actually met my future husband, I was chilled with horror.

I was not left alone with him, for which I gave thanks to the gods. His mother accompanied him. All the while she was with us, her sharp eyes took in every detail of me and our house. Whether she approved of either, I had no idea.

Her son sat by her side, looking glum. I am not tall, but this boy was smaller than I was. He was...not fat, but certainly sturdy. When I watched the way he gulped his food, I could see why. Also, he ate with his mouth wide open and spoke while he was eating. He ignored me completely, speaking only to Father, and then his tone was condescending, as if he was aware of his higher status. I disliked him instantly. I knew without knowing how I knew that Father didn't like him either, but Mother—who had come out of her apartment for the occasion—treated the boy as if he was a young lord. He reveled in her attention.

I was so naïve that when he went, I thought that would be the last time I would see him until we were married, surely many, *many* years in the future. And who knew what might happen before then? I could hardly believe it when he turned up again a few months later. And then again. Even worse was to come. On my thirteenth birthday—yes, yet another birthday!—I was taken to visit his parents.

It had been bad enough when Yuto—my betrothed—and his mother had visited us, but at least then I was in surroundings I was familiar with, and that was comforting. Here, I knew nothing and nobody. I felt sick with nerves.

Their house was nowhere near as grand as ours. That gave me a certain courage, and I managed to keep my head up and answer the many questions that were put to me by my future mother-in-law.

She took me aside as soon as I had taken my zori off in the entrance. I stared entreatingly at Father, but he simply nodded, so I followed Ai-san. Mother and Father were ushered into a cramped reception room by a well-dressed older man who—as he was not introduced to me—I had to assume was my prospective father-in-law.

Ai-san led me through to her apartment and kneeled on the tatami, leaving me standing uneasily in front of her.

"So, Mi-san, I am to lose my dear son Yuto to you."

She paused, clearly expecting a response. I had no idea

what was expected of me, so I took refuge in simply agreeing.

"Yes, Ai-san."

"Yes? That is the best you can do? Are you not overwhelmed with pleasure at such a great match? I can tell you, I am not at all happy about it. My husband tells me that your father is a very rich man, but is that enough? What about the fact that your family are no better than merchants? My own family have farmed the land since time began. I was pleased to marry Hideki-san, even though I had barely met him before the marriage ceremony. And why was I pleased?" She paused, although whether to draw breath or give me a chance to answer, I had no idea. I stayed silent. "Because Hideki-san was also a farmer, that was why."

"Yes, Ai-san," I answered promptly. I was beginning to grasp that whatever I said would not satisfy her. I was right.

"Is that all you can say?" she demanded. I kept my eyes fixed on the tatami. "Well, I suppose you are at least polite."

I was shocked as she reached out and fingered my kimono, rubbing the excellent silk between her fingers.

"That is expensive. Far too good to waste on a child. Your father must be wealthy to throw his money away like that. I hope you are not going to be extravagant, child."

There was no answer to that, so I made none.

The questions went on and on for so long they gave me a headache and I was grateful when we set off for home. As usual, Father said very little, but Mother was unusually animated.

"What an excellent family! Everything done exactly as one would expect, don't you think?" Father grunted, but

Mother was not deterred. "Ai-san told me how both her family and her husband's have been farmers for many generations. When they married, with Ai-san's dowry, the size of their estate almost doubled. And Yuto is the eldest son. I do hope Mi realizes what a fortunate child she is."

It seemed to worry Mother not at all that neither Father nor I made any reply.

Although I thought things with Yuto could not get any worse, I was wrong. About half a year after my visit to his family, we received an urgent message to say that Yuto was gravely ill. He had caught the speckled monster, and it was not certain if he would live or die. I am ashamed to say that I prayed to the gods that he would not survive—I was a mere child, how was I to know what a terrible thing I was asking?—but alas, the gods did not listen to me. In hindsight, I suppose that was a good thing, as in later years, no doubt my conscience would have troubled me deeply had he died.

But he did not die. He made—according to the message that finally came from his mother—a good recovery. Or so she said.

When I saw my betrothed again, I was appalled. Yuto may have recovered, but the speckled monster had done its worst to him. Never handsome, now his face was deeply pocked by the scars of the terrible disease. His skin seemed to have hundreds of fish eggs bubbling under the surface. The thought might have made me want to laugh if it hadn't been for his eyes. They were half-closed, and it was obvious that one eye was blind. The iris was completely white, a sickening, bone-white that made an unlovely contrast to the true white of his eye.

Even Mother was lost for words for a moment, and then she tried to hide her shock by gushing out her pleasure that Yuto had been returned to health. She needn't have bothered. He was still more interested in his food than anything else and only spoke grudgingly to her when politeness demanded it.

And I was to marry this nasty...thing? I shuddered at the thought. Then, with the resilience of the very young, I took refuge yet again in the knowledge that our wedding was many years in the future. If the gods were kind to me, who knew what might happen before then?

Tanaka's question had brought all that back to me, and I was so lost in the past that I did not answer immediately, and he had to repeat his question, his tone brisk.

"You are betrothed, are you not?"

"Of course. But even when—" *If* I corrected myself firmly. "—I am a married lady, surely it will be good for me to be able to assist my husband in any way that I can?"

I seemed to have hit on the right answer. Tanaka nodded thoughtfully.

"You may be right, Mi-chan. We live in troubled times, to be sure. When I was a young man, everybody knew their place and stuck to it. Now, all is changing. And not for the better."

I thought he must be talking about how many gaijin were in Japan now, and I nodded dutifully in agreement. I had seen them in the streets of Edo frequently.

I caught myself up hurriedly as I realized my thoughts had strayed again. Tanaka had his head to one side, clearly waiting for my answer.

"You are right, of course, Tanaka-san," I said quickly. "So much is changing. Who can be sure of the future anymore? And that is why I want to learn to read and write. With so many changes happening, surely it would be good for me to be able to support my future husband in any way

I could. I'm sure Father would be pleased as well," I added craftily.

"Perhaps so." Tanaka clearly liked the idea of pleasing Father.

So did I.

CHAPTER

SEVEN

When I was a child,
I loved to play hide and seek.
But those times are gone

I assumed that Tanaka would teach me to read and write, just as he had taught me how to use the abacus.

I was wrong.

Never one to waste time, once the decision was made, he called over my head and I was astonished to see the young messenger he had sent for my chopsticks walk toward us briskly.

"Gen, you are excused from your duties for the rest of today. I wish Mi-san to be taught to read and write." *Tanaka* wanted me to learn to read and write? I closed my lips firmly on my surprise. It didn't matter how I achieved my ambition. The important thing was that I got what I wanted. "Your calligraphy is excellent. You will teach her to write—and read—as well as you can.

"You may both go up to the archive now. You will have

quiet and privacy there. I will inform the clerks that the archive is closed today so nothing will distract you. Come back to me at home time and tell me what Mi-san has learned today."

That was it; the thing was done. A clerk came over with a slip of paper and Tanaka bent his head to it at once. Realizing we had been dismissed, I got to my feet and followed Gen.

I had often wondered what happened on the mysterious second floor, but as Tanaka had never mentioned it, I did not ask. I was delighted by this unexpected turn of events. Not only was I going to learn to read and write, but my curiosity was about to be satisfied.

"This is the quietest place in the whole building, Mi-san," Gen called cheerfully over his shoulder. "It's part of my job to file everything here each day, so if I am here already, we will be left in peace." He laughed, clearly finding his own comment amusing. I stared back stonily, suddenly feeling I had been cheated in some way.

I longed to be able to read and write. I found it difficult to explain even to myself, but I felt that the more knowledge I had, then the better it would be for me in whatever my future held. I guessed that Yuto could neither read nor write, and I used the thought to justify my own desire to learn. If I had to marry Yuto, surely he would be delighted to find that his bride could be useful in ways that he had never dreamed of. Or at least I hoped so.

But to be handed to a mere messenger boy for instruction! That had not been my plan at all. Somehow, it spoiled the moment for me. Made it second best.

I would not tolerate this.

I spoke curtly to his back. "You can read and write well, I suppose? I want to learn properly."

"That I can." Gen was wandering around the room, humming absently to himself. "If that was not so, would Tanaka-san have given me the honor of teaching you? Of course, I am his favorite out of all the messengers, but that has nothing to do with it."

It was grossly rude of me, but I couldn't help it. I laughed loudly. Gen was Tanaka's favorite? Tanaka seemed to only ever speak to Gen to scold him.

"Really?" I asked. "It seems to me that Tanaka-san is angry with you all the time. I've never heard him speak to the other boys like he does you."

I chose the word "boys" deliberately to show Gen his true position. He was, after all, nothing but a messenger. I was annoyed when he seemed not to notice.

"Quite right," he said cordially. "But then again, how often have you heard him speak directly to any of the other messengers? He doesn't waste his time on them. He expects their superiors to keep them in order. But he likes me, so he takes the time to ensure that I do things right. He knows I am going to be important one day, and that I will remember his instruction when I was nothing. I am honored by Tanaka-san's faith in me. Especially in entrusting Kono-san's daughter to me for instruction."

I glared at him but could find no words that would slice through his absurd confidence. Gen seemed not to notice my annoyance. Even though he appeared to be passing the shelves that lined the huge room from ceiling to floor casually, I noticed that every now and then he paused and ran his fingers over the spine of one of the many leather-bound volumes.

Each book had kanji on the spine, embossed in gold. I stared at them hungrily, annoyed that whatever their secrets were, they were hidden from me. But not for long!

"What is this place?" I demanded. Gen turned to look at me, his expression amused. He glanced around and then turned back, his eyebrows raised as if to say, *isn't it obvious?* I felt intensely stupid, and because of my embarrassment I snapped at him. "If this is where you work, it seems to me that you must have very little to do. A bit of dusting, perhaps? Keep everything tidy? Or does Tanaka-san send you up here to punish you when you've been particularly annoying?"

I looked around as I spoke and reluctantly began to wonder at what I saw. Each shelf was full of leather-bound volumes. At first sight, each seemed to be approximately the same size and thickness, but as I walked further into the room, I saw that the books in the furthest corner were much thinner and that the bindings were far less rich. Impulsively, I tugged one of those books out and allowed it to fall open in my hands.

The paper was very old, so old it was yellowing and the ink on the pages was brownish rather than black. I turned the pages gently, afraid they would come apart in my hands. Each page was full of kanji, some almost invisible with the passage of time.

Before I could really take in what I was looking at, Gen took the book from my hands—quite gently—and put it back on the shelf in its allotted space. I was annoyed at once. This was my father's business. Who was Gen—a mere messenger boy—to prevent me from looking at whatever I wished?

"I am sorry, Mi-san." He smiled pleasantly as he spoke, and my temper dropped a notch. "That particular ledger is very old indeed. In fact, it was part of the original business before your honorable father purchased it. It is very fragile and has to be handled carefully."

My attention was caught at once. Father had bought this business from somebody else? I spoke impulsively, glancing at the slim volume Gen had taken from me.

"Father must have made the business far more prosperous than it was when he purchased it." I had the pleasure of watching amazement make Gen's eyes widen. "That old ledger is thin compared to the ones that look much newer, so the business must be far busier now than it was when Father took it over. That is so?"

Gen nodded. He breathed out before he spoke. "Mi-san, I have had the honor of working for your father since the year of the dog. In all that time, neither of your brothers has expressed any interest in this place." He waved his hand around the room. "Nor have they ever asked anything about how the business works."

I swelled with pleasure. "I am not my brothers, Gen-san. I want to know everything that is important to my father. Explain to me about this place, please. Tell me what each book contains, and why they are treasured."

EIGHT

Come, land on my hand,
Little bird, and sing to me of
Wonders you have seen

Gen paused, and I guessed he was choosing his words carefully.

"This room is the heart of Kono-san's business."

Already, I was shaking my head. How could that be so? The room was deathly quiet, unlike the hustle and bustle of the floor below us. Was Gen trying to make his role here far more important than it truly was? I smiled indulgently.

"I think you are exaggerating, Gen. This place is..." I tailed off, suddenly aware that I had no real idea of what it was. Gen jumped in eagerly.

"It is the archive. Every transaction that takes place, no matter how small or large, is here. Look." He removed one of the fatter ledgers with almost reverential care and allowed it to fall open at a random page. I saw three columns of kanji, with an empty column suggesting that something might need to be added later. But it all meant nothing at all to me, so I shrugged in irritation.

"So? What does it say?"

Gen colored, obviously comprehending his mistake. "I am in error, Mi-san. Please, allow me to explain. This first column is the name of the client. The other columns are the sums of money borrowed and the dates they were repaid. The empty column is there to record the very rare times that money is not repaid on time."

Money borrowed and repaid? My confusion deepened and I looked at Gen helplessly, wordlessly waiting for him to explain. His expression was equally puzzled for a moment, and then I was sure I saw a glint of laughter in his eyes. Perhaps I was wrong as he spoke quickly and courteously.

"These are your father's account books. Kono-san is the most successful and important moneylender in the whole of Edo."

I thought about that and found myself vaguely disappointed. Moneylending had none of the allure of what I thought of as business. Real things. Thing that could be bought and sold. Jade and silk and pearls. *Nice* things. But moneylending? Where was the joy in that?

"And that is good?" I asked dubiously.

"Anything to do with money is good," Gen answered firmly. "There are many moneylenders in Edo. But Kono-san is the most successful by far."

I shrugged, still not convinced, and Gen's expression was suddenly sharp. When he spoke, his voice was so harsh I almost jerked back from him.

"You do not understand the value of money, Mi-san,"

he grated. "I am the only child of a poor widow. Mother is not a strong woman. She manages to do laundry for those of our neighbors who are better off than we are, but it does not pay a great deal. If I do not work, then Mother would not be able to pay the rent on our little house. If I did not work, we would have no food. Have you ever known what it is to be hungry, Mi-san?"

"No," I said cautiously. "I have never been hungry. But I can't help that."

"No, of course not." Gen was smiling again as though his outburst had never happened. "Please, forgive my unconsidered words. You are not interested in the life of a mere messenger boy. I should have explained that it is because Kono-san lends money to people that you do not go hungry." He paused and spoke slowly, as if to a child.

"He does not do it out of the goodness of his heart. When he lends money, he expects to get it back at the end of the agreed term, together with a little extra because he has not had use of that money himself. If he lends somebody a lot of money, then he will get a lot extra back. That is why he is a wealthy man.

"That is how business works, Mi-san. And that is why your father is one of the wealthiest and most honored businessmen in the whole of Edo. And because of that, I am proud to work for him."

I heard what Gen said, but there was so much to take in that my head was spinning. I would think about it all later, very carefully. At the moment, I was humbled to discover that a mere messenger boy such as Gen could be so very wise in the ways of the business world while I knew nothing.

I took the ledger from his hands and flicked the pages.

Although the kanji meant nothing to me, I sensed the power in these pages. *These* were where my lovely clothes came from. *These* were what enabled Mother to buy her expensive gaijin furniture. *These* were what allowed my ungrateful brothers to bet on sumo bouts as often as they wished.

These books *were* money.

And I could understand nothing that they said.

Suddenly, I was hungry. I had hoped to learn to read and write so I could please Father. Now, I understood that my initial thoughts had been only the first inkling of something much greater. These books were both the past and the future. Anybody who could read them could chart Father's business from lowly beginnings to great wealth and beyond. I wanted—wanted more than anything I could recollect—to be able to understand what they contained.

To be part of it.

I would learn, just as I would learn to read and write. I had mastered the abacus easily enough, and if all the clerks in Father's business could read and write, it couldn't be so very difficult.

I glanced at Gen. He was staring longingly at a heap of loose papers on the shelf nearest the shoji. I recognized them at once, the slips of paper the clerks passed to Gen and the other messengers. I pushed aside the sweeping thoughts that were whirling in my mind.

"Gen." He was startled by my voice and jumped and turned to me reluctantly. "Those are the slips of paper that the clerks complete. What do they say? Why are they here?"

He lifted his head. I could see he was pleased by my question. "I, and all the other messengers, bring them up here each day. Each slip is a record of a transaction. They either record an amount of money loaned, or an amount repaid, or—very rarely—money that is overdue for payment. At the end of each day, I enter the information they contain in one of the ledgers. At the end of each month, Tanaka-san looks at the ledger entries for the previous month and..."

He paused, and I guessed he was trying to explain what Tanaka did in terms I would understand. I nodded encouragingly. "Tanaka-san balances the figures. He adds up how much has been loaned and how much has been repaid. That—less a little for loans that should have been repaid but have not—is the profit Kono-san has made for the month."

That was easy enough to understand. I was delighted by my grasp of the complex world of my father's business.

"You have a very responsible job," I said, and I meant it. Gen beamed at my words.

"I am honored to work for Kono-san."

I nodded, but suddenly I was tired of all this talk. I wanted to learn to read and write. Not tomorrow or the next day—now. I wanted—no, I needed—to be able to comprehend the hidden world that lay inside these closed books. These books that represented everything Father had achieved. If they were important to him, then they were important to me.

"That is all most interesting, Gen. But you were released from your duties to teach me to read and write. Can we begin now, please?

A slow grin spread over his face. "We will begin today, certainly. But reading and writing are very difficult things, Mi-san. It will take much longer than a single day for you to learn anything at all."

I glared at him. He was wrong, of course. I was my

father's daughter, and I would achieve anything I set my mind to. If a mere messenger could master the art of reading and writing, how could it present a challenge to me?

A short while later, I understood that it was I who had been wrong.

Listen to the breeze!
Has it been sent to lure me
From my given tasks?

"No, you're holding the brush all wrong. It's not a chopstick. Hold it like this." Gen took the calligraphy brush from me and held it delicately balanced in his fingers. I took it back and copied him, but the brush felt awkward and wrong in my hand.

"Show me how to write something," I demanded.

Gen shook his head. "What's the point when you won't know what you've written?" He spoke reasonably, I supposed, but I was still sulky.

"Then teach me how to read," I demanded.

By the time of the mid-day meal, I was near to despair. Gen was patient, but I wanted to know everything all at once. When he started to explain to me about the one thousand and twenty-six kanji that I had to learn first—*first!*—I put my hands over my ears and refused to listen.

Gen spoke gently. "It is not easy, Mi-san. But if you truly want to learn, then it will happen."

I glared at him. "Can my brothers read and write?" I demanded.

"Of course," he said promptly. "How else could they hope to inherit the great business your honorable father has built up?"

I burned with jealousy. If my brothers had mastered this dreadful task, then so could I.

"Show me." I picked up the brush and held it poised over a sheet of paper. I held it very firmly, fearing that it might twist and turn in my grip like a living thing.

"Some kanji are very easy to remember." Gen picked up his brush and made a single, horizontal line. "What do you think that means?"

I shrugged, angry that I had no idea.

"It means one."

I nodded. That made sense. Gen added another straight line beneath it.

"And that?" he asked.

I thought for a moment and then said cautiously, "Two?"

"Quite right. And this?" He added another line beneath the first two.

"Three." I was more confident now and my voice barely asked the question.

"Yes, three. Now, try this one."

His brush moved fluidly, and I stared at another four lines. Three of these lines were perched on top of a single line lying down, and the middle line was longer than its friends.

For some reason, the sea came into my mind, and I said tentatively, "A wave?"

"No, it is a mountain. See how the middle peak towers over the other two?"

I was entranced. Of course, that made perfect sense. If this was all there was to reading and writing, then it was nothing. I was delighted.

"That's easy," I said confidently. "Are all kanji as simple as this? Show me some more."

"You only know four words, Mi-san." Gen's voice trembled with laughter. "I told you, children must learn over a thousand kanji. Once they have mastered those, there are many more to learn. And some kanji sound the same, but are written differently. Also, some kanji look the same, but depending on what you are trying to say, they mean different things." He must have seen my unhappy expression as he went on quickly. "But you have done very well. In only a few moments, you have learned to read and write four kanji. I will show you more. I will put them on paper and tell you what they mean, and then you can copy them."

Gen had a fluid grace with the brush and ink. Next to him, I felt clumsy. I did not enjoy the sensation and retreated into a sulky silence. I copied his kanji grimly, all the time repeating the meanings to myself silently.

"Draw me the kanji for arrow, Mi-san."

Gen had been silent for a while and his voice startled me. *Arrow.* Yes, I remembered that. I drew it carefully and was annoyed when Gen shook his head.

"No, that is the kanji for misplacing something. Look." He brushed two kanji quickly on the paper and I stared at them. Reluctantly, I shook my head.

"They both look the same to me."

"Look closer. See—the difference is in the central stroke."

And so it was. I rubbed my hands over my eyes. After

staring at black kanji on white paper for so long, they felt gritty and painful. But I would not give in. I copied the arrow symbol again and then inspected it carefully. It would do.

Gen seemed to agree with me. "You have worked very hard, Mi-san, and learned a great deal. The kanji are very beautiful, aren't they? And they will be even more so when you can make sense of them. It will be worth it, I promise you."

I looked at my clumsy efforts alongside Gen's elegant script and wondered. Suddenly, I wanted to see kanji that meant something, that were not just odd words scattered on the page.

"Write something for me," I demanded. "Something that makes sense."

Gen paused, nibbling the end of his brush. Finally, he wrote something—it seemed to me with far more care than he had used before. None of the kanji were familiar to me. I waited for him to explain to me what he had written, and—grudgingly—asked when he remained silent.

"So? What does it say? Something nice?"

"I think it is something very beautiful."

Gen's voice was almost tender, as if he was speaking of something—or somebody—he loved. I was jealous. Not because of the unknown somebody, but because a few words scattered on a piece of paper could distract him so easily. With the emotion came a flash of insight far older than my years. If so much could be achieved by ink on paper, then this was a very important skill indeed. Perhaps even more important than learning how to make the abacus obey me.

Much as I hated it, I would master the art of reading

and writing. Not just a thousand kanji, but I would force every kanji that had ever been written to bow to my will.

"Tell me what it says," I demanded again. "Tell me what each kanji means."

"It doesn't work like that," Gen said apologetically. "The same kanji can mean something different entirely, depending on where it is placed. But I will tell you what it says. It is a haiku."

I had no idea what a haiku was. Something else that I must learn about. As Gen seemed to take it for granted that I knew, I stayed silent so as not to lose face in front of this mere messenger boy. Anyway, I would pick it up from his words. I would make sure of it.

Gen's voice was normally quite loud. I supposed it had to be in order to be heard over the constant murmur of voices around him. But now, he spoke softly, with a gentleness that surprised me.

"See the spring ocean,
Swaying gently too and fro,
All the whole day long."

"Isn't that beautiful?" he asked. I didn't answer at once. The words were pleasant enough, but I couldn't see that they meant anything much. Had they spoken of business, of the clash of abacus beads adding and subtracting, I would have liked them far better. But I didn't want to be rude, so I nodded.

"Lovely. Did you write it?"

Gen laughed so loudly I was startled.

"I could never compose anything as meaningful as that. No, it was written many, many years ago by a very famous poet named Yosa Buson. I will lend you a book of his poems. I know them all by heart, but when you can read better, you will enjoy them greatly."

"Thank you," I said dubiously. I doubted I would enjoy such silly ramblings, but if it helped me to read better, I would not refuse the offer. Besides, I now knew that a haiku was poetry, and the knowledge pleased me.

"Would you like to try and write a haiku, Mi-san?" Was he making fun of me? I glanced at Gen, but his expression was open and encouraging. "As you can see from this one, all haiku have seventeen syllables. Traditional haiku all comment on nature in some way." He must have seen my bored expression as he added quickly, "Hundreds of years ago, in the Haen period of our great history, all great ladies were experts in writing haiku. It was a talent that was viewed as essential as being able to play an instrument or sing. It's an odd thing, but I've noticed that many gaijin seem to love haiku."

I cared nothing for all the dead years that had gone by, but if the gaijin liked haiku, then I was determined to master the art. The mention of gaijin reminded me of Dickson-san. I felt that meeting him had been very fortunate for me. That it was because he had taken an interest in me that Father continued to bring me back to Edo. I stared hopefully at every gaijin who entered Father's place of business, but I never saw Dickson-san again.

Thinking of the gaijin brought an interesting question to my mind. Haiku could wait; this was something that required an answer.

"Perhaps I will try to compose a haiku later, when you have taught me to read and write properly. Tell me about the gaijin, Gen. They must be rich men or they would not be here, right?"

I meant, what were the gaijin doing in Japan? And what business did they conduct with Father? But I was so eager for the answer that the words tumbled out any old how. Gen seemed to understand what I meant.

"They come to Japan to trade with us. They think they are very wise, that they are far cleverer than we are, but really they are fools." Gen's voice had taken on a hard edge. I stared at him fascinated, wondering how he had come to learn so much at such an early age. He was surely no more than three or four years older than I was, but next to him, I felt as ignorant as one of the gaijin he dismissed so lightly.

"You know how they forced their way into our country? How they sailed their great iron ships into Edo harbor and demanded to be taken to see the shogun?" I had no idea what he was talking about, but I didn't want to disturb his train of thought, so I nodded anyway. "Before then, our beloved country had been sealed against the outside world for many hundreds of years. The shogun had no wish to change that, but he was a wise man and saw that we could not fight such powerful invaders. He promised the gaijin the world, then as soon as they left us in peace, he forgot all about them. But they came back the next year, with even more of their warships, and the shogun understood that they could not be put off.

"That was the very start of all the changes that have been imposed on us. The gaijin insisted that the emperor be restored to power. That the gaijin should be allowed to come and go as they pleased. And—the important thing for men such as Kono-san—that Japan must trade with the outside world once again."

He had spoken so passionately, he had to pause to

catch his breath. I was fascinated. All of this had happened before I had been born. I had no notion what life must have been like before the gaijin forced their way into our country. But it seemed to me that the one essential thing in all of this was that, somehow, it had been a good thing for Father. For his business. If that were the case, then I wanted to know how and why.

"I see. But why is all that so bad, Gen? If the gaijin who come to trade are stupid, then surely that is good for us? For Father, especially, as he does so much business with them."

"They have no place here." Gen almost spat the words. "They do not want to help us in any way. The only reason they forced us to open our country to them was because they thought they would be able to make money off us. That they would force us to take the goods they make while charging us the earth for them."

"We are not fools!" I interrupted indignantly. "How could they ever think we would take their goods? None of them can match the quality of things made here in Japan. What need do we have of anything the gaijin make?"

"If only that were so." Gen's temper had cooled. He looked at me consideringly, as if he was not sure it was worth explaining to me. I held his gaze unflinchingly until he spoke. "I told you we had had no contact with the rest of the world for many hundreds of years. Well, in that time, things had moved on everywhere else, but not here in Japan. We had no idea of any of that until the gaijin came with their great, black ships. We had nothing like those ships, Mi-san. Nor did we have the weapons the gaijin possessed. Nor things they clearly took for granted—the great power that could be achieved with something as simple as steam. The ability to navigate across oceans. The means of communicating across great distances, as if by magic. Great factories that produced more in a day with just a few men than a thousand of our men could make in a year. Even medicine that could heal things we had no cure for. We knew nothing of any of it. So great were their weapons that they could have mown us all down like stalks of rice falling before a sickle and thought nothing of it.

"The shogun had no choice but to appear to bow down to the gaijin, and they were pleased. They came in the thousands. But in spite of their great knowledge, they were really fools. We took the things they wanted to sell us, and then we took them apart to see how they worked. And we sold them our goods in return. The gaijin want things that have no power. Pretty things. So we sell them what they want—pearls and jade and ivory trinkets and boxes crafted from gold and silver. Things that part them from their cash but do not matter to us in the least.

"And the gaijin are pleased. They think they have achieved what they wanted—they have a new market for the goods that they churn out by the million. They think we have bowed down to their might and given up."

"We have not!"

I could contain myself no longer. I had thought Dickson-san to be a nice man. Now I knew he was no more than a monster in human form. I was furious with myself for being taken in by him. For a moment, I even thought of throwing my Victoria down the well, but then I reconsidered. Father said it was valuable. Where was the sense in discarding something like that for the principle of the thing?

"Quite right." Gen smiled. "All the time, the gaijin thought they had us under their power, but secretly we were learning to fight fire with fire. We smiled at them and bowed and were polite to their faces. And they were greatly flattered and agreed to allow our brightest young men to go to their countries and learn their ways. Doesn't that just show you how stupid they are? Those young men came back here, not just with the secrets of the gaijin's weapons, but also the understanding of how their great machines worked. So now, we are beginning to make the things the gaijin want to sell to us for ourselves. Because we are clever, we make them for less cost than the gaijin can. We no longer need to buy their machines and their weapons. In years to come, we will be great again, Mi-chan. Then we will achieve our rightful place in the world again. Japan will tell the gaijin what to do, and they will obey us. They will have no choice."

"Yes!" I was so enthralled with his words that I didn't even reprove him for calling me Mi-chan.

Also, I was pleased for another reason entirely. Today had been a great day for me. I had not only begun to read and write, but I had learned a great deal about the world of business. Things I'd had no idea about yesterday.

Smugly, I wondered if my idle brothers either knew or cared about all I now knew. I doubted it. They were fools, I decided.

I was not a fool.

Yet two things still nagged at me. One could wait for another day, but the other concerned me.

"It seems to me that Father shows the gaijin great favor." I hesitated, choosing my words carefully. "If what you say about them is true, surely that is not a good thing?"

For as long as I
Can see and hear, then surely
I will learn each day

Gen stared at me as if I had suddenly appeared from nowhere. I was so bewildered by the way he was looking at me that I put my hand out and touched his sleeve timidly.

My touch recalled him to the moment, called him back from wherever his thoughts had taken him. Surely, far away! He smiled—a polite sort of smile that had no warmth in it.

"I am so sorry, Mi-san." His voice was suddenly formal, almost groveling, as if he had suddenly recalled that he was a mere messenger and I was his employer's favored daughter. "I forgot myself for a moment. What was it you asked me?"

"You were talking about Father," I reminded him. "If the gaijin are bad for our country, is it good that Father does so much trade with them?"

"Oh, yes. Most certainly." Gen's answer was so prompt and stiff I doubted it could be true. "Your honorable father takes a great deal of money off the foolish gaijin, money they use to buy expensive trinkets from us. Naturally, that has to be good."

There was something odd about his reply, but I could not work out what. I decided at once that the fault was mine and I had been foolish to ask. Father was an honorable man. Anything he did must also be honorable.

"I understand." I glanced down at the brush, still in my hand. "Will you teach me some more kanji, please?"

"It must be nearly time to eat, and I'm certain there will be many slips building up for me to enter into the ledger. Perhaps it would be better if you were to eat and then help Tanaka-san. We can continue next time you are here, and you can take the kanji we have written this morning home with you to study."

Gen spoke very humbly. So how did I know that even if I argued with him I would not be able to change his mind? I didn't bother. Instead, I gathered up my papers and—almost as an afterthought—a stoppered jar of ink and my brush. I would practice with the hated kanji until I could write them perfectly. Next time, I would learn more.

Tanaka-san found me an absent companion that afternoon. My thoughts were on what Gen had said, and when a gaijin I had never seen before was ushered into my father's private office as if he was the most important of men, I wondered all over again.

But I was very young, and my life—hitherto without incidence—had taken such an exciting turn that I quickly forgot about my worries.

Once a week—sometimes more, if business was quiet —I was taken to the office to work with Tanaka-san and

Gen. To my surprise, I found the allure of the abacus no longer held me in its spell. Doing sums with the flying beads was too easy. Even Tanaka-san admitted I was as fast and as accurate as any of the clerks and he could teach me nothing more. But reading and writing, that was different. That was difficult, and I was determined it would not beat me.

Gen and I were no longer allowed the privacy of the archive. Tanaka-san shook his head regretfully but was firm.

"I am sorry, Mi-san. When you used it the first time, a number of important papers became disordered because they could not be filed at once. That cannot be allowed to happen again. But I have made a space for you and Gen in the corner there, where you will not be disturbed."

The loss of the archive bothered me not at all—I knew its secrets now and it had nothing else to teach me. But I was put out by the thought that Gen could be called away from me at any moment.

And he was, often. One morning he was gone longer than usual. When he returned from collecting papers from the ever-busy clerks, he sat down again and scratched his head.

"Now, where were we, Mi-san? I've lost track."

I pointed silently at my paper, where I had been practicing writing the last kanji he had taught me.

"Excellent. You have quite a neat hand with the brush."

"Perhaps so, but how am I supposed to learn when you keep getting called away?" I was annoyed and wanted him to know it.

Gen raised his shoulders helplessly. "I must do as I am told, Mi-san. Perhaps it would be better if Tanaka-san had a word with your father and persuaded him to hire a professional tutor for you. That way you could learn undisturbed, at home."

I suppose the words were meant kindly, but I was appalled. Do away with the joy of coming into Edo with Father? Lose the immense pleasure of watching his world? And—I was near to tears at the thought—above all, lose the time I spent with the worldly-wise Gen, who knew so much more than I even understood? And although I could hardly bear to admit it, I was deeply hurt by his offhand words. I had thought Gen was my friend, but here he was casually suggesting that I would be better off at home!

I was so wounded by the thought that I lashed out blindly, without thinking. "I expect you're right. After all, you're nothing but a messenger. I don't really know why Tanaka-san thought you could teach me properly."

Gen was quiet for so long that I was on the verge of apologizing for my outburst. As whatever I said would doubtless have made things worse, it was probably best that I stayed silent.

"You are quite right, Mi-san." He stood and bowed formally. Although he did not move, it was suddenly as if there was a great space between us. "Naturally, you would not want to learn from a mere nobody. I will tell Tanaka-san that there is no more that I can teach you and that you deserve a real teacher. I believe one of the clerks is trying to attract my attention, I must go. Perhaps you would like to practice the kanji I have showed you today."

Gen bowed again and then walked away. I couldn't see a clerk trying to attract his attention, but he went up to the archive anyway. I wanted to go with him, to be able to touch the wonderful ledgers with their history of wealth. I might not be able to understand their contents, but I was already beginning to think of them as not just records of money, but almost of money itself.

I was angry with Gen but could do nothing about it, which made me even more angry. Finally, I decided that rather than have Gen speak to Tanaka-san, I would speak to him myself and tell him that I did not feel Gen was teaching me at all well. That I would prefer somebody older, somebody in a superior position, to teach me. I was rather pleased with my solution. I would still be able to come to work with Father, and I could continue to learn without having to put up with Gen's rudeness. It would also reflect badly on Gen. I knew I was being spiteful, but I was hurt and wanted my revenge.

I was surprised by Tanaka's reaction. He seemed very startled and I recalled—too late—Gen insisting that he was Tanaka's favorite.

"If that is what you want, Mi-san. But I can assure you that Gen is a master of the brush. There is nobody here who can read and write better than he can."

I was astonished. Gen was only a little older than I was, and nothing but a messenger. How could this be so?

"Why is he only a messenger, then?" I demanded.

"Everybody must make a beginning," Tanaka said reasonably. "Gen's late father was a calligrapher—the very best in Edo. His workmanship with the brush was exquisite. He did a great deal of work for your honorable father over the years. Fortunately, he passed on his skills to Gen."

"So why didn't Gen become a calligrapher?" I hid my remorse behind a mask of disdain.

"He didn't want to follow his father." Tanaka shrugged. "It is often the case with young men these days. What was good enough for their father is not good enough for them."

I was sure he glanced slyly at my brothers, who were sitting idly and staring into space. I felt a slow, deep blush spread across my cheeks. I longed to defend Gen—he was not a lazy boy, like my brothers. He was willing to work. He had not even shied away from teaching a sulky, ungrateful girl child to read and write. But after my decision, how could I say that?

"So, Gen became a messenger for my father instead?" I said lamely.

"He came to Kono-san after his father died and begged to be taken on here in any capacity that was available. At the time, your father had no need for any more staff, but he agreed to employ Gen both because he respected his late father and because he felt the boy was very intelligent and eventually would be an asset to his business. I think that will be so, if Gen can tear his thoughts away from all his nonsense about politics."

"Oh." Gen had not been bragging, then. It appeared that both Tanaka and my father thought well of him. "In that case, perhaps I was too hasty in saying I wanted somebody else to teach me to read and write. I will be pleased for Gen-san to help me. If he wants to."

"I will speak to him tomorrow," Tanaka said kindly. There was a distinct twinkle in his eyes that made me blush even more. "I'm sure he will be delighted to continue to teach you. He told me after your first lesson that he had never known anybody more determined to learn than you were. He even said that in his opinion, it was a great pity that you had been born a girl and not a boy."

For some reason, I was not at all pleased by the great compliment that Gen had paid me.

Had I known what was waiting for me before I would see Gen again, perhaps I would have appreciated his words a little more. But I did not, and no man—or woman—can see the future. I rode home in front of Father, humming happily to myself, clutching my papers and inkpot and brush tightly against my chest.

I regretted speaking to Gen as I had. Kindly, I decided I would take him to one side the very next time I saw him and apologize for my hasty words. Naturally, had I known he was truly a master of the art of writing and reading, I never would have spoken to him so hastily. I would tell him that I was wrong and ask him if he would continue to teach me.

Reluctantly, I admitted to myself that part of my decision was pure selfishness. I really did not want to have a stuffy, old tutor to teach me. It would not be nearly as enjoyable as learning from Gen, who was nearly my own age and knew so many, many things about the world that I did not. Besides, was it possible that if Father did get a tutor for me, he would forget about taking me with him to Edo and leave me at home to my instructions? The idea filled me with panic, and the knowledge that if it did come to be it would be all my own fault was no comfort at all.

This could not be. I would not let it happen. I would seek out Gen as soon as I possibly could and apologize most humbly to him. I was sure he enjoyed teaching me, and even if I was wrong, would he really want to disappoint his employer's daughter?

Of course not. Having decided my course of action, I set my worries aside and concentrated on enjoying the ride home.

I was so happy, I had even forgotten that it was my birthday very soon, and because I had forgotten about it for the first time in many years, I did not dread the event.

Ironically, it was also the only birthday that I can—even now—remember nothing at all about, good or bad.

It was the birthday when the most dreadful thing happened to me, and after that, nothing in my life was the same ever again.

Hide from me while I
Count the heartbeats until I
Must start to seek you

My amah said that summer was going to be very hot. I was too old to still need an amah, but Anzu had been my brothers' amah before I was born, and she had been about the house for so long I suppose it was taken for granted that she should be there. In any event, it had never occurred to anybody to either send her away or find her another job.

Anzu tended to ramble on, so I nodded absently, barely listening to her as I waited to see if Father would summon me. When I heard the sound of his horse clattering away—the shoji had been left open in the hope of catching any breeze that arose—I sighed and paid her some attention. I had nothing else to do.

"How do you know it's going to be hot this summer?" I asked lazily. "It seems the same as last year to me."

"Oh no, Mi-san, it's much hotter already. The river is

very low, and the kitchen maids say the well water is so low they have to put a large stone in the bucket to weigh it down to get any water in it."

In spite of the fact that she had cared for me since the day I had been born, Anzu was still stiffly formal in my presence. She did everything for me, from bringing my meals to hanging up my clothes and soaping and rinsing me before the bath. I liked her well enough, except when she wanted to chatter about nothing at all, and then I quickly became irritated with her. One day, when I had been very bored, I had tried to show her how the abacus worked, and she had reduced me to fury in moments with her total bewilderment. Now I shrugged and answered absently.

"Oh, I daresay it will be hot this year, then."

It meant nothing to me. As far as I was concerned, all the days when I did not accompany Father to Edo were dross. I spent my time copying the kanji Gen had left me with over and over again until I was sure they were perfect. Only then did I allow myself the pleasure of playing on my biwa or doing increasingly complex calculations on the abacus for my own amusement.

Whatever I did, Anzu watched me with breathless admiration. I realized how much I missed Edo when I found myself wishing that Gen had ever given me a fraction as much praise as she did. Even more did I long for Father to acknowledge that I was useful. Tanaka-san said that I was as quick on the abacus as even the best of Father's clerks, and perhaps even more accurate. Had he, I wondered, mentioned that to Father?

If he had, Father did not speak to me of it.

There was no reason for me to be hurt by his silence. As far back as I could remember, Father had been a quiet sort of man. Naturally, I did not see him that often at home. If he was back from Edo in time, the whole family took the evening meal together—unless Mother was feeling unwell, which was often the case, and then she chose to eat alone in her apartment. Father ate in silence, acknowledging any comment either of my brothers made with a nod of his head or a grunt.

The day after my disagreement with Gen seemed like any other. Mother did not join us for the evening meal. It made little difference. When she did eat with us, she was generally quiet, concentrating on her food rather than joining in the conversation. I, of course, was not expected to speak.

For some reason, Father did not like to have the servants present during a family meal, so I handed round the dishes they had left when one of my menfolk asked for something, and I made sure the tea bowls were full. In between, I ate my own food quickly before it went cold.

But I listened. Carefully. Young as I was, it seemed to me that my brothers were much given to idle chatter. Both of them were very fond of sumo wrestling and often spoke of bouts they had seen or how their favorite wrestler was performing. Father—as politeness demanded—appeared to listen but rarely commented. But now and then, even his patience was exhausted and he would demand abruptly how much cash Ichiro had lost betting on the wrestling matches.

Whenever that happened, a dreadful silence would fall in the room. Ichiro and Satoru would exchange glances until one or the other of them—usually Ichiro, who held the responsibility of being the eldest son—would reply meekly.

"Honored Father, the whole world attends sumo

matches. It is an excellent place to make contacts. Naturally, one has to place a bet now and then. If one did not, then the other patrons would think we were short of money, and that would mean loss of face for the family business."

It was a smooth answer, and generally Father chose not to question it. But now and then he persisted, and both my brothers would eat the rest of their meal in sulky silence.

That day, Satoru had, I think, taken too much sake after his meal. He had become loud and boastful, talking of how he had persuaded a foolish gaijin to borrow a large amount of money to buy inferior pearls from one of Satoru's cronies.

Father heard him out quietly and then spoke calmly and softly. Even so, his words bit like a sword-blade.

"It is you who is the fool, Satoru. The gaijin will find out he has been duped and he will not trade with us again. Even worse, he will advise his fellow gaijin not to trade with us. You may have made money on one transaction, but you will lose it ten times over in future trade."

I was so startled by Father's bluntness—to call his son a fool was a deadly insult and very uncharacteristic of him—I was quite frightened and dropped my chopsticks. I was grateful for the diversion. It meant I could pretend to search for them and not look at the men.

"Father..." Satoru began to protest and then thought better of it. Instead, he held his sake cup up, clearly expecting me to jump up and fill it.

"I think you have had enough to drink, Satoru-san." Father spoke so formally, I understood he was very angry. "And in the future, if you want anything to eat or drink, then either get it yourself or call for a servant. Mi-chan has better things to do with her time than serve you two."

My brothers glanced at each other, and Ichiro shrugged fractionally. I recognized the message that passed between them. *Oh, Father is annoyed with us over nothing. Smile and nod and all will be well.*

But they were wrong.

Father stared at both of his sons, then turned to me and spoke so abruptly I was startled.

"How many clerks do I employ, Mi-chan?"

I was relieved the question was easy and answered quickly.

"Not counting Tanaka-san or the messenger boys, you have thirty-two clerks, Father."

"And if I gave you an abacus and told you how much I paid each clerk each day, would you be able to tell me how much the salary bill was for all of them each year?"

"Of course, Father." I was mystified but replied promptly. Father nodded and then turned to face his sons. His voice was very even when he spoke.

"Ichiro-san, Satoru-san, did either of you know how many clerks I employ?"

"Of course, Father," Ichiro spoke quickly, smiling as if it was a foolish question. "And I think Mi-chan is wrong. I believe the number is thirty-three."

It was Ichiro who was wrong, not me, but I dared not correct him. Father did it for me.

"Mi-chan is correct," he said sharply. "Could either of you calculate their yearly salaries?"

"Given an abacus, naturally," Satoru said.

Ichiro had become very sullen. He reached across for the warming vessel and helped himself to more sake. He filled the cup to the brim and exclaimed angrily when a few drops fell on his robe.

"I could do it easily. But as I do not have an abacus at hand ..." He shrugged and sipped his sake.

The silence lingered for so long I began to be frightened. I stared at my bowl, longing to eat but not daring to move. Finally, Father sighed and shook his head.

"Do either of you know that Mi-chan is learning to read and write? Tanaka-san tells me that she is an apt pupil and shows great determination in pursuing her studies."

Satoru stared at me as if he had never seen me before. Finally, he threw back his head and laughed.

"Why? Why would a betrothed girl ever want to learn to read and write? Mi must surely have inherited her talent with the abacus from you, Father. And naturally, it is always useful to have another clerk, particularly an unpaid one. But a woman who can read and write? What's the point? When she marries Yuto-san, he will knock all that nonsense out of her head."

My spirits had been soaring high. Tanaka-san had spoken to Father. And Father had, in his own quiet way, complimented me on my achievement. I was so happy I almost cried with pride. So very happy that even the mention of Yuto could not depress me.

But the moment was snatched from me almost before I had time to savor it.

"I suppose you are right, my son." Father sighed and picked up his bowl. His anger was always as quickly forgotten as it was infrequent, and this evening was no exception. "But it is a great shame that Mi-chan was born a girl. Had she been a boy, then who knows what she might have achieved."

Both my brothers chuckled at the thought.

I ate my cold food miserably in spite of the great compliment Father had paid me. I had the beginnings of a headache—I supposed caused by the argument—and was pleased when dinner was over and I could go and lie down in my bedroom.

The night felt very sultry, and I tossed and turned on my futon, searching for a cool spot. Anzu might be right, I thought. The summer was probably going to be very hot.

I never found out if she was correct or not.

TWELVE

With great age comes great
Wisdom. But I will not wait for
My old age to learn

I did not sleep well that night. I blamed poor Anzu for telling me how hot it was going to be. I was certain if she had not put my mind to thinking about the heat, I would not have noticed it so much.

As it was, I thrashed about until my kakebuton was a wrinkled mess. I was sticky and sweaty and thirsty. My thoughts flitted here and there and I could not quiet them. I wiped my hand over my forehead and stared in surprise when I found it came away wet. My headache was much worse as well. I was astonished. Apart from the time I dislocated my shoulder, I was never ill. In fact, Mother often sighed in despair about my robust good health, telling me it was unnatural for a girl to be so healthy. Girls should be delicate and need to be taken care of by their husbands.

Yuto-san, she said, would undoubtedly expect me to be

fragile and dependent on him. It was the man's place to be strong, not the wife's. I agreed with her, as was only polite, and did my best to look frail whenever I was in her presence.

I thought wryly that Mother would be proud of me at the moment. I needed a drink of water. I turned over and tried to get up, only to fall back on my futon with a thud when my back and neck felt too stiff to bend. I wanted to call out to Anzu, but I could make no more noise than a very small kitten mewing.

Still, I was not greatly alarmed. Whatever I had would pass, I was sure. Perhaps it had been the argument between Father and my brothers that had upset me. I lay back down, watching the shadows on the ceiling until morning came. Anzu came in as always at first light to call me to the bath. I croaked at her—by then my fever was so bad I had no idea what I was saying—and she made a small sound of distress and crouched down by my side.

"Mi-san!" How very high-pitched her voice was. It drilled through my head and gave me great pain. "What is it? What is the matter?"

When I tried to speak, my teeth chattered together as if I was very cold. But I was not cold, I was hotter than I had ever been in my life. Anzu put her hand cautiously on my forehead. Her touch increased my pain still further and I shrieked at her not to touch me.

"Can you stand up, Mi-san?" Anzu's eyes were huge, her lips puckering nervously. I managed to shake my head and she stood up and backed away from me. A moment ago, I had wanted her to go away. Now, I plucked at the air, trying to tell her to stay, not to leave me. "I will get some help, Mi-san. Kono-san has not yet left. I will ask him to come and see you."

I longed to be able to speak, to tell Anzu not to bother Father. If he took the time to come and see me, he would be late getting to Edo. I was not important enough to delay him. The thought made me want to cry, but I was finding it difficult to breathe and I could not find the strength to tell Anzu not to go.

I can remember Father standing over me. He asked me questions—I think he asked how I felt. Did I have any pain?—But I could not answer him. My vision was wavering, but I was aware that Father had gone away and then he came back, literally pushing Mother in front of him.

"What is wrong with her?" he demanded. "Is she very ill? Would it be best to send for a physician to treat her?"

I can remember to this day the sensation of shock I felt at my father asking Mother for advice. It was then that I understood how very ill I must be.

Father stood at the side of my futon, looking down at me. How very tall he was. He towered over me like a tree. Mother was at his side for no more than a moment, then she backed away, her hands held out in front of her as if warding off an evil spirit.

"Look at her!" she shrieked. "She is burning with fever. She can barely breathe. Can you move?"

I realized Mother was talking to me and expected an answer. With an effort that made my chest hurt, I drew a breath, but no matter how I tried, all the sound I could make was a croak. A frog could have made more noise. Still, I tried. I managed to lift my arm a hand's width from the futon, but lacked the strength to hold it there and it fell back at once.

"Look! She's nearly paralyzed as well! We must get away from her. Now!"

Father caught her arm and held her in place. "She is

very ill. I can see that. But what is it? Do you know what is the matter with our daughter, Emica-chan? If you do, tell me at once."

There was such concern in Father's voice that I longed to speak to reassure him. This was surely nothing more than a summer chill. Mother had caught Anzu's hysteria. I would be fine in a day or two.

"She has paralysis of the morning. I have seen it before. It can kill her." Mother's voice was a screech. It pierced my head and suddenly I wanted to vomit. That would never do. I swallowed and forced the nausea down with an effort of will that left me shaking even more. "We must leave her. She can pass it on to us, and everybody knows the disease is much worse for adults than it is for younger people. She could kill us as well as herself, I tell you."

Mother tore herself from Father's grasp with surprising strength. She was gone in a moment. My vision had become very dark. I thought sweat had got into my eyes. Father was no more than an outline. I heard him instructing Anzu to send for the physician at once and I wanted to both thank him for his kindness and beg him to go to Edo immediately. The family business was far more important than any illness I might have picked up.

After that, my world became very strange.

I had pain. Much pain, especially in my legs. It was difficult to breathe. I could hear my breath rasping in my chest, but I did not understand that it was me who was making the noise. There were many times when I thought my last breath really was going to be my last breath, and when that happened, Anzu put her hands on my breast bone and pushed rhythmically for a very long time, until she was panting for breath herself from the effort. It made me very sore, but it helped me to breathe, and if I had been able to speak, I would have thanked her. As I could not, I held the regret inside me and prayed that the day would come when I could tell Anzu that I was truly grateful for all she had done for me. I had been an ungrateful child. I had taken her attention for granted just as much as my brothers had done, and that made me deeply unhappy.

I was vaguely aware that the physician had arrived. It was the same man who had put my shoulder right when I dislocated it. He had been kind, I remembered. He was kind now, but his voice was very grave, and I wondered if perhaps I was going to die. I was so ill and in so much pain that the thought did not seem at all dreadful. Anzu clearly thought it was—she sobbed constantly from the moment the physician began to speak until he left. Father must have been there as well, as I recall hearing his voice.

But he should not have been at home. His place was in Edo, meeting clients and overseeing the workplace. Without him, my brothers would do as they liked. Even Tanaka-san would not be able to control them. And if the business failed, then it would be my fault. The knowledge made me weep, but I had such a high fever the tears went unnoticed on my face.

"I am sorry, Kono-san. Mi has morning paralysis, as your wife thought. There is nothing that can be done at this stage. If she survives, then we will see. She is a very healthy child usually. There is hope for her."

Both men walked away from me, and I could hear their voices as if from a distance. Only one thing stayed with me —*if* I survived? How could this be so? I was young. I had my whole life before me. Suddenly, for no reason at all, I thought of my betrothed, Yuto. He had never shown any interest in me. Would he be pleased if I died? I was sure his mother would be—she could then choose him a bride who was more to her liking. Ridiculously, the knowledge made me determined that I would not die.

I would not give the dreadful Yuto and his mother such satisfaction. I would live if just to spite the pair of them. I must have muttered something out loud, as Father came back and looked down at me. His voice echoed my thoughts.

"Mi-chan will not die," he said calmly. "She is too strong. Too determined. She is my daughter and the best of all my children. Do what you can to help her, please."

Even though my thoughts were flying like leaves in the autumn wind, I grasped Father's words to me and held them tightly, feeling my chest ease with the joy they gave me. He was right. I would not die. I would not allow myself to die.

I would live, and not just to annoy Yuto and his mother. I would live to please Father, and myself.

The physician's voice was very quiet as he replied. "Paralysis of the morning is a dreadful disease. We have no idea what causes it, or why it is most often caught by children. I must warn you, if Mi-chan survives, she will be very fortunate. And the disease may well cause lingering problems. In any event, until the fever breaks, I can do nothing but give her opium to relieve her pain. She must drink plenty of water." He paused, and in a moment of clarity, a memory from what seemed long ago came to me—something Anzu had said about the water in the well being so low that the bucket had to be weighed down before it would bring up any water. It seemed to me that the house water had tasted nasty for some time, and suddenly I did not want to drink any more of that water.

"Tea," I rasped. Both Father and the physician went

quiet, and I felt them staring at me in astonishment. "Please, tea. Not water. The water is bad."

My tongue dried then and I could say no more. But I heard Father chuckle softly and then what he said to the physician before my fever took me and I sank beneath it.

"You see? This illness will not claim Mi-chan. She will not allow it to get the better of her. I am proud of her."

I was very happy.

I was not going to die, and even better, Father was proud of me. What more could I ask of this life?

THIRTEEN

Will the sun still rise
And the birds still sing if I
Do not know of them?

I had no way of knowing if Anzu's prediction about the heat of the summer was correct or not.

It seemed to me that I slept deeply. My dreams were bad for the whole of that long, long night. There was pain, pain that almost—but never quite—brought me to full wakefulness. I couldn't understand it, but whenever the pain got so bad that I screamed in my sleep, somebody held a cup of hot liquid to my lips and kept it there until I drank it. The liquid tasted almost like tea but carried an undertone of sweet muskiness that helped it to slip down my throat easily. After a while, I began to like the strange tea very much, as when I drank it the pain went away, for a while at least.

Apart from the pain, there was also terror. People loomed over me, staring down at me with worried faces. People I knew well, but who were somehow distorted.

Their familiar faces wavering until, had I had enough breath, I would have begged them to keep still. Father and Anzu, even on one occasion Mother. Other people I thought I recognized but who I could never quite put a name to. I desperately wanted all these visitors to speak to me, but they never did. Occasionally, I heard them whispering when they moved away from my futon, and I tried so very hard to call out to them, to ask them to tell me what they were saying, but they never did.

Anzu was my constant companion. Whenever I clawed my way up from the depths of my sleep, I knew she was at my side without opening my eyes. I could smell her. Always she carried with her a sweet, rather musky odor that recalled memories I had thought long forgotten. Memories of the time when I was very, very young when she would sing nonsense rhymes to me and coax me to eat my rice when I wanted nothing more than to be out in the bright sunshine. If I had resented her preventing me from escaping then, now I hated her for it.

In my muddy thoughts, I was sure that it was Anzu who was keeping me beneath my kakebuton when I wanted to throw it off and run outside into the sweet fresh air. I know I fought her sometimes, pushing and shoving at her to throw her to one side and weeping at my own pathetic lack of strength.

Far, far worse was being washed from head to toe by my faithful amah. The touch of the wet sponge was hateful. It made my skin burn as if the sponge had been dipped in boiling water. It was agony when she turned me over. I wanted her to go away, to leave me alone. What did it matter if I went unwashed for a single day? When I awoke from this terrible dream, I would visit the bathhouse and let the hot water wash away my dirt.

And more terrible than anything were the occasions when I half-awoke and found I was lying on a wet patch. I knew my bladder had betrayed me in my sleep when that happened and I cried and cried, hating the weakness that had caused me to become a helpless babe again. I hated it even more when Anzu rolled me over gently and pulled my bedding from beneath me, somehow tugging me back when she had replaced the soiled shikibuton with a fresh one smelling deliciously of jako.

Anzu was at my side whenever I cried out, whenever I so much as opened my eyes. She must, I thought, be sleeping at the foot of my futon for her to be with me so promptly. I found the knowledge disturbing, as I couldn't understand why she felt the need to be close to me again, as she had been when I was a young child.

It was a long night. A night that was so very long that even in my confusion I began to wonder if something was very wrong. But the thought never stayed long enough to take root as the fever claimed me time and time again and I slipped away into its hot, demanding grip.

Mine was not a sudden awakening. Rather, very gradually, I became aware of who I was once again. I felt light on my closed eyelids. Light that lacked the intense, humid heat of summer. Light that sat easily on my sore eyelids and felt soothing. I wanted to open my eyes, and that surprised me.

It seemed to me that during the long night that I had been asleep it had been far better to keep my eyes closed in case the monsters that had chased me in my sleep were actually there at my side. But now, the temptation called to me, and I took my courage in my hands and tried to open my closed lids.

But I could not. My eyes were sealed shut, and no

amount of effort could pry them apart. I found this deeply distressing and I cried out loud. I was startled by the sound of my own voice. It was so high-pitched, I thought it was the cry of a seagull battling against the wind.

"Mi-chan, lie still." Anzu's voice. But not the annoying, persistent voice that had echoed in my dreams. She sounded firm, almost commanding. I wanted to laugh at her overbearing tone, but suddenly I found it was an effort to breathe, and I had to concentrate on that instead.

I was annoyed. This would not do at all. With a huge effort, I forced air into my lungs and spoke in a rush, my words running into each other in my haste to get them out while I still could.

"Anzu, is it morning? Have I overslept? Has Father gone to Edo without me?"

"It is morning, Mi-chan. You have slept for a very long time, but do not worry. You have been very ill, but you will get better now."

Something hot and wet dripped on my face. I licked it away with my tongue and it was salty. For a moment, my memory refused to tell me what it was, then I understood from the huskiness of her voice that Anzu was crying, and it was her tears that were falling on my face.

I was bewildered, but still one thing above all was important to me and I persisted. "Has Father gone, Anzu? Did he ask for me?"

"Kono-san has not been here for some time, Mi-chan. You...you have been asleep for a very long time. Be still. I will send a messenger for the physician, and I will bring you some tea. Would you like something to eat?"

Her tone was the soothing coo of a mother comforting a very small child. I was bewildered—what need did I have of a physician? I rubbed my eyes fiercely, but still I could see nothing. Suddenly, I understood Anzu's concern. Somehow, I had gone blind in the night. That was why she wanted the physician to attend me.

"Anzu! I cannot see! What has happened?"

Anzu clucked at me—it was a sound of distress I had heard many times over the years. It was the noise she reserved for when I worried her. When I insisted on going out on my pony when a storm threatened. When I returned home and showed her a particularly bad graze or cut. Suddenly, I remembered her making that noise on the day I had dislocated my shoulder so very long ago. Had I done something equally silly now, only this time to my eyes? I was distressed at the thought and rubbed my eyes fiercely.

"Mi-chan, keep still. I will help you."

I felt a warm, wet sponge being rubbed very gently across my eyes. I tried to blink again, but my eyes were still glued shut.

"You're not doing any good." I sounded petulant and I was immediately sorry. Anzu was clearly doing her best to help me.

I found that speaking the few words had left me short of breath and I was forced to keep quiet as Anzu scrubbed again and again at my eyes.

"Try and open your eyes again, Mi-chan," she said after a while.

I did as she instructed, but as soon as my eyes opened, I shut them again. The light was so very bright it was painful.

Anzu moaned with me and jerked to her feet. I could tell from the sound of her movements that she was pulling a shoji shut. She kneeled back at my side and spoke encouragingly.

"Try again, Mi-chan."

I opened my eyes a fraction at a time. They felt very gritty, and I rubbed at them carefully, feeling something brittle between my fingers. I was relieved. This had happened to me before. My eyes must have watered in my sleep and the tears had hardened and glued my eyes together. Anzu's sponge had solved the problem. I wanted to laugh out loud with delight at the ease of it—I was not blind. How very silly I had been to think something so bad could have happened to me.

I stared around in delight and then blinked.

The light was all wrong. Yesterday had been bright and sunny. The sun had set reluctantly, giving promise of another hot, clear day. But even through the shoji I could see that the weather was cloudy, and my bedroom was so cool I shivered and drew the kakebuton around my shoulders.

"I will leave you for just a moment." Anzu got to her feet and winced as her knee cracked. I stretched and winced with her as sympathetic pain shot through my left leg. "When I come back, I will bring you some tea."

I lay back and watched her scurry away, her feet making crisp patting noises on the woodblock floor.

While Anzu had been with me, I had resisted the desire to feel my body, particularly my left leg, which seemed to be lifeless. I knew she was watching my every move, and if I showed the least sign of distress, she would cluck over me like a mother hen, which in turn would annoy me and make me feel worse. I was sure there was something wrong with my leg. No matter how I tried to move it, I had no sensation in it. Had I laid on it too long and it had gone to sleep and not awakened with the rest of me? I supposed I must have had a restless night. My skin felt as if it was as wrinkled as my shikibuton, and my bones ached as if I had woken up an old woman.

It was silly, I knew, but as soon as Anzu had gone I was reluctant to even touch my left leg. Instead, I began with my face and started to work downward.

My face felt alright, although the skin seemed rather dry to me. My hair, on the other hand, felt horribly greasy. I would wash it carefully in the bath as soon as I rose, before I even thought about eating. I ran my hands down my body and was relieved to discover that my stomach seemed to be in good order.

Obviously, I had allowed my night frights to affect me far more than was good for me. I was smiling at my own foolishness as I stretched luxuriously. My right leg moved.

For all my efforts, the only thing my left thigh did was cramp. Hard. The pain was so unexpected and severe that I screamed.

FOURTEEN

I always thought that
Morning could heal bad dreams. But
Then I grew older

I couldn't scream for long. My breath emptied from my lungs so quickly I was reduced to gasping for air.

But Anzu heard me and came back as fast as her kimono would allow her to run. She knelt at my side, forcing me to lie down with gentle strength, and began to knead rhythmically at my chest.

"Slowly, Mi-chan. Take slow breaths. Do not try and gulp for air." Her voice was so commanding I automatically did as she instructed and, to my relief, I found I could breathe a little easier.

"Anzu, my leg. What's happened to it? It won't move and it hurts at the top when I try to force it. I can't feel the rest of it at all. It's as if it's not there. It was fine yesterday. What's happened to it?"

I was frightened and bewildered. How could this be? I had been a young, healthy girl when I went to bed last night. How was it possible that in that short time something had happened that had left me as weak and helpless as a mewling babe?

I stretched my leg again, but very cautiously, and immediately the cramp in my thigh came back tenfold. My lips stretched wide in a silent shriek and I forced myself to relax, feeling the pain ebb slowly, so very slowly, as the limb went back to where it wanted to be.

Panic flooded me. Tears clouded my eyes and I blinked them away frantically. I would not cry with my pain. Tears were for small children and their nursemaids. Tears were for Anzu. I would not show her such weakness. I took a deep, shaking breath—proud that I had managed it—and spoke with only the least amount of tremor in my voice.

"Anzu, I don't understand what has happened to me. I can't breathe properly. My leg...I can't feel most of it, not at all. I'm sweating—do I have some sort of fever?"

Anzu shook her head. She would not look at me, and I understood that something very terrible had come to me. I waited a heartbeat and then repeated my words.

"Anzu, tell me. What's happened to me?"

"I have sent for the physician, Mi-san," she whispered. "He is the right person to explain to you, not me. Please, allow me to get you some tea."

Anzu could be incredibly stubborn when she chose to be. I glared at her even though I knew full well she would not answer me. Very well. I would wait for the physician to arrive.

My lips were terribly dry. When I tried to lick them, my tongue felt too large for my mouth. I was starting to shake —no doubt with the shock of finding out that I was truly ill. I decided quickly that tea would be very welcome. I nodded at Anzu and she almost ran out of my bedroom.

Alas, the tea was a disappointment to me.

I inhaled the steam. I knew at once that it was not what I had expected and looked at it suspiciously. I recalled tea that was sweeter and more aromatic than this, with an under-taste that I had welcomed in my dreams.

"Drink it, Mi-san." Anzu was hovering anxiously, ready to take the bowl from me should I let it fall.

"It doesn't taste right," I said firmly.

I handed it back to her half-drunk. A moment later, I was glad I was no longer holding the delicate, porcelain bowl.

With no warning at all, I began to shake violently. I bit my tongue, hard, before I realized it was between my teeth. It hurt, but the hurt was nothing at all to the pain in all my joints. Everywhere hurt. My shoulder that I had dislocated so long ago felt as if it was on fire. My stomach cramped so violently I folded over on myself and I could feel my skin streaming with sweat.

What is happening to me? I thought I had shouted the words out loud, but I could see from Anzu's confused expression that I had said nothing. She wrapped the kakeb-uton around me and then put her own arms around my shoulders, holding me tightly and rocking me back and forth just as she had done when I had been a very small child who could not sleep for fear of the shadows dancing on the ceiling.

She stayed exactly where she was until the physician arrived, then let me go with obvious reluctance.

Either time or Anzu's attention had done some good by then. I was still soaked with sweat, but the pains in my poor body had subsided to a dull ache and my stomach cramps were no worse than the pain I had most months when my courses were due.

The physician barely glanced at me before he laid down his silk furoshiki and picked at the knot with his long fingernails. I watched him miserably, too sunk in self-pity to even speak.

"Anzu, get a fresh bowl of tea, and make sure it's hot. Quickly." As he spoke, he took out a pottery jar and shook it, obviously assessing the amount that was in it. "So, you have awoken at last, Mi-san. And very well you look, if I may say so."

He could say what he liked if he told me what was happening—what had already happened, I thought sourly. But my chattering teeth kept the rudeness behind my lips and prevented me from speaking.

Anzu must have run to the kitchen and back. She presented the tea bowl to the physician and he pulled out the stubborn cork from the jar with his teeth, spitting it neatly into the furoshiki. He took a long sip from the tea himself—*my tea!* I thought indignantly—and then topped up the bowl from the jar.

"Mi-san, drink this down quickly and you will soon feel a great deal better."

I sipped at the tea cautiously and, finding it far more to my taste than the weak brew Anzu had given me earlier, I gulped the rest of it down eagerly.

The physician stood smiling at me all the while. He was beginning to irritate me—so many questions I needed answering, and all he could do was stare at me—but suddenly a great tranquility began to wash over me. I smiled, then laughed out loud as I felt the remains of my pain recede. I lay back down and watched the outline of the tree outside my shoji flicker back and forth. The movement looked as lazy as I felt, and I wanted to congratulate the tree on our kinship.

"That tea is good. Can I have some more?" I asked.

I was disappointed when the physician shook his head. "No more at the moment. Later, when you have pain, Anzu will give you some." He glanced at Anzu and asked, "Do you still have some of the tincture?"

It seemed to me that Anzu was not at all happy, but she answered politely, with a downcast gaze. "Yes, sir, but only a little. Should I give Mi-san the same amount as before?"

"To begin with, yes. When your jar is empty, you may begin to give her a very little less each time. But be very careful. It would not do to give her too little too soon. If you find that the amount you are giving to her does not take away her pain fully, then go back to giving her the full dose at once. It may be a long time before she can manage without it. I will give you a full jar before I leave."

I stared from one to the other, baffled. Why were they talking about me as if I wasn't here? Perhaps he caught my puzzlement, as the doctor finally turned his attention to me. "Now, Mi-san, I am sure you find everything very odd. But you have been ill for a very long time, and that is only to be expected. I must congratulate you on your recovery. I was very worried about you."

I smiled at him. My pain had gone completely. Not only that, but I felt wonderful. My futon was as soft as a cloud, the air that I had found unpleasantly chilly earlier caressed me like a cool kiss. I stretched and wondered almost lazily why my leg had no feeling in it at all, as if it no longer belonged to my body. Never mind, that could wait. I must explain to the physician that he was wrong, that if I had really been ill, it had been only for a very short time.

"But I saw you only yesterday." How very long it took for the words to come out. When they did, I was sure I could see their shapes in colors on the air. How wonderful! "You were here with Father and Mother."

The faintest touch of alarm sounded in my mind. Mother, here? I was sure I had seen her. But if she had been in my apartment, then truly I must have been very ill. But if I had been very ill, what could have persuaded Mother to be close to me? The conundrum circulated in my mind for a moment and then vanished like smoke before a breeze. It didn't matter. Nothing mattered. I was so very content, so very *languid*. Yes, that was the word. Languid. I rolled it around my tongue and tasted it.

I was vaguely annoyed when the physician's voice broke in on my tranquility. But the moment was fleeting; I was too content to allow anything to disturb me.

"Can you hear me, Mi-san?" I realized that my eyes had closed, and it took a great effort for me to open them. And an even greater effort to nod. "Good. Now, please, listen to me very carefully. What I have to tell you is important. You did not see me yesterday. Or rather, I was here, but you were not aware of it. Do you understand?"

I smiled, wondering lazily what he was talking about. Of course I had seen him yesterday. I was delighted with myself when I managed to speak.

"Yes, I understand." I would agree to anything if it made him go away and stop nagging at me.

"Excellent. You have been ill for a very long time, Mi-san. What is the last thing you remember?"

That was easy enough. I remembered the physician, together with Father and Mother, all standing around my futon, looking down at me. Mother was very upset. The memory disturbed me, and I didn't want to think about it, but I supposed he would persist until I answered.

"You and Father and Mother."

"Good. And when was that?"

"Yesterday."

Even as I said the word, I knew it was wrong. Yesterday had been hot and sultry, with—as Anzu had forecast—the promise of a humid, over-heated summer to come. The very air had felt heavy and unpleasant. Now, my bedroom was crisp and cool. The sun shining through the shoji was at the wrong angle and was barely warm.

A shiver of doubt ran down my spine. I looked hopefully at the tea bowl, knowing instinctively that my salvation from all that was disturbing me lay in its depths.

"Listen to me, Mi-san." The physician was suddenly stern. I hunched my shoulders, trying to block out his voice. "You have been ill for a long time. It was spring when you were taken ill, now it is late autumn. You have had paralysis of the morning. You are very fortunate to be alive."

I could hear him still speaking, but I had to concentrate to not smile widely, which would have been inappropriate at that moment. I had been fortunate? Indeed, I had. But far more fortunate than the physician would ever understand.

My fifteenth birthday had come and gone, and I had survived without even knowing about it.

FIFTEEN

I will close my eyes
To the world and hope that it
Forgets I am here

I made my face serious until he had gone, apparently satisfied with me and pleased with himself. I had heard what he had to say, but little of it made sense to me. Later, when my mind was working properly, I would ask Anzu to explain the matter to me.

For now, the physician had exhausted me with his serious face and words. I wanted to sleep, deeply, with no dreams. And no pain.

But I could not.

The wonderful world I had entered such a short time ago had already given way to growing irritation. The soft breeze annoyed me. I was too hot, but as soon as I threw my kakebuton aside, I was too cold. A bird singing outside my shoji sounded shrill and its song threatened to give me a headache. I called for Anzu. I knew what would help me. I was very thirsty. I wanted some more tea, with some of the physician's magical tincture mixed with it.

I could hardly believe it when Anzu shook her head at my harmless request.

"Do you have any pain, Mi-san?" She kept her gaze on the tatami, but her voice was unexpectedly firm. I thought about it, then shook my head reluctantly. My leg still felt wrong, but I tried not to move it and I found that if I kept still, it didn't hurt, just felt strange. The only way I could explain it to myself was that it felt as if it wasn't my leg, as if it was foreign to my body. "Then I cannot give you any more opium. The physician said I was not to give you any unless you were hurting."

It was obvious that Anzu was lying to me. I was so startled that my wits sharpened and I began to regret not listening to all that the physician had told me. But no matter. I wanted more tea, and I was not going to let my own amah deny me.

"Anzu, I think you misunderstood him. I am thirsty. I want some tea. Tea with the tincture in it."

Anzu hesitated, then shook her head. Two red spots burned on her usually pale cheeks, and I stared at her in astonishment as she blurted, "Mi-san, I am sorry. I will give you some tea, of course. But it is not good for you to take too much opium. In fact, it is not good for you to take opium at all."

"Why not?"

It was a reasonable enough question. Most men indulged in opium from time to time. My brothers certainly did. I had smelled the sweet, seductive smell of opium pipes wafting out from their apartments from time to time. Although Father did not take opium himself, he had never forbidden my brothers. If Father did not think it was wrong, then surely there could be no harm in it for me.

But Anzu was having none of it. Her lips were set in a straight line, her expression stern.

"You have had paralysis of the morning for a long time, Mi-san."

I sighed impatiently. I knew that. Although I could still barely believe it, I supposed I had to accept it was so.

"And it has caused you to suffer very greatly. Without the opium, you would have had so much pain, it would have been very terrible for you."

My attention was caught at last. If what Anzu was saying was true, then I had surely been very brave. I was pleased with the knowledge and smiled graciously.

"Then it must be a good thing for me to have opium," I said slyly. "I know the physician left a fresh jar with you. Please, make me some opium tea, Anzu." When she did not move, I tried the effect of a little cry of pain. "Oh, but my leg hurts. Quickly, Anzu, get me my tea before it gets really bad."

She did not move. My temper began to rise and— unforgivably—I shouted at my loyal amah.

"Don't just stand there. I want some opium tea. Do as you're told, Anzu, or I will ask Father to move you to working in the kitchen."

"No."

The single word stopped me dead. I put my hand over my mouth, appalled with my behavior. This was my amah I was shouting at. The woman who had cared for me ever since I was old enough to leave my wet nurse. The woman who I knew had never left my side for more than a moment for the whole of my illness.

I began to tremble with remorse for my unspeakable

rudeness and also from the dawning of a hurtful knowledge. I understood that it was not the real me who had shouted at Anzu. Somehow, my longing for opium had turned me into a stranger to myself. It had blinded me to everything but my need for its sweet oblivion. It had turned me into a monster who thought of nothing but myself.

It was all so very unfair. Not only had I been desperately ill, but now it seemed I had been damaged by a drug I had neither wanted nor asked for. For a terrible moment, I thought I had gone blind as my vision wavered. Then, I understood that I was weeping.

Anzu knelt at my side at once and put her arms around me, rocking me back and forth just as she had done when I was much younger and had taken some minor hurt. I was finding it difficult to breathe again, but I forced myself to gasp out my apologies through my sobs.

"I am so sorry, Anzu. I don't understand what has happened to me. Is it my illness? Has it affected my mind?"

"No, Mi-san." Anzu spoke softly. Her mouth was so close to my ear that her words tickled and, in spite of everything, I wanted to giggle. "It's not you at all. It's the opium that has taken control of you."

Her words cut any desire to laugh dead. I was no longer in control of myself? Something outside of me had taken over my mind? This could not be so. I would not allow it to be so. I disentangled myself from her arms and pulled far enough away so I could see her face.

"Opium has taken control of me? How can this be so? I didn't even know I was taking opium."

Suddenly, I felt deeply unsure of myself. My thoughts reeled. I longed for just a sip of opium tincture. It would steady me, I knew. Enable me to gather my wits and discuss things sensibly. And it could not really be bad for me. The physician would not have told Anzu to give it to me if it was. Clearly, my naïve amah had misunderstood what he had said.

I was about to explain all that to Anzu when, with startling suddenness, I knew I was lying to myself just as much as I was prepared to lie to Anzu. I caught my breath with an effort and tried to gather my thoughts.

I ached in every joint and was nauseous. But above everything was the longing for opium. Just as it had done when I first awoke, I felt my whole body shriek its demand for the drug. My stomach hurt. My muscles cramped. I began to shake and was uncomfortably hot. As a further minor irritant, my nose began to run uncontrollably. When Anzu wiped my nose carefully with a large, cotton tenugui, the minor compassion made me burst into tears all over again.

"What's happening to me, Anzu?" I cried pitifully. "I don't understand. Lots of people take opium. I'm certain Mother takes a tincture of opium when she gets her headaches, but it has never hurt her. How has it come to claim me like this?"

Even as I spoke, I wondered if I could somehow use Anzu's pity to my advantage. Surely, if she could see how distressed I was, she would let me have some opium tea just once more? Once I was properly calm, I would have no further need of it, I was sure. It was the shock of being told that I had been ill for an entire summer, that I was fortunate not to have died, that was what was causing this terrible, gnawing need.

I was deeply relieved by the knowledge, but not for long. My illusions were broken cruelly by Anzu.

"You have had much pain, Mi-san. More pain than even

a strong man could bear. And you could not breathe; it was dreadful to listen to you fighting for air. The physician told me to give you opium the very first day he came to you. He said it would relieve your pain and relax you so that you could breathe better. I did not want to give you so very much, but…" She paused and licked her lips, obviously distressed. Finally, she spoke in a rush. "You cried out with the pain, night and day. It was not your fault, not at all. You were barely in the land of the living, and you had no idea you were calling out.

"After the first few days, Emica-san sent a maid to bring me to her. She shouted at me and said I was not doing my job properly. That I must keep you quiet. She said the noise you were making was unbearable and that soon she would be as ill as you seemed to be if you weren't kept quiet. She demanded to know if the physician had left any medicine for you, and when I told her he had given me a tincture of opium to relieve your pain, she became even angrier.

"'What? The doctor has given you opium for my daughter and she still cries out with pain? Clearly, you are not giving her enough. Double the dose. Give it to her whenever she begins to feel pain. I cannot be disturbed like this. If I do not get some rest, I will be far more ill than Mi.'

"I didn't dare go against your mother's wishes, Mi-san. So, I did as she told me and doubled the dose. Very soon I began to know when you were about to feel pain, so I gave you the tincture then, rather than waiting until you were hurting. I knew it was not good for you to take so much opium, but I had no choice. When I told the physician what Emica-san had instructed, he said it was the right thing to do." Tears were running down Anzu's face. She wiped them away with the back of her hand and I noticed absently how tiny and delicate her hands were. They were a lady's hands, not those of a servant. For some reason, the thought made my stomach constrict into a hard ball of sorrow. "They expected you to die, Mi-san, that was why nobody cared how much opium I gave you. I knew you would live, but nobody would listen to me. I'm sorry. It's all my fault that the opium has you enslaved. I should have been strong, just as you always have been, and given you just a little, just enough to ease your pain."

I concentrated on my breathing. I felt my chest labor with each breath I took and felt the relief when my lungs emptied. As I persisted, breathing became a little easier and I was able to concentrate on what Anzu was telling me.

Had I really been so very ill that I had been expected to die? And if that was so, how was it I was still on this earth? Anzu had said I was strong. If it weren't for the fact that I knew it would upset her, I would have laughed at the idea.

How could I be strong if the wretched opium had me enslaved? Suddenly, I felt very sorry for myself. I had not died, but was it any better to live with no will of my own? I was only a young girl, but I had lost so much time already. Was this to be the remainder of my life from now on, waiting and counting the moments until I could tell Anzu to bring me my "special" tea, caring for nothing else? Surely it would have been far better if the paralysis of the morning had killed me when I was young and happy with all my future before me.

I began to shake as the pain in my joints made me curl inward and I hugged myself in an effort to lessen it. Anzu stood up quickly.

"Emica-san and the physician are right, Mi-san. I am the most foolish of women to think I know better than them. I will bring you opium tea at once." She gabbled the words; her face contorted as if she shared my agony. "It will ease your pain. That is the most important thing."

My teeth were clattering together so hard I could not understand my own words. Neither could Anzu—she had turned and was halfway across the room. I tried again, louder.

"No. Stay here with me. I do not want any more opium. Ever."

Anzu flinched, her distress obvious. "But the opium will help you. Perhaps if you took just a little?"

"No." The word juddered abruptly from my lips. "No more. Never. Even if I ask you for opium, do not give it to me. Bring me tea, Anzu. Lots of tea. But just tea. You understand?" I saw hope dawning in her face and I managed a deep breath. "And then bring my abacus."

SIXTEEN

They say that cats purr
Even when they are in pain.
I will smile instead

I could see from her expression that Anzu thought my mind was wandering. I wondered myself, to be truthful.

She brought a full pot of tea for me, and I gulped bowl after bowl, desperate to conquer my raging thirst. When I had wrung the last drops from the pot, I set down my tea bowl regretfully and picked up my abacus in its place.

My hands were trembling. My sight was so blurred I could see both the abacus and a ghost of it as well. I placed my fingers firmly on what seemed to me to be the more solid of the two images and began to move the beads back and forth. I was appalled to find that I could recall nothing of how my abacus worked.

I paused and took the deliberate decision not to force my memory. For a while, I simply flicked the beads back and forth, allowing the soothing *click-click-click* to reassure me. Gradually, without any conscious effort on my part, I began to work on both levels of the abacus. Simple additions at first, and then—as my fingers remembered their forgotten skills—more complex subtractions and multiplications. When I reached the stage where I had to think to follow my calculations, I realized my breathing was easier. Even better, the pains in my joints had died away to a dull ache. I was quietly pleased. I guessed I had a long journey in front of me to throw off the grip of the opium, but if I had conquered it once, then I could do it again, and again, for as long as it took to be free.

But with the relief from acute pain came an annoying discomfort. All the tea I had drunk in such a hurry was demanding to be released. I needed to go to the lavatory, and quickly. The ordinariness of my need was pleasurable, a reminder that some things in my life had not changed. A distressing recollection of being so weak I had wet my futon stole into my mind, quickly followed by relief. Surely, I had to be getting back to health if I could worry about passing water in a proper manner?

I put my abacus down carefully and bunched up my legs, ready to rise. Immediately, I knew something was very wrong.

My balance gave way as soon as I tried to put any weight on my left leg. I put my hand down hurriedly to stop myself from falling to one side. I tried again, only to find that my left leg was refusing to obey me.

A creeping sense of foreboding chilled me to my very bones. What was wrong? Was this yet another sly attempt by the opium to keep me under its rule? I stared at Anzu, my lips working, but only a sigh came from between them. I had not enough breath to speak. My chest was tight and I was panting shallowly. The pain in my chest felt like a large stone had been placed on my ribs. All I could do was gesture frantically at my leg, at the same time tugging at the kakebuton that entangled me.

Instead of helping me, Anzu squatted down and grabbed my frantic hands.

"Gently, Mi-san." Her voice was unsteady. I stared at her, shaking my head silently. I needed to know what was wrong with my leg, yet at the same time, I wanted to put off the moment for as long as I could. Finally, I found my voice and forced myself to rasp my question.

"Anzu, my leg. What has happened to my leg? It doesn't hurt, but it won't move. Is it broken?"

"No, Mi-san. Not broken." Anzu paused and I was certain she was going to tell me that my leg was gone. That I was imagining that I had touched it. That there could be no sensation as there was no leg to feel it.

I knew that could not be so, but at that moment, it made perfect sense to me. My illness had taken my leg from me. I wanted to howl my grief out loud, but instead, I bit my lip so hard that I drew blood. I tasted the coppery flavor and bit harder still, concentrating on the small pain until I was certain I had control of myself again.

"Have I lost my leg, Anzu? Has the paralysis of the morning taken it from me while I was ill?"

My voice barely shook. I took pleasure in the minor triumph, but Anzu's reaction to my question threatened to undo my composure.

"No, Mi-san, your leg is still there, I promise you. But..." She cleared her throat and stared miserably at the kakebuton. My efforts to move had stretched the covering tightly, and as I followed her gaze, I finally understood that while both legs were still there, something was very wrong with the left one.

My right leg was clearly a leg. Its shape was a defined curve beneath the kakebuton. My left leg was not. It seemed to me that its length did not match the other leg—it was the width of a man's hand shorter. And it was surely much thinner and lay at an odd angle.

"Let me see it," I demanded.

Anzu hesitated and then—when I reached clumsily for the kakebuton myself—pulled the cover away gently.

My sleeping robe was open and rucked around my hips. My gaze was pulled as if by magnetism to my legs. To my left leg.

I felt my heart jolt, in the way that it does when you dream you are falling. I rocked back and forward without knowing I was doing it, my breath catching in my throat as I stared at the nasty, warped thing that had once been my left leg. My long, slender, perfect leg.

It was definitely shorter than the other one. It had not shrunk, as I had feared; rather, it was shorter because from the knee down it was twisted to one side. For a horrifying moment, I thought it had somehow twisted so far round that it was back to front. I stared again, tracing the angle of the joint with my gaze and slumped with relief as I saw that I had at least been spared that horror.

But my foot stuck out at an unnatural angle. Very cautiously, I tried to move it back to a more normal position, but nothing happened. Panting violently with the effort, I relaxed. Then, tentatively, as if I was truly touching a dangerous wild animal that might bite me, I ran my fingers down my shin.

My muscles were so flabby I could feel the bone through them. I had expected to have no sensation at all in the withered leg, but I was astonished to find that I could just feel my own touch on the flesh of my thigh. I stared at it and forced myself to be calm, assessing the damage as best I could.

"Has the physician seen this?" I hissed in horror. Anzu nodded. "And what did he say about it? Will it get back to normal? Tell me what he said, Anzu." My voice rose to a shriek. I was, I knew, being unfair in asking my poor Anzu the question, but I had to know.

"He said it often happened in cases of paralysis of the morning," she said miserably. "Especially when young people catch the disease. But he said the important thing was that you were able to breathe. And that he would do what he could for your leg when—" She hesitated, and I knew she had substituted "when" for "if" at the last moment. "—when you've recovered a little."

"I see. Well, I have recovered." My voice shook, but I managed a smile for my poor amah. "The important thing is for me to get my leg working properly. But far more important at the moment is my need to go to the lavatory! Will you help me, please, Anzu? I seem to find it a little difficult to stand at the moment."

How casual my voice sounded! Anzu's face was working, and I prayed she would not begin to cry. If she did, I would join in her tears and that would not do. I knew that if I began weeping, I would never stop again.

Anzu had said that Father was not at home. So, the important thing was for me to be as normal as possible when he returned. The thought gave me courage, and I managed not to so much as a moan as my amah bent down and put my arms around her neck. The movement was so very practiced that I guessed she had done this many times during the summer.

I tried not to put too much weight on her slight body, but Anzu lifted me effortlessly. I leaned against her, balancing carefully on my right leg, already hating the way my other leg simply hung at its ridiculous angle. I was tempted to lean to one side, to try and put some weight on it, but I decided against it. I sensed I could do myself great harm by using the leg in ways it did not want to go. Surely, it would be far wiser to wait for the physician to give me some medicine that would cure it. I would tell Anzu to send for him at once, as soon as I had completed my toilet.

"Ready, Mi-san?" Anzu asked courteously.

"Ready."

She moved very slowly. Even so, for the first few steps, I hung on to her fiercely, terrified that I was going to unbalance and drag us both to the tatami. I discovered very rapidly that the only way I could make any progress was by hopping on my good leg and using Anzu's support in place of the other leg.

By the time we reached the lavatory, I was streaming with sweat again and as tired as if I had been walking for hours. I was deeply grateful that this dependence on someone else was going to be very short-lived. The sooner the physician did something to cure my rebellious leg, the better.

Reluctantly, I began to consider that it might be possible that medicine on its own would not cure my leg. I wondered if he might have to break my knee and set it straight again. I had never heard of such a thing, but I supposed it was possible. It would be very painful for a while, but that bothered me very little. Refusing the opium tea had caused me huge pain—what did a little more pain matter if both my legs were straight and serviceable again? If Father could look at me and see his beautiful, healthy daughter once more?

When I hobbled into the lavatory, I began to understand the challenge that lay before me. I stared down at the washiki in mute horror.

The washiki was basically a hole in the floor, surrounded by a porcelain oval. I had never so much as given a thought to it before. Occasionally, the night soil men would come and empty the pit beneath it, but as these were burakumin—the lowest class of untouchables—nobody ever gave them a thought either. At that moment, I could think of nothing else but the washiki.

To use it, I would have to squat. Even with Anzu hanging on to me, I knew I would never be able to bend sufficiently without losing my balance and falling over. I could not think of any way that would allow me to leave my left leg stuck out and at the same time bend on my one good knee without collapsing in a heap. I gulped back tears of weakness and despair.

Anzu saw my distress. She tugged me forward very gently. I fought against her grip, but she was having none of it. Once more, I was the baby she had nursed through every childhood illness, and I was both pathetically grateful for her help and infuriated by my need for it.

"Like this, Mi-san."

Once she was sure I could balance for a moment by leaning against the shoji frame, she stood over the washiki and leaned forward from the waist, barely bending her knees at all.

I laughed at her antics. I had to—it was that or cry. Anzu put her arm around my waist and pulled me into place gently. When she was satisfied I was positioned correctly, she lowered herself, taking me with her, and then turned her head discreetly to one side.

I jerked aside the skirts of my kimono and held on to

Anzu with the strength of a drowning man. My aching bladder did the rest on its own.

In the whole of my life, I had never felt a greater sense of achievement. Anzu was clearly proud of me. I was proud of myself.

I cleared my throat and tried not to let my weakness show. "Anzu, would you send a servant for the physician, please?"

"At once, Mi-san."

I tried to pretend I did not notice the depth of pity in her glance as she slid her arm around my waist so I did not trip over the lip of the washiki when I moved.

SEVENTEEN

It must be autumn.
The geese fly to warmer climes.
Please, take me with you!

I was sure the physician would be pleased with my progress. In the weeks that had passed since his last visit, I had made sure I was eating and drinking well. More importantly, I had resisted the allure of the opium tincture with its false hopes. Although it took my pain away for a short while, I was certain that it also caused a far deeper, more subtle agony than the pain it relieved in my leg. I knew that did not make sense, but in my own mind, I knew it to be true.

My first day of full consciousness had been very terrible. Time after time, the pain in my joints came back. I sweated and felt nauseous, my breath stuck in my throat and seemed determined not to reach my lungs. Anzu hovered at my side, her eyes wide with worry. But she did not offer me opium tea, and I did not ask.

The second day was a little better, and by the third day

I felt brave enough to ask Anzu to help me into the bath. I had mastered the washiki, surely the bath could not be any worse. Alas for my hopes, it was. In common with all baths in private houses, our tub was a deep, fairly short, wooden affair. It had never occurred to me before my illness to notice how high it was, and when I finally managed to hook one leg over the side, I would have fallen in headfirst when my treacherous leg refused to support me if Anzu hadn't been hanging on to me.

No matter. I was clean, at last. And I felt infinitely better for it.

Truly, that third day was one of surprises.

I was exhausted after the effort of taking my bath, and I slept deeply. And I dreamed. A dream that was so real I might almost have been awake and conscious of everything that was happening around me. It seemed to me that Mother had come into my bedroom and was staring down at me with Anzu at her side. I even heard her speak, her voice doubtful.

"So, she survived the paralysis of the morning. My husband said she would, even though the physician doubted it. She's lost a lot of weight, but other than that, she looks quite well." Mother sounded surprised.

"Mi-san has been very brave, Emica-san," Anzu murmured. "She has had much pain, but she has borne it without complaint. The physician says the gods must have smiled on her for her to recover so well."

"Pain! Don't talk to me about pain! If she suffered from headaches as I do, then my daughter would know what pain feels like. She is completely recovered, you say?"

Anzu hesitated, and then I felt my kakebuton being twitched aside, very gently. I heard my mother's hiss of indrawn breath.

"This is completely well? She is deformed. Oh, what will Ai-san say about this? She was never happy about her precious son being betrothed to Mi, in spite of the fact that we could buy and sell her family any day we choose." She took a deep, trembling breath. When she went on, I thought dreamily that she was talking to herself rather than to Anzu. "She has asked about Mi several times while she has been ill. I'm sure she was hoping she would die and relieve her son of his obligation. I will send her a message and tell her Mi is completely recovered. They will surely come to see and we will brazen it out then. In the meantime, that good-for-nothing physician must do what he can for her. We're paying him a fortune—he must be able to do something to make that...that *thing* better."

Even in my sleep, I wanted to cry out to Mother. To tell her I didn't want to see either Ai-san or her son.

But in my dreaming state, I could neither move nor cry out. And in any event, Mother turned and walked away abruptly. Anzu said nothing about my mother's visit when I finally woke up, so I assumed I really had dreamed it.

The physician came the next day, and from his first words I began to wonder if Mother really had come to see me. His whole demeanor had changed. Rather than addressing me as if he was talking to a child, his face was serious and his voice concerned.

"Mi-san, how very well you look. Do you still have much pain?"

The answer was an undoubted "yes," but I bit back the reply. If I admitted it, I was sure he would insist I take the opium tincture again, and that I would not do. I was regaining my true self at last. I would not give that up.

"Hardly any," I lied.

"Excellent. Now, Mi-san, may I look at your leg?"

I pulled my skirts aside and turned my head away. I found it was easier to bear if I did not look at my own leg. I hated it. I did not want to own that it was part of my body. In my dream, Mother had said it was deformed. She was right. I would be happier without the hideous thing. Better half a normal leg than to carry this hated burden for the rest of my life.

The physician ran his hand down my leg. It tickled and I twitched in response. He seemed surprised.

"You felt me touch you? There?" He did it again and I nodded, suddenly hopeful.

"Yes, I felt it. Is that a good thing?"

"It's unusual. In most cases of paralysis of the morning, affected limbs do not have much sensation." He took my misshapen foot in his hand. "Can you push?"

I tried. I tried so hard I grunted with the effort. I felt no movement at all, but the physician seemed pleased.

"There was some response. You have been ill for many months, Mi-san. In all that time you have not moved. Your muscles have wasted because of that. That is chiefly the problem with your leg now."

He nodded wisely, but I was not deceived. My other leg had also not moved in all that time, but it was still strong enough to bear my weight. I knew I should not argue with an adult, especially a wise man like the physician, but I was so angry I could not contain my skepticism.

"I don't believe you," I said flatly. "My knee looks as if it's turned backward. My foot is pointed toward the ground and I cannot straighten it. Although I can feel your touch, when it is left alone, my leg from the knee down might as well not be there. I have no feeling in it at all. I can just touch the floor with my great toe, but that is no use at all in helping me to walk. Tell me truly, please, will it ever get better?"

He was going to lie to me. I felt it in the anxiety that roiled from his body. I tensed, waiting for the words that would condemn me to a lifetime of horror. I would not flinch. When he spoke, his voice was measured and slow.

"You are fortunate to be alive. I have never seen a case of paralysis of the morning as bad as yours where the patient recovered. But your leg will never be as it was, Mi-san." He held my gaze as he spoke, and I saw the truth in his eyes. I wanted to weep, but I would not allow myself the weakness. Instead, I met his eyes and waited to hear what he had to say with as much calmness as I could find. "If I had been able to do something for your leg earlier, perhaps something more could have been achieved. But it was too dangerous. Anything that distracted from keeping you alive would have been a grave risk."

He nodded at his wisdom and spoke quietly. "Thank you for saving my life." My words were a lie. I would rather have died than been cursed to a life where I was unable to walk, where even I found my withered limb repellent. Where I would be an object of pity for everybody who saw me. I shook my self-pity off and spoke briskly. "But as I am alive, what can be done for my leg now?"

"There are a number of things we can try."

Try? I shook my head. I did not want half-measures. If nothing could be done, I would ask him to sever the lower half of my leg as soon as I was strong enough to bear the pain of the knife. I would learn to walk with a crutch. Anything but bear the horror of knowing this ugly, deformed thing would be with me for the rest of my life.

"Have these things been proven? Are you sure they will help?"

"I am certain," he said quickly. Too quickly for my liking. He began to reel off a list of treatments, ticking each one off on his fingers. "To begin, exercise is vital."

"I cannot even walk on my own," I protested. "How can I hope to exercise?"

"You can, and you will."

Oh, but I liked that tone much better! I began to listen carefully. If my malformed leg could be persuaded to a semblance of normality, I could put up with any amount of pain.

"But at the moment, you still have difficulty breathing. To begin, we will concentrate on that. There are many exercises that you can do that will help your breathing when you are lying down, or—with Anzu to help you—standing up. I will explain them to you before I go today. Spikenard oil will help you to breathe more easily. Sprinkle a little on a tenugui and inhale the scent, but be sure not to let it touch your face. It is too fierce for that. Also, a few drops of it mixed with a tea bowl full of sweet almond oil will be excellent to rub into your leg. It is very good for overheated joints and will be soothing.

"Now, to assist your leg, the bath is very important. Make the water as hot as you can stand, and get Anzu to add a good handful of almond meal and mix it with the bathwater. When you are in the bath, massage your leg vigorously, from the knee to your toes. Try and stretch the limb as well.

"Each day, apply a poultice of dry muriate of quinine to your knee. It will be hot when you apply it. Leave it in place until it is cold. I will leave you the spikenard oil and quinine. Your kitchen will have everything else. For the moment, I believe that is all that can be done."

He paused, tapping his lips, and I repeated all he had

said to myself. I was concentrating so hard on his instructions that I missed the physician's final words, and it took me a moment to understand he was asking me if there was anything I had not understood.

"No, thank you," I said hurriedly. "If you could just show me the exercises to help me breathe better, there is nothing else."

To show him how serious I was, I struggled to my feet, almost falling flat on my face when my great toe refused to hold me. Anzu was at my side at once, and I leaned on her gratefully.

"Be careful, now. One must learn to walk before one can run." The pompous fool cackled at his own wit, and I smiled politely, wanting him gone.

Walk? I was certain that I would be running in no time at all. The grim shadow of reality made me shiver before I could push the thought away. At least, I would if I kept my leg.

CHAPTER

EIGHTEEN

Sometimes, one does not
Need words to know what another
Person is thinking

Mother disliked anything out of the ordinary intensely. Unexpected noise and fuss brought on her most violent headaches. As a result, everybody in the family did their best to avoid distressing her.

Perhaps my brothers sensed that today would be one of Mother's difficult days, as they both gulped their morning meal and set off for Edo much earlier than usual with no more than a nod in my direction. Neither of them had so much as mentioned my illness, and I was grateful to them for their unintentional consideration.

I had expected the roughest of teasing from them, so to be treated as if nothing at all had happened to me was a huge relief. And also, in an odd way, it was a comfort. If my own brothers, suave, iki, men-about-town as they were, saw nothing strange about me, then surely there was hope that the rest of my small world might also come to accept me as well.

Mother always took breakfast in her own apartment. I was astonished when she appeared in the main part of the house even before I had finished my own meal.

"Mi, you are up and about already. Good. Lady Ai and Yuto will be with us later this morning. I need to speak to you before they arrive."

My stomach clenched as I stared at the tatami in silent misery. Mother either didn't notice my distress or chose to ignore it.

"The furniture from my apartment is going to be moved in here. Naturally, Ai-san will expect us to receive her and Yuto here in the reception room. You haven't seen them, but your father has purchased two other pieces of furniture for me. They are called *chairs*."

She pronounced the short but difficult word carefully. Feeling something was called for from me, I asked dutifully, "Are they like your sofa, Mother?"

"Similar, but smaller. Each one seats only one person." I was relieved as I had obviously struck the right tone with my question. "They are very, very expensive. But naturally, one has to pay a high price for items that are extremely fashionable. I have heard that even the emperor has them in the imperial palace. None of the gaijin know how to sit properly. They fidget all over the place if they have to sit on the tatami, so of course the emperor has purchased their own style of furniture to ensure they are comfortable in his presence."

I remembered Gen's anger at the way the gaijin appeared to be taking over our country, and at that moment, I understood and even shared his fury. If it was possible that they could dictate to the emperor in such a small matter, what else was changing to accommodate their strange customs?

Mother appeared to be waiting for me to say something, so I said colorlessly, "Yes, Mother."

She glanced at me suspiciously and then sighed and put her hand to her forehead. If Mother had a headache coming on, then it was wise to retreat. Quickly. But I could go nowhere without preparation. My crutch was in plain view, but I dared not grab for it. Mother followed my gaze and shuddered theatrically.

"That thing must be hidden. Ai must not see it."

I shared Mother's revulsion, but I could not move a step without my crutch. I hated it, but for the moment, it was vital. It was an ugly thing—a lump of wood with a padded handle. The estate carpenter had made it for me, and I suppose I should have been grateful. But it was as clumsy in use as it looked, was almost as ugly as my withered leg, and was far more visible. But I would not, I prayed, need it for too much longer.

I practiced my exercises every day in spite of the pain they caused me. I massaged my leg with spikenard oil and inhaled it often. I massaged my leg again and again in the bath. I had begun to be despondent when I could see no change until Anzu pointed out gently that not only my great toe but also my second and third toes could now touch the ground, together with the pads beneath those toes. Small progress, to be sure, but something. If I could manage that, then anything was possible. Or so I told myself.

Alas, my small triumphs counted for nothing at this moment. Mother's word was law. I jerked myself to my feet with the support of my crutch and watched as two of our gardeners moved the gaijin furniture into the room. The sofa must have been heavy as they grunted under its weight. But Mother was not yet finished. She ordered the furniture to be moved back and forth until she was finally satisfied.

"Mi, sit on the sofa. At the far end. You—" She gestured at one of the gardeners. "—take that thing away and put it in the kitchen."

The gardener gawped at her until Mother pointed at my crutch and flicked her finger at it disdainfully. He seized it obediently, holding it clumsily, and instantly I was filled with fear that he was going to break it. Before I could call a warning to take care of it, both men bowed and shuffled out.

Without my crutch, I felt as if something was missing from my body. I was deeply puzzled. I hated the thing—to me, it shouted to the world that I was a helpless cripple. Yet as soon as it was taken from me, I wanted it back. With a flash of instinct that left me cold I understood that I had already come to depend on the crutch. At once, I decided I would increase the times I performed my exercises each day. I would not allow myself to be dependent on anything —especially not an ugly lump of wood.

Mother's voice broke in on my thoughts. "Sit on the end of the sofa, Mi. Put your legs to one side. No, not like that. Watch me." She sat down gracefully—I was deeply envious of her elegant movement—and tucked both her legs neatly together, on a slant. My own efforts were less successful. She rose immediately and pulled my legs about until they pleased her, and then spread the skirts of my kimono care-fully across them. "That will have to do. If one doesn't look too carefully, your left leg looks almost normal. It will seem very strange that you don't rise and bow to Ai-san and her son, but I'll think of something to explain that. They should be here soon, they've spent the night at a local ryokan. Don't move."

I was uncomfortable and wanted to fidget. Even worse, before long, I needed to pass water. I hoped tea would not be served; that would make my plight desperate, indeed.

"Please, do come through Ai-san. How lovely to see you and Yuto-san after so long. And how very well your son looks! He has grown into a man since I saw you both last."

Mother's voice was high-pitched and sounded artificial. I realized with astonishment that she was nervous. And then Ai and Yuto came into the room and I forgot everything—even my manners—in my horror.

Lady Ai looked exactly the same—a prosperous farmer's wife, dressed in excellent quality but old-fashioned clothes. But Yuto!

Mother had said he had grown into a man. She lied. He had grown alright, but sideways rather than upward. He was grotesquely fat. His head appeared to sit directly on his shoulders with no neck to intervene. His belly bulged out of his robe and when he sat—awkwardly—on the chair Mother indicated, I heard it creak with distress.

His face was as round as the full moon, and rather than reducing the appearance of his pockmarks, they seemed to be deeper than ever. His eyes were almost buried in fat, as was his nose. Only his lips stood out, thick and repulsively red.

As if he sensed my inspection, Yuto turned his head to stare at me and I saw at once I had been wrong about one thing, at least. He did have a neck; the back of it was covered in rolls of fat. I swallowed hysterical laughter and managed to find a smile even as I turned my head away from him hurriedly. Surely even Mother could no longer wish me to marry this mountain of a young man. The thought held me rigid. I could not. I would not. I would rather the paralysis of the morning had killed me when I still had hopes of a normal life.

Everybody was silent when Mother stopped speaking. Both Ai and Yuto were staring at me, Ai with raised eyebrows. I blushed as I understood she thought I was being terribly impolite by remaining seated and I glanced imploringly at Mother.

"Please accept my apologies for Mi-san. Her illness has left her a little delicate. But that will pass, naturally," she added smoothly. "Could I offer you both some tea, Ai-san?"

Ai's response was so curt it was rude. "Not just at the moment. I understand from your letters that Mi-san has had paralysis of the morning. A bad case, was it? She's certainly lost weight."

Had I? I had been so worried about my leg I had not bothered to consider the rest of my body. But now that Ai had mentioned it, I did have to pull my obi much tighter than before my illness.

"My daughter may have lost a little weight, but I think it suits her greatly."

It was, I was sure, the first compliment I had ever had from Mother. I glanced at her in surprise. She was sitting very straight, her expression set. Ai was staring back at her without blinking and I felt the tension thrumming between them. It was exactly as if some sort of silent battle had been declared.

Yuto spoke unexpectedly, and all three of us turned to look at him. I was sure he flinched back from our stares, but he was the only man present, and it would have caused him too much loss of face to back down.

"I think it suits her as well, Mother." Any pleasure I

might have taken in his words withered as he licked those full, red lips greedily.

"Yes, dear," Ai answered indulgently, as if he was a child. A very large child. "But it is not always a good thing to be very slim. It can be a sign of a weak constitution." Mother gasped indignantly as Ai went on relentlessly. "There has never been a case of paralysis of the morning in our family. We come from good, healthy stock. But I have heard that the paralysis often leaves those who survive deformed. Is Mi still whole in her body?"

Mother glared at Ai as if she had been insulted. Which I supposed she had been. Ai glared back at her. Yuto had lost interest in the conversation and was picking at a scab on the back of his hand.

"Mi-san has a little trouble with her left leg," Mother said icily. "But the physician assures me that it will pass in no time."

Ai was smiling, a smile that said—as clearly as words—*I knew it!* I expected Mother to placate my future mother-in-law and my mouth fell open when she turned her head and nodded at me.

"Mi-chan, please be so good as to show Ai-san your left leg," she purred. I was aghast.

"Mother?"

"Your leg, Mi-chan."

Both Ai and Yuto were staring impatiently at my skirts. After a last, appealing glance at Mother, I fumbled them aside.

I could not bear to look at my own deformity and watched Ai and her son instead. Ai's hand flew to her mouth so that I could only see her eyes, but I was certain they held a look of triumph. Yuto shocked me. He stared at my leg, and his expression turned greedy. He rubbed his knuckles over his mouth and smiled.

"And you say *that* will recover?" I was right, Ai's voice resonated with triumph. "I must tell you, Emica-san, if it was not for the fact that my Yuto has formed a very dear affection for your daughter, I could not consider ever allowing him to marry a girl who is crippled beyond hope. As it is, I must discuss this matter with my husband. At the very least, he will demand a far higher dowry if we are to take Mi off your hands at all. In fact, it would probably be far better if Yuto took her as his second wife in due course. There would be a ceremony, of course, but I really could not condone my dear son taking a cripple for his first wife."

She might as well have slapped me across the face. Knowing that Ai was watching me closely, I kept a closed face. I would not allow her to see what distress she had caused to me. And if Yuto did not stop staring at my leg with such greedy interest, I would hurl the fat cushion that was supporting me at him. I wished I still had my crutch to throw. That really would have hurt him.

But this was truly a day of surprises. Mother was smiling and nodding as if she had expected nothing more. When she spoke, her words were so at odds with her expression it clearly took Ai some time to realize what she was saying.

"I am so glad we have had the chance to have this little chat, Ai-san. Now that I have seen your son again, I realize that I could not let my beautiful daughter marry him under any circumstances. Her leg may recover, but alas, your son will always be an ugly, bad-mannered lout." Comprehension began to dawn on Ai. Her face flushed a bright, mottled red. She began to speak, but Mother simply carried on as if she had remained silent. "And as for a dowry, if *you* were to offer *me* all the rice in Japan to allow my daughter to marry *him*, I would still refuse." She clapped her hands loudly and a maid appeared at once. "Umi, please show my guests out."

Mother's politeness to the maid was in stark contrast to her rudeness to her visitors. Ai stood at once and pushed her way past the astonished maid. She was almost at the door when she realized Yuto was not following her and turned and gestured to him impatiently. He rose with obvious reluctance, his greedy gaze still fastened on me.

I heard his whining voice as Ai shooed him through the shoji. "Why can't I marry Mi, Mother? I like her far better now than how she was before. I like thin girls. And her leg doesn't bother me at all. She couldn't move very quickly with a leg like that, could she?"

I exhaled on a long breath and stared at Mother with a new respect. She waited until she was sure that Ai and Yuto had left the house and then stood, brushing her hands one against the other as if she was flicking dirt off them.

"I will ask the men to clean my lovely chairs very well before taking them back to my apartment. Who knows what sort of mess those farmers brought with them?" I nodded, speechless. "When your father gets home tonight, I will tell him that he must commission a new crutch for you. The finest one that money can buy. If you must use one, then it must be of the best."

"Mother..." I paused, searching for words as she waited. "Thank you."

"For what?" She was tapping her foot impatiently on the tatami and I stayed very still, wondering if she was angry with me. "Ai's family may be higher caste than we are, but in this day and age that counts for very little. We have money, and because of that, we have power." The effect of her words was spoiled completely for me as she added, "In any event, as you are only a girl, I thought it would be a good enough match for you.

"Had one of your brothers wanted to marry a girl from a good family who had no money, that would have been a different matter entirely. In any event, that woman presumed too much. She and her precious husband do not understand how things have changed since the gaijin forced their way into our country. Farmers and landowners and even samurai no longer have the power they used to wield. It is men such as your father whose voice matters these days. Don't worry too much, child. We will find you another husband, in spite of your deformity."

I bowed my head, both from habit and to hide my rebellious expression. I did not want a husband found for me. Especially one who was prepared to overlook my withered leg.

Any husband I took must want me for who I was, for *what* I was. Of that, I was determined.

CHAPTER
NINETEEN

I do not need a glass
To see your image in the
Shadows of evening

I was overjoyed to find I could still ride a horse. Not as confidently as before my illness, but once I got over the awkwardness of a groom helping me into the saddle, it was not as difficult as I had expected. And I was sure that my pony had missed me. Like the dreadful Yuto, she had grown fat in my absence. That would soon be cured; a few brisk rides and she would be back in excellent shape.

Anzu worried. Had I allowed it, she would have walked alongside my pony wherever I decided to go. She offered to find me a servant to ride alongside me, but I refused. I wanted to be out of the house and, above all, alone.

It was a great delight to me to be able to move quickly and easily again. My deformity was far less noticeable on horseback. I thought the withered leg just appeared to be held at an odd angle, as though I had sustained a minor injury. Not that it mattered. There was nobody to see me except the peasants working in our fields and they always cast their eyes down at the approach of a person on horseback.

I slowed my pony to a walk and allowed my thoughts to wander. I was still amazed by Mother's stand against Lady Ai. If she only knew it, she had gifted me life itself. I would have died rather than marry a man who liked a woman who looked as I now did. Or, for that matter, a man who looked like Yuto.

Did I want to marry anybody? Or rather, would I want to marry anybody who wanted to marry me? Most definitely not, but what was the alternative? The answer was bleak. I could either live with my family until Mother and Father died, and then hope one of my brothers would allow me to live with them as a dependent, or decide my own future and join a monastery.

Either option made me shudder.

Still, at least I would not have to spend the rest of my life with Yuto! By the time I turned my pony toward home, I had begun to wonder if a third way might be open to me. I wasted no time and approached Father after the evening meal the same day.

Every day since I had awoken from my long sleep, I had hoped that Father would send for me and congratulate me on my recovery. He did not. When I recovered sufficiently to take the evening meal with him and my brothers, he simply treated me as if no time at all had passed since he had last seen me and that nothing had changed.

Each morning when he set off for Edo, I waited for him to send a servant to tell me I was to accompany him. The word never came, and I was bitterly hurt. But I could understand Father's reluctance to have his clients see me as I was now. Surely even the children-loving gaijin would be distressed to be introduced to a cripple like me.

I pushed the hurt aside with brutal determination. I was helped by the fact that I had never quite forgotten the feelings that the archived accounts had raised so tauntingly in me, and now I found I was hungry again. Hungry for the knowledge they contained, and through that knowledge—power. Power I could only access if I was able to read their contents.

I took it as a good omen that my brothers were in a hurry to get away that evening after their meal. An appointment with friends, they said. Probably gambling, I thought cynically.

As soon as they had gone, I rose as gracefully as I could with the aid of my crutch and poured Father some more tea.

I spoke with my head lowered, watching for his reaction beneath my eyelashes.

"Father, I think Tanaka-san may have told you that I was learning to read and write before my illness." Father nodded without looking at me and I went on quickly before his thoughts could stray to more important business matters. "Gen was teaching me, and Tanaka-san said I was doing very well. Obviously, I cannot go with you to Edo at the moment." I paused hopefully, but Father said nothing. My spirits sank, but I went on anyway. "It seems a shame that I should not finish what I started. If it isn't too much trouble, I wondered if perhaps I might have a tutor to teach me to read and write here at home, where nobody can see me?"

The last words came out of my mouth without me meaning to say them. I curled up and died inside, but it was said and I could do nothing about it. It was down to Father, now.

He drained his tea bowl and stood up, stretching. How I envied that simple movement! When he walked away without speaking—as was usual for him when we were alone—I knew I had failed. I was so sunk in misery, I thought at first that he was talking to one of the servants when he called over his shoulder without so much as turning his head.

"If it would give you something to do, I don't see why not. I can't spare Gen to attend to you. The office is very busy, and he is far too valuable for me to release him to attend you. But I will arrange for a tutor to come to the house. Learning to read and write is a difficult business, especially for somebody as old as you are. But if you are certain it is what you want, I will get an appropriate person to come here. If they say that you are a diligent pupil and it is worthwhile to teach you, then it shall be so. But—" He raised his finger sternly. "—if you are not inclined to learn and waste the tutor's time, then he will no longer come. I will not waste money on a whim, Mi."

I blurted my thanks to his retreating back. My heart was galloping. I put my hand to my chest as if I could force it to slow. My future depended on this. Could it really have been so very easy? I spared a moment to dare to dream, my pleasure so great that for a moment I saw myself seated close to Tanaka-san, my gaze flicking over the slips of paper passed to me by the obedient clerks, sorting out what was important enough to concern Tanaka-san and deciding what I could deal with myself. I saw Tanaka nod his head at me, his expression pleased, and I dared to wonder if one day—when the venerable chief clerk retired—I might even be able to take his place as Father's most trusted employee. Would it be possible that I could be the one who looked at the accounts each month and told Father how much he—*we*—had earned in that month?

I was excited at the thought but forced myself to come back to earth. Even if I could not rise so very far, surely it would be possible for me to become a reliable—and relied-upon—part of Father's business, to the extent that when Father finally handed the reins of power to Ichiro, he would advise my eldest brother that I was a worthwhile addition to the business and should be valued in the future. I had no doubt that Ichiro would be delighted to agree to anything that made his life easier.

Such a thing was unknown, of course, but in this time of change, why should it not come to pass that a woman would work for a living? Not just as a yujo, a woman of pleasure, or as the proprietor of a teahouse or brothel, but in an office? I sighed and shook my head as my dream left me. That was all in the future…I hoped. First things first. I hobbled as quickly as I could to my room. I had put my precious kanji papers in my chest. They were there, along with my brush and ink. I stared and stared at the kanji, tracing my finger over them and repeating the meaning of each one time and again.

Would my tutor come tomorrow? I should have asked Father. I almost dared to go to his apartment and ask, but common sense called me back and I sat happily, rolling my brush between my fingers to familiarize myself with it again.

TWENTY

To and fro I go,
Busy as the hummingbird
That tastes each blossom

Some of life's lessons are learned at great cost. Of all people, I should have known that. The evidence was before me every waking moment and even—when my dreams were cruel—at night.

As the proverb goes, "Be careful what you wish for, you may get it." Even though—in common with most girls of good families—I had lived a sheltered life, even I had heard this said. Generally by my brothers, who would tease me with it when I asked to be allowed to join in their games when they were younger. To prove their point, they would occasionally allow me to join them, and I always emerged battered and bruised afterward as they seemed to take great delight in using me as their target. Needless to say, when the game was a small-scale reenactment of the legend of the Forty-Seven Ronin, I was invariably cast as the villain, Kira. Not only did I lose my head, but it seemed to me that my brothers took great delight in mistreating me in ways I did not recall hearing in the legend.

Eventually, I learned that I had nothing to gain except pain from annoying my elder brothers in this way, so instead, I simply sat and watched them.

I had never contemplated that I might ever regret asking Father for a tutor. But all too soon, I wished I had stayed silent as my hopes dwindled and died when he did not speak of it. As the days went by, I became sure that he had forgotten my request. I did not dare ask again. Father was an important, busy man. He surely would not welcome me nagging him over such a small thing. To distract myself, I copied Gen's kanji over and over again until I became so dispirited, I put my brush and paper away.

Even my abacus lost its allure. For the first time since I had fallen ill, I retrieved my biwa and began to pluck at its strings. My music sounded melancholy to me, and even the recollection of Tanaka-san saying that being good with figures and musical talent often went hand-in-hand did not cheer me at all. If anything, the recollection of the happy times I had spent in the hustle and bustle of Father's offices made me even sadder.

Naturally, that train of thought led me to Gen. My music became slower and slower as I wondered if he had ever asked after me. Was it possible that he might even miss me…just a little? I plucked a wrong note and put the biwa down angrily. For all I knew, Gen might not even work for Father anymore.

I had seen that he was an excellent calligrapher. Such men were in great demand in Edo, where it was still common for even well-off people not to be able to read and write. Women were not expected to be able to do either, and many calligraphers did little else but write flowery love letters for women whose suitors appeared to be losing interest.

For some reason I could not name, the thought of Gen writing love letters for unknown women made me angry. I brushed the notion aside. I was being ridiculous. Gen was nothing to me, just one of the many messengers Father employed. Had he not been such an excellent calligrapher, I would never even have learned his name.

I would forget him, just as he had no doubt forgotten me. The only difference between us was the fact that Gen no doubt had plenty to occupy himself with, whereas I had nothing at all.

On a day that had nothing to distinguish it from any other, I lingered deliberately over my morning meal, eating my rice slowly. I was at the stage of boredom where I couldn't be bothered to do anything, not even play my biwa. I was startled out of my apathy when a maid entered and then stood aside, bowing a stranger into the room.

"Mi-san." A man strode forward so confidently he obviously thought I expected him. And he even knew my name. How strange! Even more bizarre, he was a monk. What was a monk doing here? My family was nominally Buddhist, but we only attended temple for major festivals. Other than that, religion played no part in our lives. "My name is Brother Tengen. My kannushi has instructed me to teach you to read and write."

I grasped the edge of the low chabudai table in front of me to rise. My time spent exercising had given me great strength in my arms, and I thought I would be able to get up, although clumsily.

"Do not stand. I understand that you have a withered leg as a result of paralysis of the morning. I will not think you impolite if you remain seated."

As he spoke, the monk folded to the tatami gracefully and set a furoshiki at his side. He ignored me as he opened it, taking out brushes and paper and an inkpot sealed with a wide cork.

He had spoken about my leg with as much concern as he might have commented that it would probably rain later. I could not explain it, but had anybody else simply accepted my deformity, I would have been grateful. Coming from this man, it seemed more like deliberate condescension. I decided at once that I did not like him.

"I am sorry I am not prepared for your visit, Brother Tengen," I said stiffly. "Father did not tell me to expect you."

"No matter. Kono-san has spoken to my kannushi, and he has instructed me to come here every second day until you are proficient in reading and writing. Kono-san is a great patron of our temple, and I am honored to be of service to him."

Father was a patron of the temple? I was astonished, but only for a moment. Naturally, Father would never speak about his donations, but it would be known of in the business community. Such things were. He would gain great face from his charity. That being so, my own wishes on the matter counted for nothing. It was a done thing whether I liked this monk or not. And I had taken an instant and no doubt unreasoning dislike to this unsympathetic man.

I stared at him calmly, so deliberately it was insolent. Tengen was preoccupied with setting out his writing implements and seemed not to notice. He didn't even raise his head to look at me when I sighed heavily. Very well. It would give me time to assess my new tutor.

I had noticed when he entered that he was tall and of slender build, yet he was not at all thin. There was a hint of muscles beneath his robe, and I wondered if he was a practitioner of martial arts. It was far from unknown for monks to be adepts of one or more such skills. Naturally, he would never fight in anger, but as he went about unarmed, it might be very useful to be able to defend himself in these uncertain times. He moved with a natural grace that was very attractive. His head was shaven, of course, but it seemed to enhance his features rather than detract from them. I wondered curiously how such a handsome young man had come to choose the life of a contemplative. His name meant "heavenly eyes," and grudgingly I had to admit it was appropriate. His eyes were truly beautiful. They had a classic almond shape and were very dark brown, and he had an odd mark like a starburst in the right one. I had never seen anything like it before, and it fascinated me.

Tengen chose that moment to speak, and his voice was so chillingly polite that I jerked to attention. I noticed that he did not look at me when he spoke to me, but instead seemed to stare over my shoulder.

"So, Mi-san, I believe you have already begun to learn some kanji." His dismissive tone of voice said clearly that he didn't believe it. "Please show me what you already know."

His voice was perfectly polite, but I felt that he disliked both his allotted task and me. No matter. I reached for brush and ink and made a start on the kanji Gen had taught me. Alas, Brother Tengen had made me nervous and my kanji seemed ragged and lacking in grace. But soon the page was full and I was pleased I had something to show him.

"It is some time since I last had a lesson," I murmured apologetically.

"That is obvious. I think the best thing is for you to forget all you have learned. We will begin again. To start with, you are not holding your brush properly. Hold it like this."

I glanced at the brush in his hand and tried to adjust mine so it looked the same. But it did not feel comfortable at all. Tengen waited for a heartbeat and then leaned across and twitched my brush until he was satisfied. He had to touch my hand to do it, and I had the oddest feeling that he wanted to flinch back from contact with my skin.

The lesson did not improve. I loaded my brush with far too much ink and my kanji were blurred as a result. Tengen said nothing, except to tell me to repeat my strokes, which unnerved me even more.

In an effort to lighten the atmosphere, I tried to make conversation.

"Are you a teacher at the temple, Tengen-san?"

"Please address me as Brother Tengen," he snapped. "Yes, I teach the young boys who join the temple how to read and write. They come to us from the age of eight, and most of them have never picked up a brush before that."

I noticed that his harsh voice softened as he spoke of the boys in his care. Perhaps he was human after all.

"And are they quick learners?" I murmured.

"Some are. Some are not." Abruptly, he was ice again. "Please repeat that kanji. It is correct, but not precise enough."

I paused for a heartbeat and then did as I was instructed. My response had nothing at all to do with Tengen's—*Brother* Tengen's command. Common sense told me that if I refused to do as he asked, then he would ensure that word got back to Father, and I would not be given a second chance. And that would not do at all.

I worked grimly, doing exactly as I was instructed.

At first, I was too smoldering with anger to actually think about what I was doing, but by the time the first day's lesson was complete, I was astonished at the number of new kanji I had learned.

Brother Tengen stood abruptly, startling me. "That is enough for today. When I return, I expect you to have remembered all of these kanji and to be able to write them all perfectly."

"Yes, Brother Tengen," I said meekly.

He glanced at me suspiciously, but I made sure my expression was sweet. Only when he had gone did I unleash my built-up anger.

TWENTY-ONE

Take me at my word
When I say I know nothing
Of the world. Teach me!

I took my frustration out on my crutch. What else did I have any power over?

On Mother's crisp instructions, my original crutch had long since been replaced. If I had not been forced to use it to walk so much as a step, I would have readily admitted that the replacement was almost a work of art. The length of it was intricately carved with birds and animals, and the bar that fitted under my arm was padded carefully for comfort and topped with a thick layer of fine silk. Alas, it was made of teakwood, so it was so heavy that if it had not been gifted to me by Mother, I would have quickly replaced it with the old one.

I found after a while that Mother was shrewder than I had given her credit for. Because the crutch was heavy, I had to force my wasted muscles to work hard to use it. I discovered that it had benefited me quite by accident. One of the maids moved my new crutch out of the way when she was cleaning my room and as my old one was to hand, I used that instead. It felt so light compared to the new crutch it was almost a pleasure to use.

At first, I was delighted, but after a few minutes I felt my joy vanish. Suddenly, I felt insecure using the lighter crutch as I became certain that it would give way. After a while I put it away and picked up the new one. Perhaps the padded top had adjusted to my form. It felt *right* and I relished the challenge of using it to support me.

Now, I forgot all about how pleased I was with my crutch. I lowered myself lumpishly to the tatami and threw it viciously away from me, almost as if I hoped to hurt the unfeeling wood. I simmered for a while and then realized I would have to stand unaided or shuffle across the floor on my rear to retrieve it. The knowledge rounded off my misery perfectly and I groaned.

I was about to work my way clumsily across the tatami on my rear to pick up the crutch when a vision of Brother Tengen's face came to me. How he would have loved seeing me admit defeat so easily! I said "no" out loud. I would not allow him—or any other man—to sneer at me. Nor would I let myself down. I took a deep, calming breath and placed both hands on the tatami at each side of my hips. Very carefully, I levered myself to hip level and then found I lacked the confidence to stand fully.

Although I knew I had great strength in my arms, my balance was far from sure. I teetered for long moments and almost sat down again before stubbornness returned. If I gave in now, the next time I faced a challenge, it would be easier still to give in. And the time after, and the time after that...?

With a grunt of effort, I staggered to my feet—or rather

my foot. I wavered frantically and then—because I had no choice as it was either that or fall over—I put my left foot down. Although my leg stuck out at a horrible angle and no more than the pads beneath my toes touched the tatami, somehow, I balanced.

I was panting with the effort, but I had come so far, I would not back down now. For a moment, I dithered. Should I try and balance on my deformed leg while I moved the right one, or do it the other way around? I held my hands out, appealing for help to the empty room and then the decision was no longer mine.

My left leg was so weak I could feel it giving way. I took the weight off it quickly and hopped rather than walked on my right leg. I felt huge triumph as I put my left foot to the floor again, briefly, and then did it again. And again.

Actually picking up the crutch was an even greater challenge. Eventually, I balanced on my right leg and allowed my left leg to swing out as I swooped down and grabbed the crutch, tucking it beneath my arm as rapidly as I could.

I was streaming with sweat and shaking. But when I glanced across the room, I marveled at the distance I had managed to move unaided. I laughed out loud with delight and even managed to spare a grudging thank you to Brother Tengen, for surely if it hadn't been for the thought of his smug face watching me struggle and fail, I would never have managed such an astonishing journey.

Immediately, I felt deflated. A few steps, and I was celebrating?

"The journey of a thousand days begins with a single step," I whispered. And then I said it again, and again. My single step had been taken. I would not turn back now.

My resolve was strengthened when Brother Tengen came back.

I had spent the whole day between his visits practicing my kanji. To my great surprise, I began to find his precise kanji more attractive than Gen's more fluid characters. It was, I supposed, rather like my affinity for figures and music. Both were equally meticulous. In any event, I was waiting for Tengen eagerly.

He looked over my efforts and placed his fingertips together in front of his chest. If I had expected praise, I was to be disappointed.

"We will move on today. I will teach you more kanji, and on my next visit I will test you on all you should have learned so far."

Should, I noticed. It didn't worry me. I would be perfect. My body might not be perfect at all, but there was nothing wrong with my mind, as Brother Tengen would find out.

And he obviously did. He made no comment, but very soon his teaching picked up pace. When I hesitated over a kanji, I felt his impatience glowing within him. I made sure it happened very rarely.

I forgot the pleasures of my biwa. I even gave up my daily rides on my pony. Soon, nothing mattered more to me than being able to show Tengen that I had learned everything he had shown me.

Anzu became anxious. "Mi-san," she coaxed. "It is a lovely day. Would you like to sit in the garden?"

"Not now. I have work to do."

She didn't understand my needs at all, and sometimes neither did I.

One day, when I had copied kanji for Tengen endlessly, rather than learning anything new, I became dissatisfied enough to challenge him.

"I know all these," I said dismissively. "I need to learn new kanji. And more importantly, I need to be able to make sense of them." Tengen stared at me without speaking. I could tell from his expression that he didn't understand what I was asking and I tried again. I pointed at my full sheet of characters. "I know all these kanji. I can write them and I can read them. But they don't matter. They are just words. I want to be able to put them together. To make them speak."

I thought my last words were rather poetic, but Tengen obviously disagreed.

"You wish to run before you can walk," he snapped shortly. "You have much to learn before you can get to that stage."

Echoes of the physician's words! Oddly, the comment had not bothered me when the physician has said it, but I had assumed a holy man would be more thoughtful. I supposed Tengen had no idea how hurtful his words were and put the incident aside.

It was pure coincidence, but a little later that day I caught the inkpot with my sleeve and the contents spilled over Tengen's robe. I stared in horror, thinking the rusty black ink looked like drying blood against the intense saffron of his robe.

I pulled a tenugui from my sleeve and tried to dab at the ink. I was astonished when Tengen jerked back as if my touch had burned him. When I persisted, all the time murmuring apologies, he grabbed my wrists tightly and held me away from him at arm's length.

His grip was so tight, it felt as if iron manacles were squeezing my wrists. I stayed still, waiting for him to release me. Strangely, he did not. He did not move at all. He was trembling with rage, and I fully expected him to forget his Buddhist teachings and strike me for my clumsiness. I would not have blamed him if he had. All monks—even those in monasteries—had no possessions. His robe was probably the only one he had, and now he would have to go back to his kannushi and explain that it was ruined.

With that thought in my mind, I blurted, "I am so sorry. I will explain to Father what happened through my clumsiness and ask him to pay your kannushi for a new robe."

He threw my hands from him so violently that I lurched back, almost losing my balance.

A maid must have heard the noise. She slid the shoji back and poked her head through timidly, her eyebrows raised in question.

Tengen sprang to his feet immediately. Even in my confusion, I had time to think that he moved with all the grace of a trained warrior. Although now was certainly not the time to ask, I thought that one day—if the day ever came when he was in a better mood—I would ask him if he was skilled in martial arts.

My small pleasure died at once as Tengen grunted with anger. I realized he thought I was laughing at him. Before I could apologize, he turned and almost ran past the maid, shouldering her aside rudely.

I smothered my mouth with my hand, lost for words. In any event he was gone before I could explain. There was nothing further I could do. Instead, I turned to practical matters and asked the maid to take up the ruined tatami and have it replaced. She bowed briefly and bent to her task, but not before I had time to catch her expression.

She was smirking, barely hiding laughter. I was so angry with myself I thought nothing of it at the time, but later, when I was alone and—of course—practicing my kanji, I wondered about it, but finally decided she had been amused by the sight of a monk losing his temper.

I only wished I had found the situation half as funny.

CHAPTER
TWENTY-TWO

Some birds delight in
Flocking together. Some are
Alone. Which find joy?

After much serious thought, I decided I would wait until Tengen came back before mentioning the matter of a new robe for him to Father. My caution was two-fold. I worried if I asked Father before mentioning it to Tengen that the monk would be annoyed by my forwardness. But also, I hesitated in case Father might be angry with me for my clumsiness in spilling the ink.

As things turned out, it was just as well I did not speak to Father.

Tengen did not come back for my next lesson. Nor the next.

I was on fire with anxiety. Was it possible that his kannushi had forbidden him to return? I doubted that. Tengen had said that Father was a major benefactor of his monastery. The kannushi would not want to lose Father's contributions over such a relatively minor incident. Then was it Tengen himself who had decided he no longer wanted to teach me? I shook my head; I could not—would not—believe that.

Finally, I decided that Tengen was trying to punish me in the same fashion as he no doubt punished his much younger pupils in the monastery, by simply ignoring me.

Once the thought occurred to me, I settled down at once. He would be back. I only had to wait. And I would surprise him when he did come back.

I borrowed ink from Father's apartment and copied out my kanji. All of them. I only stopped when I was certain I could no longer improve on them. Then I put my brush and paper aside and delved into my chest.

On the last occasion I had seen Gen, he had given me a book of haiku written by Yosa Buson. I had never so much as looked at it since. There was no point. I couldn't read any of it. Now, I pulled it out and turned the pages carefully.

I realized the book was very old indeed. The cover was of leather, so aged that it was beautifully soft and almost warm to the touch. The pages inside were bound in a way that I had never seen before. Each page was folded double with printing on both sides. The only bound books I had seen before were Father's ledgers, and they were nothing like this. His, I supposed, were very up to date, perhaps even gaijin in style. They were also practical, containing nothing but rows of kanji, with the same symbols repeated often.

This book was simply beautiful.

It contained not only kanji, but illustrations. As I turned each page reverently, I rejoiced in its beauty. Why, I wondered, had I never looked at it before now? Was it because I had thought it would be no use to me until I could read, or was it because I did not want to admit that I was defeated by it? I shrugged the thought aside. No matter, I was looking at it now.

I gazed at the wood-block illustrations with pleasure and dawning excitement. Each one must surely indicate the subject matter of the haiku it represented. That would make it much easier for me to be able to understand the many kanji I was not yet familiar with. I turned to the first page and began to explore.

It was not quite as easy as I had hoped. I became exasperated with the book very quickly, as I found significant gaps in my knowledge. Kanji I recognized were scattered here and there, but seemed to make no sense. I sat back with an exasperated sigh. I was about to close the book and replace it in the chest until the day came when I could truly understand it when an echo of something Gen had said came back to me. The thought was elusive, and I had to relax and deliberately empty my mind before it would come to me.

Then, I had it. Not one thing, but two.

Haiku, he had said, were all about nature. I glanced again at some of the illustrations and nodded to myself. Yes, I could see that. Like an echo to that thought came another: *kanji do not always mean the same thing. They can have different meanings depending on the kanji on either side of them and the subject matter.*

The knowledge was almost as exciting as my first attempts to learn how to use the abacus. I took a deep breath and looked at the haiku again.

They didn't exactly make perfect sense, but when I allowed my eyes to simply skim over the text without forcing myself to understand every word, I found I could at least get an idea of what each haiku said. I was delighted and barely noticed Anzu when she brought me tea.

"Oh, that is pretty, Mi-san. Is it very valuable?"

"Probably." I closed the cover of my book quickly, as though I was jealous of anybody else reading it. Unexpectedly, a wave of regret made me deeply sad. I had accepted the book from Gen as though it was nothing. It had never occurred to me that it might be valuable, and now I felt very guilty. Gen was no more than a humble messenger. This book could well have been the most precious thing he owned. To distract my thoughts, I asked, "Can you read, Anzu?"

She laughed at the question. "Read? What use would reading be to me, Mi-san? Anyway, I am not clever like you. I would never be able to understand all those kanji."

Me, clever? I found the idea delightful, even though I did not believe it.

"I'm only learning. Brother Tengen is an excellent teacher, but it is still difficult." I added moodily, "I think Brother Tengen was very angry with me when I spilled ink on his robe." I hesitated and finally spoke the words I had been denying to myself. "I wonder if he will come back?"

I did not expect an answer, and I was surprised when Anzu answered me quickly. "Oh, I'm certain he'll be back."

I glanced at her, and I was sure I saw the same slyly amused expression on her face that I had seen on the maid's when Tengen rushed past her. I was tempted to demand why Anzu was so sure, but I felt it was beneath my dignity to gossip with my amah, so I did not.

In any event, she was right.

I had almost unraveled the riddles of my haiku. The more I read them, the easier they became. I exclaimed with delight when I understood how the same kanji could mean something completely different depending on the context. Even better was being able to read something that made sense, that was not just isolated words.

That was a key to everything for me, and I read and reread the poems with growing pleasure. There were still kanji I could not be sure of, but that did nothing to destroy my pleasure. The only thing that did trouble me was the knowledge that I had taken something so precious from Gen with barely a word of thanks.

Hard on the heels of that thought came another. I could, I supposed, give the book to Father and ask him to return it to Gen. I recoiled from the idea at once. Father was far too important to spend time seeking out a messenger. But I could ask him to give it to Tanaka-san. I could, I thought, manage to write a simple note and put it in the book, asking Tanaka-san to give it back to Gen.

I could do that. But I chose not to. Somehow, it seemed to me that it would be terribly rude to return the book in such an impersonal way. No, I would wait until the day came when Father called for me to go with him to Edo, and then I would hand it back to Gen myself. With suitable thanks, of course.

My daydream was so pleasant I had no idea Brother Tengen had come into the room. It was not until Anzu stood up quickly and bowed that I realized we were no longer alone. When I saw that Tengen had returned, I was so pleased that my greeting was over-blown and sounded false.

"Brother Tengen! But this is such an unexpected pleasure. I am so pleased to see you again. I quite thought you had forgotten all about me."

As I gushed the entirely inappropriate words, I could not resist glancing at his robe to see if the ink stain was still visible. It was not, and although the robe was perfectly clean, I thought it was also far from new. Its vivid saffron—I thought of the lovely color as sunshine through clouds—was faded slightly, and some of the hems of the material were slightly frayed. Instantly, I cursed myself for my selfishness. Just because I had feared telling Father about my clumsiness, Tengen had been forced to wear somebody else's cast-off garment. I was appalled.

"My kannushi instructed me to return to give you your lessons."

How very formal he sounded, very cold. Suddenly, I was no longer clever. I felt exactly as one of his young pupils must feel when he had made a stupid mistake.

"Then please convey my thanks to your kannushi," I murmured politely.

"I will do so should the opportunity present itself," he replied curtly. "I see you have been practicing your kanji. We will begin where we left off."

He sat down as stiffly as his words, with none of the fluid grace he usually showed. I noticed he seated himself on the opposite side of the chabudai to me, almost as if he wanted to put as much physical distance between us as he could without actually being discourteous. I watched him covertly as he picked up my untidy pile of papers and shuffled them firmly into a precise stack.

It seemed to me that each movement was causing him discomfort. I recognized his actions. I had been exactly the same when I had first begun to exercise, intensely reluctant to move a fraction more than necessary as I anticipated the pain that would follow.

"Are you well, Brother Tengen?" I asked cautiously.

He did not reply at once, and I was about to repeat my question when he answered me.

"I have a little stiffness in my back. It is nothing."

At once, I was intrigued. How had a teacher come to get a stiff back? Were my first thoughts correct? That this monk was not just a teacher of small boys, but also a practitioner of martial arts? Had his pain been acquired in combat on the dojo? Before I could ask, he handed me the inkpot and brush and began to bark out a series of words.

Without realizing I was doing it, I had stiffened in response to his tone. My back began to ache in protest at my posture and I blushed as I understood how very wrong I had been. Tengen had not been punishing himself with too much exercise. He was simply stiff with the effort of ensuring both his body and his tone of voice were as formal as possible.

What a fool I was. Tengen raised his head and stared at me with his eyebrows raised. I was sure he had read my mind, and I lowered my head and began to brush my kanji quickly.

It was very fortunate that I had practiced my calligraphy so much that it was second nature to me now. I had no need to think about the shape of kanji that I already knew. I was very grateful for that.

TWENTY-THREE

A bud unfurls in
The breeze, using its perfume
To entice the bee

I kept my head bowed as I tried—and failed—to concentrate on my kanji. I was unsurprised when Tengen spoke to me abruptly. I had expected to be scolded for my lack of attention, but his words were not what I had anticipated.

"What is this?"

I was startled by both his tone and his lack of formality. He was holding my book of haiku in his hand. I had dropped it in surprise when he entered. It must have fallen under the chabudai. I must have disturbed it when I reached for paper.

"It's a book of haiku," I said promptly, "by the poet Yosa Buson."

"I can see that. But what are you doing with it?"

Tengen sounded bewildered. It was the first time I had ever seen him when he was less than in total command of himself, and I was intrigued. I considered my words carefully before I spoke.

"It was loaned to me by a friend. I'd hoped it might help me with my reading, but alas, I cannot make much sense of the haiku. Still, the illustrations are very beautiful and I enjoy looking at them."

I was surprised how fluently I lied. I was raised to believe that telling the truth at all times was important, but it was clear that Tengen was deeply interested in the haiku. Apart from the odd occasions when he spoke about his pupils, it was the only time his coldness had cracked, and I decided that, just once, I would fib. If I could get him talking, who knew where it might lead?

"Your friend is quite fortunate to possess such a beautiful thing, as are you to have it in your possession. It is very old. I think it is possible that the master Yosa Buson created the woodcuts for the illustrations himself."

He sounded very envious. I was astonished, and—quite ridiculously—jealous. How could a book, a thing of paper and ink that could not even speak, raise such passion in a man who was usually as calm as a frozen lake?

"It is lovely," I agreed. Suddenly, I wondered if it was possible to turn Tengen's passion to my advantage. "I only wish that I could read some of the haiku for myself. Could you..." I hesitated, as if I was aware of the intimacy of my request. "Could you perhaps read some of the haiku to me, Brother Tengen? If you could show me the kanji at the same time, I am certain it would help me greatly."

I expected him to hesitate, probably tell me that such a thing was far in excess of my capabilities. I coughed to hide my astonishment when he nodded at once and moved to my side, close enough so I could see the open book in his hands. Hands that trembled.

Now it was I who felt uncomfortable. Tengen's robe was thin. We were so close, I could feel his body heat through it. His sleeve brushed against my hand, and I felt a shock run through my flesh.

I sensed he had noticed nothing amiss and fought to keep my gaze from his face. Unlike me, all his attention was on the open page. I was concentrating so hard, his voice startled me.

"This one is particularly beautiful. It might benefit you if you also looked at the illustrations; they will give you a clue as to what the haiku is about. Also, you must remember that all traditional haiku speak of nature in some way."

Gen had said that. Still, I nodded thoughtfully as though the knowledge was new to me and moved as if to ease the position of my leg. Tengen was close, too close for me to be able to concentrate on anything other than the smell of his body—incense mixed with clean flesh—and the sensation of feeling his breath on my neck. Even though I knew it was nonsense—the man was a monk; I was no more to him than an irritating pupil he was forced to instruct—I could not stop my pulse beating loudly in my ears and my face was flaring with heat.

Tengen appeared to notice nothing. He was stroking the page with a single finger, his lips moving as he read the haiku to himself silently. I wanted to snatch the book from him, reclaim his attention no matter what it took.

Hysteria rose in my throat and I swallowed laughter as I thought of the contrast between this man and the awful Yuto. How could I ever have contemplated being forced into marrying a man like Yuto, with his rolls of fat on his neck and his greedy eyes on my leg? His expression had puzzled me at the time. Now, I realized it was the excited look a small boy would wear when he was contemplating doing horrible things to an imprisoned insect. I shuddered and Tengen glanced at me with raised eyebrows.

"Something must have startled me," I said lightly. "As if a bird had flown up beneath my feet."

Tengen nodded absently and leaned forward so I could see the book better. I wondered if he would feel how rigid my body was.

"This haiku is particularly beautiful. You see how the illustration represents a field in blossom? What do you think the haiku might be about?"

Tengen spoke in his school master's voice. At once, I was irritated. What, did he think me one of his young boys that he had to ask me such a simple question?

"Summer crops in bloom?" I spoke sarcastically, but he missed my tone entirely.

"Quite right. The haiku says,

"Field of mustard blooms.
In the east, the moon rises;
Sun sinks to the west."

He spoke the words lovingly, running his finger across each kanji. Although it seemed to me that the haiku was no more than a statement of fact, I took a deep breath and nodded enthusiastically. At least I had learned something. I had tried to read this particular haiku myself, and I had puzzled over the kanji for mustard. Now, I spoke the words aloud to ensure that I understood the kanji perfectly.

"Yes, that's correct. But you are reading the words as if they are from a ledger rather than as poetry. Do you not feel the essence of nature that the poet has captured here?"

"Of course," I said enthusiastically. Even as I lied, a glimmer of what Tengen meant came to me. For a moment, I could see the field of yellow blossoms shimmering coldly in the cool light as they paused before closing their blossoms to the night air. Tengen leaned a little closer to turn a page and any sensation of coolness left me abruptly.

"This book itself is a thing of beauty," he murmured.

His fingers caressed the leather binding as so many other fingers must have done down the many years. As I reached across to touch it myself, my fingers accidentally brushed against his wrist.

At once, Tengen started back. He stared fixedly at the book. I sensed that he wanted to jerk as far away from me as he could, and that only politeness was keeping him still. I was so elated, I cared nothing for his obvious discomfort.

"That was so very kind of you, Brother Tengen. I am certain it would help improve my skills if you would read some more of the haiku to me. I am afraid that this is the only book in the house, apart from Father's accounting ledgers. Father does not have time to read for pleasure, and my brothers are not interested in books."

Another lie. My brothers were very interested in a certain kind of book, but not one that contained words. When I was much younger, being bored one day, I had wandered into their apartment in search of something to amuse me. The maids had not yet cleared away the futons or tidied the apartment. My brother's clothes were strewn about the tatami, and I sighed in annoyance at their untidiness. I was distracted when I found a book face down on Ichiro's rumpled kakebuton.

I picked it up eagerly and it fell open in the middle. I glanced at it and my mouth fell open in shock. There were no kanji, just a single illustration that covered both pages. On one side, a man—a samurai judging by his hairstyle—was looming over a woman whose robe was thrown aside. He appeared to be trying to thrust something into *her* body that was growing out of *his* groin.

Suddenly, I was overwhelmed with embarrassment. Both my brothers were in Edo, but what if a maid came in and found me looking at this distasteful thing? I thew it down as if it had grown hot and fled from the room.

The recollection of the disgusting pillow book was so strong, I glanced instinctively down at Tengen's lap. If his tree was as enormous as that of the samurai's, it was well hidden. By the time he looked up, I had reminded myself that he was a monk, and as far above such worldly matters as a cloud is the earth. I was ashamed of myself.

"Perhaps we could read some more on another occasion."

He would return, then. My pleasure was clouded by the fact that I felt quite silly. No doubt I had made something out of nothing.

"I would like that," I said simply.

"If you continue to make good progress with remembering your kanji—" *High praise indeed!* "—we will read some more of the haiku together."

I was certain that Tengen regretted saying "together" as soon as the word left his lips. For my part, I pretended not to notice and watched as he put the book down very carefully on the chabudai.

"Would you like to borrow it, Brother Tengen?"

I thought he would be pleased by the suggestion, but I had another motive entirely. If he had something that belonged to me, I knew he would come back, if only to return it.

His reaction surprised me. He glanced at the book, and then at me. His face showed the warring emotions in his thoughts. I saw longing flicker across his expression, followed by anger.

"I am a Buddhist monk, Mi-san," he said finally. His voice was calm and entirely without passion. "I have no possessions other than the robes on my back, the waraji on my feet, a razor to shave my head, and needle and thread to mend my robes should they become torn. The monastery provides my food, so I have no need of even an alms bowl. It would be very wrong for me to take possession of your book, or anything else."

He rose and bowed formally, obviously preparing to leave. I was abruptly determined that he would not walk away from me so easily and put my hands flat on the tatami on each side of my hips and pushed myself to my feet. I teetered for a moment, finding my balance, and bowed in return. For a terrible moment, I thought I was literally going to fall flat on my face. And so did Tengen. His hand shot out and cupped my elbow, steadying me.

His touch did not linger. He removed his hand so quickly, I was left wondering if I had imagined it.

"Thank you, Brother Tengen." Was I thanking him for the lesson he had given me, or for his touch? "I did not understand that you could have nothing personal, even it was only loaned to you. I will look forward to exploring more of the haiku with you next time."

He was looking around the room. Searching for my crutch, or to avoid looking directly at me? I solved the problem for him by nodding silently to the corner where my crutch was waiting for me. He moved with such lithe quickness to get it for me that I sighed out loud. A lifetime ago, I too had been able to move without worrying about each step.

I snatched my crutch from him with a grunt of thanks and stood slightly to one side, waiting for him to pass me. I was bitterly pleased that courtesy demanded the man must always go first—monk or not. It meant he would not see the ungainly lurch that was the only way I could walk, even with my crutch.

At the shoji, I bowed again and watched as he walked briskly out of our garden. Only then did I lean heavily on my crutch, gasping at the effort that the oh-so-short journey had taken me.

I clenched my robe in my hands, angry when the thick silk stopped me from tearing at the flesh of my withered leg. For the first time since I had awoken from my long sleep, I had no hope at all for the future. And with the contrariness of youth, I blamed Tengen for my unhappiness. I was sorry he had not gone for good.

CHAPTER
TWENTY-FOUR

I do not recall if
Your touch was ever as sweet
As the evening breeze

Called for Anzu and then—unreasonably—called again, louder, when she did not appear at once. She came at a run, alarmed at the urgency in my voice.

She fussed around me, scolding me for walking so far and offering her arm for support. I took it readily. I was so sunk in self-pity, I wanted nothing but to be comforted.

"What were you thinking of, Mi-chan, to walk so far? Did Brother Tengen help you?" she demanded as we walked down the corridor. Anzu was not tall, but I was still shorter than she was. Unreasonably, that annoyed me as well. I was fifteen, had I stopped growing? Was I fated to always appear as nothing more than a child?

I answered sulkily, "I had my crutch. I didn't need his help."

"I'm sure he would have been glad to support you." The anxiety had fled from Anzu's voice. Instead, I heard the smothered laughter I had noticed before when she talked about Tengen. She slid open my shoji and helped me through. "There, sit down. Shall I bring you some tea, Mi-san? Or perhaps you are hungry? With Brother Tengen arriving so unexpectedly, I didn't want to interrupt to ask if you wanted to eat at mid-day."

I had not even realized I had missed the meal. I was hungry, but my appetite was dampened when I recalled that I had not offered Tengen any food as I usually did when his stay coincided with a meal. The temple was at least an hour's walk from our house, even for a strong man who could set a good pace. I was aware that temple monks had one meal a day. If that were so, if he had missed the mid-day meal today at the temple, he would have to starve until noon the next day. Immediately, I felt intensely guilty.

"I am not at all hungry," I lied. Anzu looked at me with worried eyes and I gave in. She would nag if I didn't eat or drink something. "Perhaps some tea," I conceded.

Before she could go, a thought came to me and I called Anzu back. "Anzu, why were you so certain Brother Tengen would come back? I think he was very angry when I spilled ink on his robe."

"Brother Tengen would never stay angry for long with you, Mi-san." She had her hand in front of her mouth, as if she was smothering a giggle. That annoyed me as well.

"Why do you think that?" I spoke firmly, hoping that Anzu would see I was not going to put up with any silliness.

"Because he's besotted with you, Mi-san. Anybody could see that."

I almost replied, *Anybody but me,* but I was so surprised I said nothing, just stared at my giggling amah.

"It's obvious even in the way he looks at you when he

first sees you. His face is tender, as if he sees you as a wounded bird that needs to be cared for. A lot of big men are like that. They adore small women, and with your leg being as it is, he thinks you need to be protected." She must have seen the disbelief in my expression as Anzu went on quickly. "It's not just me who's noticed. All the housemaids think the same. And they think it's a wicked shame that a handsome man like Brother Tengen should be a monk. None of us can understand that. Such a waste!"

"Then you and the maids should be ashamed of yourselves," I said sharply. "It's nothing to do with any of us why Brother Tengen became a monk. He is, and that's all there is to it. And as for him being besotted with me, I've never heard such nonsense. I'm his pupil, and I can assure you that is how he thinks of me. Now, go and get my tea before I get really angry with you."

Anzu turned obediently, but not before I could see she was still smiling broadly.

I shook my head in disbelief. Anzu and the maids were silly girls who obviously had too much time on their hands. If they could see how Brother Tengen was with me when we were alone, they would soon change their opinion.

I drank my tea without tasting it. No matter that I knew it was nonsense, I could not quite disbelieve Anzu's words. Or was it just that I didn't want to? I was embarrassed at the very thought. Brother Tengen was a holy man, a monk. How had they arrived at such a ridiculous conclusion, based on nothing at all? And yet, I was tempted into wondering.

Was it really just me who had felt the prickle of excitement between us when we had touched? And Tengen had come back no matter how angry he had been with me. I laid my palm flat on my left thigh, feeling the ugliness there and grimacing at it. What nonsense all this was. What man—apart from the dreadful Yuto—could find a cripple attractive?

Tengen saw me as a wounded bird? Someone who needed to be cared for? I shook my head angrily. It was nonsense. It really was. Apart from anything else, there was no getting past the fact that Tengen was a monk. He had dedicated himself to a life of religious devotion. It was not possible that he should even see me as a woman.

But if he did, what then? I pulled my kimono away from my withered leg. It disgusted me so much that I looked at it only rarely. But now, I stared and wondered. The repulsive Yuto had looked at me with lust in his eyes when he had visited. Innocent as I was, I had seen that and guessed that to him I was not a thing to be treasured and cared for, but something he could tease and—yes—hurt.

But he had not looked at me with any interest at all before my illness. Was it possible that he had, in the nastiest of ways, found my deformity attractive? And if Yuto had found my withered leg enticing, then who was to say whether Tengen might also find it alluring? A wounded bird, Anzu had said.

Fury built in my belly, leaving me feeling sick. Any man who found me attractive was beneath contempt, monk or not. Somehow that train of thought led me to understand how Anzu—and the maids—had come to misinterpret how Tengen looked at me.

They thought themselves so very worldly, and me so innocent. But it was they who were wrong, not me. Brother Tengen was a Buddhist monk. To him, all life was sacred. I didn't doubt for one moment that the fact that I was deformed distressed him. Naturally, it did. He would know that I could never be healed, that I was fated to limp through life, attracting nothing but pity from anybody who looked at me.

Wounded animal? Yes, that was exactly how he saw me —an ugly, broken animal.

At that moment, I hated Brother Tengen as much as I hated myself.

TWENTY-FIVE

The sun will rise in
The morning whether I will
It to shine or not

"I'm sorry, Brother Tengen, I find it a little difficult to concentrate today. Perhaps you could go a little slower?"

I spoke with lowered eyes, my voice humble as I concentrated on brushing my kanji. My outlines looked ragged, as though I no longer cared about perfection.

I couldn't help it. As soon as I saw Tengen, all I could think of were Anzu's words. The more I tried to push them away from me, the more embarrassed I became. Even though I knew her to be mistaken, the thought that Tengen felt nothing but pity for me made me cringe. I was so self-conscious that I found it difficult to remember even kanji I knew well. My brush trembled, and my kanji bled through the paper.

I realized that I had suddenly become what Tengen had no doubt anticipated I would be—a timid, courteous pupil who listened to her tutor and did everything he instructed without question. Without a doubt, he would be delighted by the transformation. But it soon seemed I was wrong. I could hardly believe it. Was there no pleasing the man?

"Mi-san." Brother Tengen's voice was abrupt, but I was sure I could detect an undercurrent of concern. "Are you quite well? Do you have pain?"

"No, I am quite well, thank you." I snapped out the words, doing my best to cover my confusion. I did not want his compassion any more than I would welcome it from any man.

"You are certain?" His voice was not the voice of the strict, impersonal teacher I knew. It was hesitant, almost tender, and it broke me.

My hand was shaking so violently, I could not release the brush. Tengen took it from my fingers and put it in the pot for me. He was silent, waiting for me to speak. He would wait a long time, I decided defiantly. I was in no mood for learning today. He must go back to his monastery. Undoubtedly his other pupils would be unhappy that they had lost a day of freedom. Well, I could not help that.

The silence grew until it was unbearable. I had to speak.

"I am perfectly well." I said the words on a gasp. When I ran out of breath, I stayed quiet, knowing that one more word would undo me and I would cry. I would not cry in front of Brother Tengen. I would not cry in front of any man. Ever.

"You are not well at all, Mi-san."

I widened my eyes to keep the tears back. *I would not cry.* I repeated the sentence to myself over and over again until it became a mantra of defiance.

"I understand that your leg must give you great distress. Tell me, what did the physician prescribe for it?"

His voice was calm again. I was grateful for the tone and found that, with a great effort, I could follow his lead. As long as I didn't look at his face, as long as I didn't catch even a glimpse of pity in his expression, I could survive this.

I spoke to the tatami. "He told me to massage the leg every day with spikenard oil mixed with sweet almond oil. Also to apply a hot poultice of muriate of quinine to my knee each day. Oh, and he gave me some exercises to do, but they were to help my breathing."

"Nothing more?"

I was so surprised I looked at him. "The physician said there was nothing more that could be done. He said I was very fortunate to have recovered from the paralysis of the morning and I should be grateful to be alive. But he can walk. How does he know what it's like to be crippled?" I burst out bitterly.

"Very little by the sound of it," Tengen said quietly.

I glared at him. "And you know better, I suppose? Do they teach you how to heal in the monastery as well as how to teach little boys to read and write?"

It was unforgivably rude of me to speak to him so, but the well of misery that had been rising in my body since I had first seen my withered leg was finally full to overflowing. I could no longer contain my despair.

"I understand what you have suffered, Mi-san. But self-pity will not help heal your leg. There are things that should have been tried as soon as you awoke. But it may be that it is still not too late to help. Not cure, but help."

Tengen's voice was gentle but contained not a scrap of sympathy. It took a moment for what he had actually said to penetrate my fury. He was accusing me of self-pity? I, who had learned to walk with my hideous crutch and had followed every instruction given by the physician without a word of complaint? I gasped in disbelief and glared at him.

Brother Tengen stared back at me with raised eyebrows, his expression politely enquiring while he waited for my response. As my temper died to cold ashes, I understood that his words had triggered an emotion I had long since lost. *Hope.*

"And I suppose you can help me, even if the most skilled physician in Edo cannot?"

I could not allow myself to give in to something that was no more than a dream. I was sure I would not be able to bear it when he smiled and shrugged his shoulders and admitted he could not do anything for me.

I thrust my face forward aggressively, my shoulders hunched like a heron hunting for a frog. I had no doubt that the posture made me look even uglier than normal, and that gave me a bitter pleasure.

"I think so, yes," Tengen answered me calmly. I shook my head. I could not believe him. There was nothing anybody could do to heal a leg as withered and useless as mine.

"You think you can heal this?" I jerked the skirt of my kimono back high to reveal the whole of my deformed, twisted leg. I could not even look at its horror myself and turned my head to one side.

"Before this happened, I was betrothed. But his mother called the match off as soon as she saw that I was crippled. I understand how she felt. I can't blame her. What mother would ever want me for her son?"

And truly, I was not lying. Had I been in Lady Ai's place,

I too would have flinched away from my son marrying the hideous thing I had become.

"And your betrothed? How did he feel about losing his bride?"

Had the question been phrased with the least expression of interest, I would have flinched from answering. But Brother Tengen's voice was briskly unemotional, so I shrugged and answered truthfully.

"Yuto seemed to like me as I had become, far more than he did when I was whole. I think he would have been happy to accept me. Perhaps not as his wife, but certainly as his first concubine. I have seen nothing of this world, but even I have begun to wonder if there are men who are strange enough to prefer deformity to perfection. If some could even take pleasure out of a woman's disfigured body."

I stared defiantly at Tengen, but he simply shrugged. I was ashamed of my outburst. What could a priest know of such things? At the same time, his calm forced words to be ripped out of me as I found myself determined to shake his composure.

"I will never marry anybody, Brother Tengen. How could I ever accept a man prepared to marry a cripple such as me?"

I was panting with the strength of my emotion. I was ashamed of speaking the way I had, but my mind was made up. I would never marry. A husband and family were not for me. The thought gave me a bitter pleasure.

"You may be right. It would surely be an exceptional man who was prepared to put up with the sort of strong-minded wife that you would be."

Tengen was mocking me. He was making fun of my deformity.

At that moment, I hated him more than I hated myself. Because of that, I spoke with great politeness.

"You must forgive me. I spoke hastily, Brother Tengen. You were right, I am not quite well. I am tired and I cannot concentrate on my work. I do not wish to waste your time. It would be better if we finished early today."

I waited for him to rise, murmuring concern for my ill-health as he left. A sudden thought came to me and I pushed it away before I could reconsider and ask him to stay to eat the mid-day meal here. This would be yet another day when Brother Tengen went hungry because of me.

He said, "Mi-san, you are not tired. Angry, yes, although whether with me or yourself, I do not know."

"Go away. You have no idea what you're talking about." My voice trembled. I hated the weakness and raised my head to stare at Tengen defiantly. "There is nothing wrong with me that a little solitude will not cure. Please go away. I will send for you if I want to learn anything else."

I realized abruptly that my kimono was still pulled away from my leg. There was no circumstance in the world where it would have been proper for me to display my nakedness to a monk. To display my deformity in such a way was even worse. It was unforgivable.

Knowing that, I was determined I would not twitch my skirt back in place until he was gone. Let him get his fill of the true ugliness of his wounded bird and then see if he was still enchanted with me.

"Your leg is badly twisted." Had he not listened to one word I had said? "But I have seen worse results of paralysis of the morning. It will never be as perfect as the other leg, but there is much that can be done for it. If, that is, you are prepared for a lot of hard work over a long period and an equal amount of pain."

"Pain? Pain does not bother me at all. I have pain every time I look at this...this thing. Nor does hard work ever worry me. If I thought that you or anybody else could help me, I would work night and day. But tell me, *Brother Tengen*—" My voice dripped with the sweetness of honey straight from the hive. "—how a simple monk, a man who is a teacher of small children, can help my leg be straight again and to support me when I walk if a learned physician has washed his hands of me?"

"My father was a bonesetter, as was his father before him, and back through as many generations that I know of. I have not followed their path, but what is bred in one through the centuries cannot be forgotten or denied."

TWENTY-SIX

The crane in the field
Stands still until his mate comes
To distract his poise

"Can you break my leg and reset go back to how it should be? So I can walk properly again? Can you really do that? Is that what you're saying?" Tengen's few words had hoisted my spirits to the heavens. That had always been the answer. I had known it in my heart. And I was right! I was so excited I was panting.

"No."

Tengen spoke gently, and it took me some time to understand what he had said. Even when I did, I refused to believe it. He had just told me his forefathers were bonesetters. Why would he raise my hopes only to dash them a moment later? I must have misheard him. Or perhaps there was another reason for his change of heart.

"I have money. I can pay you for your services. I have a gold coin. It is gaijin cash, but Father told me it is still very valuable. You can have it if you will heal my leg for me." I added craftily, "I know you aren't allowed any possessions of your own, but your kannushi will surely be delighted if you can give him such a valuable gift."

I stared at Tengen, willing him to agree. When he shook his head, I was bewildered and so disappointed I itched to grab his robe and shake him until his teeth rattled. How could any man—still less a monk who should show kindness to all—be so cruel?

"Mi-san, listen to me. I could break your leg and reset it." I jerked toward him, my expression begging him to say he would do that for me. But he shook his head. "I could, but I will not."

"Is my gold coin not enough? I can persuade Father to give you more. Much more."

That was the problem, I was certain. Although Father called himself a Buddhist, his real religion was gathering money. I understood that. Without money, no man had any place in this world. What was the point of being a samurai if a person had not a coin to his name? Better, surely, to be a wealthy peasant than a poor lord.

"Money means nothing to me." I stared at Tengen incredulously. What nonsense was this? Even his kannushi had been pleased to accept Father's money in exchange for Tengen's teaching me to read and write. "The Lord Buddha tells us that we should perform acts of random kindness for no reward in this life, but to help us in future reincarnations."

He seemed to feel this was explanation enough. To me, it was nonsense and made no sense at all.

"Then don't take my cash. Do it for your own sake."

Tengen sighed. He put his palms together in front of his

face and closed his eyes. Was he about to meditate? I was so frustrated I almost screamed out loud. When he finally spoke, his voice was deliberate. Careful.

"You asked me why I thought I could help you when your physician could not. I told you my forefathers were bonesetters to answer your question."

"Yes, and now you're refusing to help me," I snapped bitterly. "Why? Why did you raise my hopes when you can't do anything?"

"I didn't say that. I said that I would not break your leg and reset it. I promise you, that would not help you. But there are other methods that could. Before I can do anything to help you, I need to know how serious the damage is. May I look carefully at your twisted leg? Touch it?"

I realized with a flush of deep embarrassment that my withered leg was still fully exposed. I turned my head away and gestured with my hand to Tengen to look, for I could not. In any event, what did it matter? I was certain in my own mind that the only way to help my leg was to reset the bone. If he would not do that for me, what was the point in him even looking at the leg?

He was silent for so very long that finally I had to look at him. He was frowning. Of course he was, my leg was hideous. I felt it twitch involuntarily when he finally touched it. His fingers were very cool and very gentle.

"Am I hurting you?"

"Not at all." As if I would have admitted it if he was. "I can feel your touch, but it doesn't hurt."

"And now?" Tengen had one hand above my knee and one below the joint and was pulling cautiously.

"It hurts," I said through gritted teeth. I hated admitting to my pain, but I had a growing feeling that it was important to be honest with him.

I took a deep breath and forced myself to look at my withered leg. At once, I had to swallow bile. It was hideous. The flesh was wasted. I could see the bone clearly. My knee looked enormous, like some bloated bird's egg. My foot was hooked like a claw. And worst of all, the leg was so twisted it looked almost as if my knee was back to front. I was so miserable that if I had been alone, I would have cried. But I was not alone, so I manufactured a smile and made myself watch Tengen.

I knew at once that he had not lied to me about his skills. His touch was confident, his gaze intent. A tiny flicker of hope rose in my mind, but I pushed it brutally down. He could—or would—do nothing. He had already told me that.

"It is deporable that your physician did not give you a program of intensive exercises for the leg as soon as you recovered from your fever. As it is, it has set itself in place, and not the place it should be in."

"Then it needs to be broken and reset," I persisted stubbornly. "If you know how to do that, why won't you do it for me?"

"Because it won't help. Not now. Look at your leg, Mi-san." I shook my head, but Tengen persisted. "Look at it. If I am going to help you in any way, you must understand what I am doing and why I am doing it. Watch."

Reluctantly, I focused on my leg. The more I looked, the more I hated it. But strangely, the very bitterness of my feelings gave me strength. I would not let my own body defeat me.

"I told you the men in my family have always been

bonesetters." Tengen appeared to expect an answer, so I nodded. "It is something that has been passed down to each generation. It is instinctive, although my father insisted that there is always something that can be learned about healing. But bone-setting is only part of the skill. There is no point in making a limb knit itself together and then leaving it alone. If one did that, then the bone would never be quite right again. It is essential that the limb is exercised and manipulated so that it can regain its former strength."

"But you will not break my bone and reset it how it should be." What was the point of this lecture if Tengen had no intention of helping me in the only way possible? I was astonished at how patient I sounded.

"It would not help you if I did." As he spoke, Tengen was performing a curious twisting motion with his hands on my knee. I could feel the joint becoming warm. I was astonished. It was the first time I had felt anything in the knee since I had awoken from my fever. "If I thought it would help, I would do it. But at best, it would do no good at all, and at worst, it could make the leg even more twisted. But that does not mean I cannot help you. I am certain that I can. It will take time, and much effort on your behalf. And when we have finished, your leg will still not be as perfect as the other one. But it will be better than this. Show me both legs, side by side."

Excitement made me breathless. No matter how I tried to push it away, hope would not be subdued. I was certain that Tengen would not lie to me, that if he said he could help me, then it would happen. I jerked my skirts aside fully and even the cruel contrast between my legs did not shrivel my spirits as it usually did. But still, I was cautious.

"How can you help? Tell me! If the bone is set too firmly

in place to be mended, how can the wretched thing be improved?"

"I can show you the way, but I cannot help you. Nobody can help you except yourself." Tengen lifted my good leg and held it in his palm. "Hold that leg steady there. Good. Now lower it slowly. And do the same with the left leg."

He hoisted it in his hand. I clenched my teeth with the effort, but as soon as he took his hand away, the leg fell lifelessly to the tatami. I almost howled with frustration.

"It's useless. I can't even feel it, much less hold it up."

"Fall seven times, stand up eight," Tengen said firmly. "Try again."

He took his palm away. My leg fell down.

"It's useless," I protested again.

"If you say so," he said amiably and stood up.

"What are you doing?" It was a stupid question. I could see what Tengen was doing—he was leaving.

"I told you, Mi-san, I cannot heal you. The only person who can do that is you. If you don't believe that your leg will improve, then it will not and we are both wasting our time."

I glared at him. Tengen smiled and waited silently.

"I cannot do this on my own," I said finally. "If you will help me, then I will do my best."

I thought that I had spoken bravely and that Tengen would appreciate my determination. I was wrong.

"Your best is not good enough. You must be certain that you will not fail. There can be no doubt in your mind. Not now, not ever. If that is not so, then there is no point in even beginning."

"The journey of a thousand days starts with a single step." How very apt the proverb was. I smiled sourly at the thought. "I will begin my journey today, Brother Tengen, and I will not fall."

"You will not fail," he corrected me gently. "You are certain to fall many, many times."

He smiled, and I realized it was the first time I had ever seen his lips set in anything but a straight line. The smile changed his whole face, making him appear younger and—the word came into my mind instantly—vulnerable. What nonsense was this? Surely it was I who was the vulnerable one, not him.

"But before we begin, I must talk to your father about what I am going to do and obtain his permission. He hired me to teach you to read and write, not heal your leg. You must understand, I can do nothing further without his permission. Or would it be better for me to speak to your mother? It may be some time before your father is here when I arrive, and I do not wish to delay any longer than is necessary. Too much time has been wasted already."

"No." Tengen was obviously startled by the urgency in my voice. I smiled and made a dismissive gesture with my hand. "Mother does not like to discuss illness. She finds it very difficult to talk about my leg. It would distress her greatly if you spoke to her. And as you say, it could well be some time before you see Father. I will speak to him myself this evening and get his permission."

I wondered if the blatant lie showed in my face. I was not used to lying, and I felt sure it must be obvious. But Tengen appeared not to notice anything.

"Good. For my next visit, please have a quantity of very hot cloths ready. And something sturdy but soft, an old obi would be perfect."

I was so pleased that he believed me that I didn't realize he was waiting for me to stand up to wish him farewell. I stood up clumsily. Normally, the lack of grace would have caused me great sorrow, but today it bothered me not at all. I was shocked when he held his arm out silently, inviting me to take it. Such an intimate touch from a relative stranger was disturbing. I took it anyway with genuine gratitude and leaned against him heavily as he walked and I shuffled to the shoji. He really was slender. I could feel his ribs through his robe, and I felt guilty all over again at making him miss two meals.

He bowed politely before he slid the shoji closed behind him. I waited, staring at the closed shoji, until the crisp sounds of Tengen's feet crunching on the gravel died into silence. Then I closed my eyes and allowed my thoughts free rein.

I had no intention of asking Father for permission. Still less would I mention it to Mother. The very thought made me shudder. At least I had not lied about that. Mother hated and feared illness in any form. Miserably, I knew that she would have preferred me to die than to live the rest of my life as an ugly, deformed cripple. She kept me out of view, as if by hiding me she could deny that there was anything wrong. Lady Ai's visit had been the only time anybody outside our household had seen me since my illness. Mother would, I knew, be appalled at the very idea of a man—even if he was a monk and, thus, not really a man—looking at my leg and touching it. Nor would she believe that he could help. If my highly paid and supposedly highly skilled physician could do nothing, how could a simple monk do anything?

But I knew Father would not react in the same way. He would probably agree to Tengen trying to help me walk again. Why not? Brother Tengen's kannushi would get his fee no matter how the monk spent his time. Yet, I did not want to ask him. I could bear my own disappointment if Tengen failed. But I could not bear seeing my dear Father endure the same sorrow. Better by far that he knew nothing of my plans. If I succeeded, we would rejoice together.

For some reason, the thought gave me great pain.

TWENTY-SEVEN

The tall grass must bend
Before the wind. Is it not
Better to be straight?

I watched as Tengen pulled lengths of steaming cloth from the basket Anzu had left. He tugged them into shape and paused with them draped over his arms.

"Mi-san, what is wrong?"

His head was tilted to one side like an alert bird. I stared at his ears rather than meet his gaze. The morning sun was streaming through them, tinting them a delicate pink, like the interior of seashells. Absurdly, I thought they were ridiculously small, shapely ears for such a tall man.

"Nothing," I said abruptly. Tengen did not move, so I spoke quickly. "If you don't hurry up, those cloths will cool."

I stuck my leg out, silently demanding that he lay the cloths over it. He moved with an elegant smoothness that made me want to howl. I, too, had once walked like that, without a second thought. The hot cloths were soothing and I began to relax.

"They are still very hot. Anzu must steam them like rice." His fingers massaged the cloths against my muscles. The sensation was delicious and I sighed with pleasure. "I will leave them on a little longer than usual. Your muscles are unusually tight."

His busy fingers were running up and down my leg as he spoke. The sensation was intensely pleasurable.

"I had the most dreadful cramp last night. I was in agony." I tried to wiggle my toes and failed. I was so annoyed with my failure I forgot about the pleasure his touch was giving me and spoke spitefully. "You must have pushed me too hard yesterday."

Tengen sat back on his haunches and stared at me.

It was the strangest thing, but when my kimono and the hadajuban beneath were thrown aside to allow Tengen to work on my leg, it did not embarrass me in the least. Yet, when he was looking at my face, rather than concentrating on my deformity, I longed to pull both layers of clothing primly back in place. I felt my face flare scarlet, but I held his gaze firmly.

"You think so? Then perhaps we should stop for a few days. Longer than that if you are still not comfortable."

His voice was toneless, like he was commenting on the weather. Absurdly, I was hurt. I had just told him he had caused me pain. Didn't he care?

"I was in great pain," I insisted.

Tengen shrugged. "Cramps can be very painful. But in this case, it is also a good thing."

Good? When I had nearly screamed out loud with the agony? When I had sprawled on the floor, mewling like an infant, unable to help myself? Was he truly incapable of empathy? I was hurt all over again, but in a way I could not explain. All I knew was that I wanted him to be hurt in his turn, so that he could understand how I had suffered. He had hurt me. I needed to hurt him in return.

"Good? You think so? I was in agony and could do nothing about it. Nothing at all to help myself. You call yourself a healer, Brother Tengen, but it seems to me that you don't know what suffering is. I thought that it was part of Lord Buddha's teachings that all his followers should respect life and care for it as best they can. Yet, you tell me that the pain you subjected to me is a good thing? I'm sorry, I don't see how that can be."

My voice was near to breaking and I coughed to hide my emotion. Tengen's face was a closed book, his expression calm, yet I was sure I could see something in his eyes that told me I had hurt him. Hurt him very deeply. A moment ago, that was what I had wanted, but now I felt nothing but remorse at my clumsy attempt at revenge.

"The fault is mine, Mi-san."

I thought at once that I must have been mistaken. He sounded perfectly polite, but not at all disturbed by my comments. When he carried on, I was certain I was right.

"I am afraid I have not explained myself very well. Naturally, I regret that you had pain. But it is still a good thing. You thought that your leg was dead. That it would never experience any sensation again. But you were wrong. Your leg resents being made to work, to live again. That was why you felt such pain in it. Truly, it is said that only through adversity may one learn."

He sat back, emphasizing the chasm between us, and smiled at me. I thought it was a satisfied sort of smile, and if I could have reached out far enough, I would have pummeled him with my fists. Anything to take that smug look off his face.

Instead, I nodded as if I not only understood what he was saying but agreed with him. Tengen was saying something. I heard his words, but I could not make any sense of them for the torrent of emotions that ripped through me.

Suddenly, I understood that I was truly in error. Not for any reason that Tengen would understand, but because I had tried to fool myself. I did not hate him for making me suffer, but I did want him to *care* about my suffering.

Without any warning, my spirit howled for comfort. I was a little girl again, a child who had been badly hurt through no fault of my own and could make no sense at all of it. I wanted to hold out my arms to Tengen and have him hold me tightly and tell me he would make everything better for me. It was an experience I had never known, but that did not prevent me from hungering for it now.

I had convinced myself that Tengen cared for my well-being, not just because it was his duty as a monk to do so, but because he cared as a man. Now, his calm response to my pain hurt me far more than the physical agony I had suffered in the night.

In addition to my hurt, I was embarrassed by my foolish error. Tengen was not a man, he was a monk. I would take great care to remember that in the future. Somehow, I managed to sound calm.

"I see. I did not understand what you meant, Brother Tengen. Thank you for correcting me."

How very steady my voice was! Tengen seemed to have noticed nothing. He simply nodded and began to massage my leg again. The cloths had cooled, so he peeled them away. I jerked with surprise as he moved his hands to my right leg, stroking it gently but firmly.

His touch was the nearest thing I had ever known to a caress, and in spite of my distress, I found it delightful.

"You are a very strong woman, Mi-san. I know you will not allow yourself to fail, at this or anything else."

That was not what I wanted to hear a. I knew I was strong, I had no need for him to compliment me on it. I was relieved I had not spoken my earlier thoughts aloud. Tengen would no doubt have been appalled to find that I was neither strong nor a woman.

"Thank you," I muttered, watching his fingers work on my flesh. His touch was almost hypnotic. Already I was forgetting how angry I was with him. I watched in fascination as he stroked and smoothed the flesh on my leg, using his thumbs to ease out tensions that had me searching for comfort every time I tried to find rest.

"It is essential that your good leg be strong enough to support you, at least at the moment." He spoke crisply, as if I had asked why he was concentrating on my right leg. He glanced up at me as he spoke and, accidentally, his fingertips brushed against my inner thigh.

I felt as if my skin had been scorched by fire. Instantly, my flesh tingled as all tranquility fled from me.

I could not look at Tengen. I could not move. For a moment that was less than a heartbeat, he froze, and then his fingers curled into his palm as abruptly as a snapping turtle catches its prey.

There had often been long silences between us. When Tengen massaged my leg, it was so soothing, I almost passed into a state of meditation. When I hesitated over a kanji, he did not speak, but waited for me to find the answer myself. Those silences did not disturb me in the least.

Now, the silence between us was anything but acceptable. The small space between us tingled as the air does when a storm is about to break. I could not understand what had happened. I was certain that Tengen had touched me in such a way before. I could not remember a specific time, but it had to be so. He was not the sort of man to skimp on a task. My massages were deep and thorough. What had happened that had made it so different this time?

I glanced at Tengen from beneath my eyelashes. Clearly, he was as disturbed as I was. His face was flushed, his eyebrows gathered together. He was staring at his hand as if it was foreign to him. The answer came to me in a flare of understanding.

When he had touched me before, it had been accidental. This time, he had meant to do it. Did he regret it? Of course he did. He was a monk. For him to give in to the need to touch a woman—any woman, not just one who was in his care—so intimately must have been anathema to him.

But he was also a man. And—for once—the man had triumphed over the monk.

I took a deep breath, and then another. Although Tengen's touch had aroused feelings in me that left me both bewildered and deeply excited, I forced my body to be still while I followed my train of thought to its logical conclusion. In my mind, I saw the beads on my abacus flicking back and forth, commuting to a logical and inevitable result.

Just as calculations on the abacus could not lie, I understood that I had done this thing. I—the wounded bird, the deformed creature that everybody wanted to hide—had aroused such longing in a holy man that he had, for a moment at least, thrown aside everything that was important to him. Because of me.

At that moment, I knew my childhood had ended. My mind made the unbidden leap from child to woman as surging feelings began to run through my body. The hair on the back of my arms stood up. Even my fingertips began to tingle.

Without any real understanding of what was happening to me, I was deeply excited. Suddenly, I was aware that the love I craved was no longer that of a child. Tengen's touch had awoken me both physically and mentally. The memory of my brothers' pillow book came back to me and I felt heat rise in my body as I imagined Tengen probing at my private parts in just the same way as I had seen in the illustration that had repulsed me so very much. But then, I had been no more than a child. Now, I wished I had taken a better look.

A much better look.

CHAPTER
TWENTY-EIGHT

My thoughts are scattered
Like pebbles on a beach. They
Are beyond counting

Had Tengen responded differently, I would have come to my senses. Would have realized that I was behaving not like the adult I thought myself to be, but more like a spoiled brat who whines for something that is beyond her reach. I would probably have decided I had placed too much weight on the incident. That his touch had been entirely accidental and that he was embarrassed by it—as I should be.

But Tengen betrayed himself, and my doubts fell away instantly.

He stood—with none of the grace that usually made watching him a pleasure—and fixed his gaze into the corner of the room as if he had discovered a cobweb there and was too polite to mention it. He spoke to the same cobweb, his voice wooden.

"I think that is enough massage for today, Mi-san. I do not wish you to suffer cramps again. Instead, I will show you some simple stretching exercises that will help loosen your muscles and should help prevent your leg from going into spasms at night."

He glanced at my futon as he spoke and instantly twitched his eyes to one side. I saw his obvious embarrassment. Clearly, Tengen the monk had shouldered aside Tengen the man.

For a moment, at least.

Tengen had never hesitated to offer his arm to help me to my feet before. Today, he did not. I smiled timidly, keeping my eyes lowered.

"Perhaps you would be kind enough to pass me my crutch, Brother Tengen?"

He moved with such alacrity, I knew he was relieved he would not have to touch me.

I used my crutch and the flat of my right hand to lever myself to my feet. I had long since mastered the art of getting up in this way by myself. Today, I took care to make it seem difficult. When I finally stood, I leaned heavily on the crutch, my left leg thrusting through my kimono. I made no attempt to hide it.

"Are you comfortable, Mi-san? It is important that you have your balance before we begin," Tengen said shakily. His gaze was no longer on the ceiling. It was drawn to my leg as if by a powerful magnet.

"I think I'll manage," I said cautiously.

"You will not fall. I promise you."

I concentrated on every syllable of the short sentence, wondering if I was reading too much into his words. I waited for him to add, *I will not allow you to fall*, but I was disappointed.

"Take a deep breath. So deep you can feel your belly rise with air. Let it out. Breath in again. No, deeper than that."

I was confused. This was not at all what I had expected. What I wanted. I tried for a little sympathy.

"May we begin the exercises? My leg is beginning to ache standing still," I pleaded.

"Not yet. First, you must see. Close your eyes."

I bit back my disappointment. As the proverb says, *The mouth is the source of disaster.* Clearly, Tengen the monk was back in charge. But what nonsense was this? Close my eyes so I could see? Bewilderment was added to my frustration.

"I don't understand, Brother Tengen," I protested. "See what, exactly? And how can I see if my eyes are closed?"

"You must see within yourself," he said earnestly. "If your mind can see you reaching your goal, then you will succeed."

Oddly, his words recalled the occasion when my elder brother had toyed briefly with Confucian philosophy, but such an improbable deviation from his usual behavior did not last long. I found out later from Anzu that he had been deeply smitten by a beautiful and very intelligent oiran. This woman had amused herself by telling my brother that she was a devotee of Confucius, and he had believed her. He had been so deeply in lust with her that he had begun to study the discipline before he realized that she was teasing him purely for her own amusement. Perhaps this was something to do with the great philosopher?

Not wanting to seem foolish, I pushed my distress with the change in Tengen's mood aside and asked hesitantly, "Is it something to do with Confucius?"

"Not at all."

I was crushed. I had hoped to sound extremely knowledgeable.

"Adherents of Lord Buddha have used the power of the mind to help guide people to better health for many hundreds of years."

This made no sense to me, so I replied abruptly, wondering what game he was playing now.

"So, if I think my leg is straight, then it will be so?"

"No." Tengen must have seen the confusion in my expression as he went on quickly, leaning toward me in his desire to explain. I swayed instinctively toward him in return, not even aware that Tengen had jerked away. I went rigid with disappointment and embarrassment. "I understand that this is a difficult concept for you to grasp. But please, do not dismiss it until I have guided you further."

"I will try."

"Now, close your eyes."

Even though I was supported by my crutch, without my sight, I felt unbalanced. I swayed slightly, and instantly Tengen was by my side, his hand beneath my elbow.

I could feel his body heat through his thin robe and became excited again. Inconsequentially, I wondered why he didn't freeze to death in winter? Was that also something to do with his mind taking control of his body fully, instructing it to obey in ways I would not have thought possible?

I was surprised to find I was becoming interested in what he was saying. Not just because Tengen felt this strange sort of meditation would help my leg, but also because the idea that I could control my own body appealed to me. I was so fascinated that I leaned against him without thinking. I was recalled quickly to reality when I felt him stiffen. I knew he wanted to break the contact but could not bring himself to do so in case I fell.

"Take a deep breath, Mi-san." His impersonal teacher's

voice again. I did as he instructed and felt the breath fill my lungs. "Let it go. And another."

This was quite pleasant. The deep breathing seemed to be relaxing me. Would it, I wonder, help me sleep on those nights when thoughts crowded my head and would give me no rest?

"Should I carry on?"

"No, breathe normally. Listen to me, Mi-san. When do you feel happiest? Most comfortable?"

The deep breaths had relaxed me more than I realized. What would have seemed an irrelevant question moments ago now sounded perfectly reasonable.

"On my futon. Sometimes, I wake in the night and for a while I forget about my leg. I even begin to make plans for the next day. At least until I remember I am a cripple and there is so very little I can do."

I was astounded. I had never thought that about myself. And if I had, I would never have shared it with anyone else. It was too personal, too painful.

"And what if you did not remember that you are crippled? How happy would you be if you continued making those plans and were able to do exactly as you wanted?"

What nonsense was this? As soon as I tried to move, my leg reminded me that happiness was no longer an option for me.

"But I *am* a cripple," I said. I tried to keep the resentment out of my voice and failed.

"If you are a cripple in your own mind, then your body will continue to fail you."

Tengen's voice seemed strange. Perhaps because I had my eyes closed, I heard more clearly than I could have when I could see clearly. His voice was trembling. The hand that cupped my elbow gripped tighter.

"Teach me not to fail," I whispered.

"I will not fail you."

His words were so close to what I had longed to hear moments ago that I was thrown off balance. My thoughts flew wildly, out of my control. I had never been so unsure of myself and cursed silently, certain that every time Tengen looked at me he saw nothing but a needy, clingy child.

I was relieved when he spoke quietly but firmly. Clearly he had not noticed my distress.

"In your mind, see yourself lying on your futon." I made an involuntary gesture toward it. On days when Tengen was not expected, the maid rolled up the futon and took it away. Because I needed to lie down for my massage, today it was still in place.

"No, I am not asking you to lie down. In your mind, see yourself lying on it. You are very comfortable, the kakebuton lying lightly on your body. Can you imagine that?"

That was surprisingly easy. I wriggled slightly, easing out an imagined crease in the futon.

"And now?" It was an effort to speak. I was so comfortable, I really wanted to drift off to sleep.

"See yourself stretching your body. Do it bit by bit. Start with your neck, and then your back. Make sure your hips are perfectly comfortable."

As he spoke, my body obeyed his words. Part of me was aware that I was still standing, supported by Tengen's hand and my crutch. But it seemed as if reality was the illusion, and that I really was reclining comfortably on my futon.

"Does that feel pleasant?"

"Very," I murmured.

"Good. Now stretch your legs. Both of them at the same time."

Tengen's voice had fallen to a whisper. It was so soothing, I obeyed him without thinking, arching my back and pushing my legs forward. I barely felt him step away from me. Hardly felt him tugging my crutch away from me.

For a moment, I was filled with content.

And then my left leg buckled and I fell to the tatami with a thud that jolted my teeth.

Humiliation filled every crevice of my body. I wanted nothing more than to curl myself into a ball, to hide from the world. Tengen had done this to me. He and his talk of needing to see myself whole and healthy. He had made a fool of me. In my distress, I was sure he had done it on purpose as some sort of revenge for his shame at touching me inappropriately.

I hated him. Almost as much as I hated myself for being taken in by the nonsense this smug monk had spun me. By the false hope he had raised.

"Mi-san, are you hurt?"

There was no trace of sympathy in Tengen's voice. He might have been asking if I thought we might have rain later. I was grateful for it. Had he sounded concerned, I would have broken and wept for the indignity of my position. But I was not grateful for anything else. I needed to be alone so I could weep with nobody to see me.

"I am not hurt," I said through gritted teeth. "Go away. I'll get myself to my feet."

"I didn't offer to help you," Tengen said mildly. If anything, his words increased my pain. "If you can get up, we can continue the exercises."

"Leave me alone. Go away and don't come back. I've learned all I need to know from you, Brother Tengen."

I might as well have saved my breath. Tengen did not move.

"No, I will not go. You are my responsibility. I will not leave you until I have done everything in my power to help you."

His voice had changed. Brother Tengen the monk had never spoken to me like with such a note of tenderness. I quickly glanced at him. His face was expressionless. His arms were held loosely at his sides, and he appeared relaxed. Yet, I could feel that his body was almost vibrating with tension. He locked his gaze on my face, appearing to look straight into my eyes.

He lied.

I knew he was hiding something, in much the same way I always knew when Anzu was fibbing to me. She did just as Tengen was doing now. Instead of looking straight at me, she focused her gaze on a point just above the center of my eyebrows. It looked as if the person you were talking to was looking you straight in the eyes with perfect honesty, and it was a clever trick, but once deciphered it was an easy way of knowing when somebody was trying to either deceive you or was not telling the whole truth. In Tengen's case, I guessed it was the latter. I didn't care. I was ashamed of my weakness and wanted nobody else to see it.

"Leave me alone," I repeated. "I'll get up when I'm ready and not before. I don't need your help. If I hadn't relied on you in the first place I wouldn't be lying here. And you are not responsible for me, I assure you."

Tengen ignored me. He held his hand out silently. I counted my heartbeats to twenty and then took his hand. I sensed his surprise that I appeared to have given in so easily.

His grasp was very strong. When he tried to pull me up,

I refused to help him in any way. Physically, I could not match this man's strength, but there had been many mornings when Anzu had tried to make me get up when all I wanted was to turn over and take comfort in my kakebuton, and I had learned that passive resistance can be as effective as the most determined physical resistance. Now, I was almost a dead weight, and the dead weigh far more than the living.

Tengen grunted with surprise and then loosened his grip without letting go of my hand. For a moment, we were in limbo.

"Please," he said woodenly. "Allow me to help you to your feet, Mi-san."

I put my hand to the floor and the next time he tugged, I pushed hard and rose as lightly as a leaf blown by the breeze.

I had won. We both knew that, and I was satisfied. For the moment, at least.

TWENTY-NINE

Cherry blossoms fall
When their time comes. But they are
Renewed with each spring

Anzu fussed around me anxiously.

"You must tell Brother Tengen he is working you too hard, Mi-chan. Even when he is not here, you are either practicing your kanji or exercising your leg. You have not played your biwa for a long time. It must be lonely without your touch."

Her face was so concerned, I hid a smile at the thought that an inanimate object could feel any emotion.

"My biwa will be waiting for me when I am ready to play it. The important thing is that I learn as much as I can from Brother Tengen while he is here."

Anzu frowned. The expression made her seem older than usual, and I wondered absently how old she actually was. She always seemed the same to me, but if she had nursed my brothers as well as me, she must be older than I thought. As old as Mother? Possibly so.

"Why? Has he said he will stop teaching you? I'm sure that's not so." But she didn't sound certain, and her innocent remark forced me to face the fact that there must come a time when Tengen would no longer be here every other day. That eventually either his kannushi would decide it was time he returned to his pupils or, more likely, Father's purse closed. And what then? Suddenly, there was a hollow place, very like prolonged and extreme hunger, in my stomach. I spoke decisively, knowing that if I hesitated Anzu would ask question after question. Questions I could not answer.

"No, not at all. Brother Tengen is determined that with his help I will be able to walk again. He will stay for as long as he is needed. But you know the saying, Anzu, that it is the high-flying dragon that repents. For myself, I think Brother Tengen is the dragon who flies too high. It is his pride that deceives him. Pride that makes him think he can help me walk. I know he's wrong. Look at my leg. Does it seem any different to you now than it was before Brother Tengen imposed his exercises on me?"

"Yes," she said simply. I glanced at her sharply, sure she was lying to please me. But Anzu's face was open and honest, as always. "Before Brother Tengen began working with you, that leg was just shapeless. Now you can see that you have muscles there again. It looks stronger, and I've noticed you don't lean so heavily on your crutch when you walk as you did before."

I stared at my leg dubiously. It looked just the same to me. Unexpectedly, I was ashamed I had snapped at my loyal amah. I smiled at her and Anzu responded with a beaming smile of her own.

I was taken aback to find myself jealous of her simple happiness. Had Anzu been cursed with paralysis of the morning, I had no doubt that rather than be miserable about the legacy of a withered leg, she would rejoice in the fact that she was still alive. I wished that I could share her optimistic outlook, but I could not.

I said, "Well, in that case, I must work it even more. Pass me that old obi, Anzu."

I took it from her and made a sling of it, which I threw over my left foot. It was made of strong silk and provided excellent support for my leg. I tugged the obi straight and began to pull the leg up and down, up and down, until it ached in protest. When I decided I could take no more, I put the obi to one side and took my foot in my hand, forcing the leg to press against my grip.

So great had been my concentration that I had not noticed that Anzu had gone. I waited, listening to make sure she was not hovering outside in case I needed her. When I was sure she was not, wondered if she was right about my leg. I ran my hands down my withered limb, laying my palm flat on my thigh. Carefully, I flexed the leg and felt it respond. Not a great deal, not what could be called true movement, but it certainly twitched.

Something, then. But nowhere near enough reward for all the effort I had put into getting such a small response. I glanced at the sun shining through the shoji. Tengen would be here soon.

I would not let him find me sitting here, apparently helpless. But first there were a number of obstacles to overcome. Getting to my feet was always the thing I hated most. I had never given it a thought before I had been inflicted with paralysis of the morning. Now, it took both a great deal of planning and even greater care with every move.

I pulled my crutch toward me and held it at an angle.

Gingerly, I put one hand on the tatami, counted to three, and then forced myself upward. My upper body strength had certainly increased. I had always been quite slim, but now the muscles in my arms and across my ribs were lean and strong. I teetered for balance, pushing into my crutch, and then forced my left foot to the ground.

Anzu was right, my foot did touch the floor a little better, and my leg was perhaps just a little less bent. But the limb was still withered and twisted, an ugly thing that had no right to be attached to the rest of my whole, healthy body. I was certain that any slight improvement had nothing to do with Tengen and his absurd instructions to watch myself walking in my mind. No, the progress had come about through nothing but my own hard work and perseverance.

I swayed slightly and stretched out my arms to help my balance, wedging my crutch underneath my arm rather than leaning on it. Once I was sure I would not fall, I relaxed and put my crutch in its proper place as I hobbled across to the shoji and pulled it to one side, relishing the cool morning air. My leg was throbbing angrily, as if it was annoyed that I had worked it so hard.

I glared at it in frustration. It seemed to me that the trouble was twofold. Most obvious was the strange angle my leg stubbornly refused to move from despite Tengen's efforts. I thought it looked exactly like an elbow when it is placed akimbo on the hip. I grunted with sour amusement at the thought. But also due to the angle of the knee and my misshapen foot, my left leg was much shorter than the right. When I walked—if the slow, dragging shuffle that was the best I could manage could be called walking—I lurched like a very fat, drunken man waddling uncertainly from the inn to his home. I made myself face the truth brutally.

Tengen's massages and the exercises I had worked at so very hard had strengthened the muscles in my leg. But it was still not enough to allow me to walk normally. Even with my crutch to lean on, I was forced to drag the leg along the floor, hobbling like the cripple I was.

The cripple I would always be.

I shook my head angrily, trying to shake the miserable thoughts away. I reminded myself again that Tengen would arrive soon. I would not allow him to find me prey to self-pity. As always when I thought about him now, my mind slid back to the moment his fingers had brushed against my inner thigh.

I shivered. It must, surely, have been the cool breeze against my skin, not the image of Tengen's face when he had touched me that had come to my mind unbidden and unwanted.

Abruptly, I grabbed for my crutch and jerked myself to my feet. Before I could become prey to self-doubt, I threw the crutch as far as I possibly could away from me. For a moment, I stood with my arms outstretched like a cormorant drying its wings in the sun and then took three uncertain steps at what felt like a run. It was nothing but a mockery of speed, but to me it was a triumph. I had achieved my goal. I was standing, unsupported, in the middle of the room. As there was no one to share my victory with, I glanced at my clutch smugly. Alas, even that small success was denied to me as I realized I could have spared myself much effort by simply using my crutch and then throwing it back into the corner. I hissed with annoyance at my lack of thought and then closed my eyes, concentrating on my breathing.

So successful was the calming effect of the deep breaths in and out—"belly breathing," Tengen called it—I had to grudgingly admit that the technique *was* helpful in calming my thoughts. It even helped me to sleep on bad nights.

Tengen's arrival took me by surprise. If I hadn't heard the slap of his bare feet in the corridor, he would have caught me with my eyes still closed. As it was, I had time to open my eyes and put a cheerful smile on my face as the shoji slid back.

"Mi-san." Tengen's tone was no more than courteous, but I thought I saw a flicker of surprise in his eyes that I was standing unaided in the middle of the room when he came in. If only he knew how much effort it had cost me! "You are standing without support. You feel no need for your crutch? You walked across the room by yourself?"

"I did." Well, I had walked three steps at least and was proud of myself. Why not admit it?

"I see."

Just two commonplace words, but it seemed to me that they carried more meaning than two simple words should. In response, my heart slowed and I could hear its sluggish pulse beating in my ears. I counted each beat, concentrating on the slow rhythm to prevent my mouth from making a fool of me. He was silent for so long, I felt the need to speak.

I said tentatively, "Tengen? Brother Tengen?" My voice was the mewing of a distressed kitten. I cleared my throat, but before I could speak again, Tengen was talking. Quickly. Cheerfully.

"Well, it is good to see that you are so much recovered. You have worked very hard, and it is no less than you deserve."

I felt like one of his young pupils, thrown a word of

encouragement for successfully completing some small task. I shriveled inside.

"If you keep on with the exercises I have shown you, I have no doubt that your leg will get even stronger, and when that happens, your balance will improve still further."

He paused and I almost mouthed the words I was expecting to hear him say with him. He was going to say that he could do no more for me, and that it was clear that I no longer had any need of his help.

I was, truly, a fool. I had been wrong all along. I had seen what I wanted to see. Tengen's touch of my thigh had been no more than an accident, deeply embarrassing for any man, even more so for a monk. To make matters worse, I had behaved like a love-sick girl, running after a man who thought of me as no more than the children he taught at the monastery.

From the corner of my eye, I saw Tengen put his hands together in the prayer position. I thought the gesture was unconscious, one he often made when he was thinking deeply. I understood that he was trying to find words to gently tell me that he had done all he could for me. That today would be the last time he set foot in Father's house. The knowledge that the blame for it was mine and mine alone was no comfort at all.

When he spoke, I was so startled by his words that my head swiveled toward his face so quickly I heard my neck creak.

"You have elder brothers, so I assume you have a dojo?"

My lips moved, but no words came from my dry throat. What did either my brothers or our dojo have to do with this? Tengen was waiting patiently, so I answered him uncertainly.

"We do. It is at the end of the garden. But what do you want a dojo for?"

"I do not want it—you do. Come, Mi-san, we will walk there. Slowly, so you do not exhaust yourself."

I did not want to go to the dojo. For me, it was a long journey. Much further than I had attempted to walk since my illness had crippled me. I stared at him, expecting some sort of explanation. I got none. He simply stood back courteously and held his hand out in a gesture of invitation.

"You say the dojo is at the end of the garden?"

I nodded silently. Already, my withered leg was beginning to throb with pain. I concentrated on that pain, trying to use it to take my mind from my humiliation.

"Quite a long distance, then, and we have work to do when we get there. Perhaps, if you do not mind me suggesting it, it would be better for you to use your crutch to walk there? I do not want to overexert your leg."

I hesitated, which was a mistake. Abruptly, I was weary. I had no energy to argue and accepted his offer with a shrug.

"If you think it would be best, then I will use it."

Tengen scooped up my crutch and handed it to me courteously. Even with the aid of the heavy crutch, walking was far from easy for me. The garden was large and traversed with carefully swept gravel paths. For the able-bodied, an easy walk. For me, it took all my concentration not to slide and turn my ankle on the loose surface. I kept my head down and counted each step we took outside the house, glancing up at each tenth step. I was relieved I could concentrate on putting one foot in front of the other as Tengen talked most of the way, mainly about the book of haiku we had read together.

"Your dojo is well-kept," he said approvingly when we

finally reached our goal. Tengen was assessing the circle of beaten earth as if he knew what he was talking about, and I stared at him, wondering what a monk would know about a dojo. Especially a monk who spent his time doing nothing but teaching small boys how to read and write.

He traced a pattern in the compacted sand of the dojo with his toe and spoke dreamily, without glancing at me.

"I came to the priesthood late in life." His expression was unreadable. "When I was a young man, I took great interest in the pleasures the dojo has to offer."

Pleasures? This was where I had dislocated my shoulder, so I associated the dojo with nothing but pain. Just as I was going to be hurt anew now. Suddenly, I was very impatient. We were here. Whatever Tengen wanted with this place, let him get on with it.

"My brothers used to use it a lot, but less so now that they are interested in the pleasures Edo has to offer. Why are we here, Brother Tengen?"

Tengen blinked. It seemed to me as if his mind was returning from a long journey. He smiled, but it did not quite reach his eyes.

"Then it is a shame that your dojo should be kept in good repair for nothing. Today, and for many days to come, we will remedy that. Will you stand in front of me, Mi-san?"

"Why?" I held his gaze, wondering at the expression in his eyes.

"You told me some while ago that you never intended to marry. Do you still feel that way?"

I watched him intently, sure there was some deeper meaning behind his words.

"Yes. I also told you I did not want to marry any man prepared to take a cripple for a wife." I spoke brutally and felt a perverse pleasure when Tengen winced. He recovered quickly.

"And that is why we are here. You are not only a woman, but a crippled woman. And by your own choice, you will have no man to take care of you."

I kept my face stone as the hurtful words tried to batter me into tears.

"There are those who will see you as an easy target. It is my duty to ensure that they are wrong. You must be strong. Strong enough to be capable of defending yourself, Mi-san, against whatever may come to you."

He was staring at me, holding my gaze. I kept my head high and tried to ensure that my expression was calm as I considered his words. They were so very different from anything we had spoken of before that I could not quite take in what he meant.

"And how am I supposed to achieve that?" I asked finally. "Even if I wasn't crippled, I am small and slim. I could never be a match for a man."

In answer, Tengen took a deliberate step away from me, and began to stretch, moving fluidly from side to side as his fingertips brushed his ankles. He said nothing but raised his eyebrows in invitation and I supposed I was to follow his actions. I held my hands out, palms up, in bewilderment. What nonsense was this?

"What are you doing? I don't understand," I said.

"Show me your hands, please."

I held out my hands reluctantly, and Tengen turned them so my palms faced upward. I wanted to snatch them away from him, but he held them firmly.

"They are very small," I said jokingly, trying to lighten the mood.

"Indeed, they are. Small and well kept. But they are also

hands that have never had any need to work, and because of that they lack strength. As do you."

"What of it? I cannot change either the fact that I am a small woman or that I am a cripple. Why have you made me walk all this way if all you want is to tell me how useless I am?" I spoke bitterly, my anger overflowing.

"I am going to teach you how to defend yourself."

I laughed incredulously. Tengen waited until I was silent before he went on and then spoke as if I had not interrupted him.

"I have taught you to read and write. I have taught you to make the best use of your withered leg. Now, I will teach you how to defend yourself. You are a stubborn woman, Mi. You do not like to fail. You will not fail at this final task."

I stared at Tengen doubtfully. He seemed to assume I needed no further explanation. His complacency annoyed me until I realized he was right about one thing—I hated failure.

Already Tengen had resumed his exercises and was moving with fluid grace. I jammed my crutch beneath my arm and tried to copy his actions. I was chagrined to find that movements he made look easy were difficult for me. No matter how hard I tried, I could not reach down to my ankles with my fingers, nor could I twist as far as he did.

After a while, my withered leg began to throb with pain. I refused to give in and continued to imitate Tengen as well as I could. The morning sun was beginning to rise high when he finally paused.

"Put down your crutch." It was less a request than an order, and immediately I became defensive.

"I need it," I insisted. "All this twisting and stretching has tired me. If I put it down, I will not be able to move at all."

Tengen held out his hand. After a moment, I understood he expected me to hand him my crutch. I clutched it closer to me and gasped indignantly when he stretched forward and plucked it away from me as if it was no more than a twig. He threw it over the boundary of the dojo and I missed its support at once.

I threw my arms out for balance. Too late I saw my fingers were hooked into claws, as though I was grasping at the air.

"Do not worry. You will not fall. I will not let you fall."

He had said that to me before, and I had believed him. Now, I was less sure.

"What now?" I wavered slightly as I spoke, but finally found a careful balance.

"Watch me. Copy what I do."

What did he think I had been trying to do all morning? I bit back the sarcastic comment and waited stoically for his instructions.

"Use your right leg to anchor yourself. Leave your left leg at whatever angle is comfortable for you."

He began again, his movements so slow, so easy, I thought that I should be able to follow him effortlessly.

I was wrong.

Each stretch, each change of direction, led him effortlessly into the next. For me, it was almost impossible.

I was so afraid of losing my balance that I soon fell out of his rhythm. I thought that Tengen had not noticed, that he was simply carrying on, but eventually I realized that he was repeating each movement several times. After many repetitions, I fell into an almost dream-like state. My attempts fell far short of his stylized grace, but at least I was making progress and I no longer had any fear of falling. At least while Tengen was beside me.

If you could learn to
Fly with the starlings, would you
Leave me far behind?

I had no doubt that Tengen's intentions were good, but I could not help find the idea laughable that I would be able to defend myself against a fully grown man. I did not voice my doubts. It was a delight to be outside the house and doing something—the more so as I found the exercises challenging—and I enjoyed the clean, fresh air of the garden.

Apart from that, I felt that being outdoors was somehow less intimate than being alone in the house with Tengen close by. He was invariably polite, even kind in his own way, but distant. Savagely, I wondered why I had expected anything more. He was my teacher. Anything else had been nothing but my own imagination.

In any event, I was sure the time I spent outdoors had brightened my complexion. I simply felt better, more confi-dent, and—yes—happier. Neither my father nor my brothers appeared to notice the difference, and as Mother never saw me, neither did she, but the ever-vigilant Anzu did. Nor was she slow to comment.

"Brother Tengen is good for you, to be sure. Your skin is glowing, and your hair shining like the sun." She sighed theatrically. "Such a pity that a fine young man like him should be a monk. Do you think he had some tragedy in his life that drove him to take up life in a monastery? If you can call it a life," she added darkly.

I sat silently as Anzu combed out my hair, enjoying the rhythm of each stroke. Absently, my thoughts wandered to Tengen. Just like Anzu, I had no idea how he came to be a monk. Was he happy in his calling? Did he ever long for his past life to be restored to him? I recalled his comment about enjoying the pleasures of the dojo and wondered how much he missed the physical challenges of his other life. From there, it was a very short journey to speculating if there might be *other* physical things that Tengen missed. Once the thought came to me, I could not shake it off.

My knowledge of what actually took place between men and women was limited to the odd comments I had heard my brothers exchange when they thought I was not listening, and of course my glimpse of my brother's pillow book. Even then, I did not believe their boasts about their successes with high-class oiran.

I found I was blushing and deliberately pushed the memory aside. It was all nonsense. Tengen was a monk. He was surely above any physical urges.

Satisfied with her attentions, Anzu put the comb down and began to massage my scalp with her fingertips. The sensation was soothing and I fell into almost a dreamlike state, not unlike the extremely relaxed and pleasant state of mind I had begun to experience when I exercised in the dojo. I had started to look forward to that. Or at least I did, until the day Tengen attacked me.

We had finished the first round of exercises. I was standing quite comfortably, my thoughts far away and my eyes closed, as I waited for him to resume the slow actions of the activity he told me was called "qigong."

"It originated in China many thousands of years ago," he explained seriously. "It is not just a system of exercise, although that is important. But it clears the mind and allows the practitioner to balance himself both mentally and physically."

Usually, Tengen was generous with his time and waited for me to signal I was ready to continue. But on that day, he did not even wait for me to open my eyes. I sensed him moving, but before I was aware of his closeness, his hands fell on my shoulders—quite lightly—and his foot hooked behind my right knee far less lightly. Less than a heartbeat later, I was lying on the floor of the dojo with the breath knocked out of me.

"What? Why did you do that?" I gasped. I was shocked and bewildered. Had it been anybody but Tengen who had laid his hands on me, I would have been terrified. As it was, I immediately assumed I had been particularly inattentive and that his patience had finally snapped. I wondered if this was the way he punished his pupils in the monastery. The thought recalled me to my surroundings. Father was paying him for my tuition. I was not one of his little orphan boys, and he had no right to treat me as if I were. I waited for him to apologize profusely for losing his temper with me.

He did not. He stepped away from me and bowed politely, his palms together in front of his chest.

"I have not hurt you, Mi-san. Your dignity may be

dented a little, but I have caused you no pain. It is time you moved on, and that was your first lesson. Qigong has improved your balance and your breathing greatly, but it has also done far more than that. It has helped to heal your mental well-being. Tell me, if you had seen me moving toward you, apparently with ill-intent, how would you have responded?"

"I would have hit you with my crutch." I was as bewildered by the question as I was by his actions, but I replied promptly. At the same time, I wondered if perhaps Tengen had gone mad. I could think of nothing else that would explain his attack on me.

"And if you did not have your crutch at your side? What then?"

I stared at Tengen in sullen anger. He knew I always had my crutch with me. Even when I was exercising, I kept it tucked beneath my arm. I was no longer as dependent on it as I had once been, but the idea of walking without it was unthinkable.

He knew that as well as I did. Was he mocking me with his question? And why, in the names of all the gods, was I still lying helpless at his feet? He *had* gone mad. That had to be the answer. And it was a well-known fact that madmen were stronger than their sane counterparts, and Tengen was very strong anyway.

I had to humor him; I did not want to think what he might do if I didn't.

"If I am standing, I need my crutch," I pointed out. "So, I will never be without it."

"And if you cannot be without it, how would you have been able to hit me with it?" Mad or not, Tengen was sly.

"I would have found a way," I said.

"You no longer need to depend on that crutch." Tengen

spoke so calmly it took me a moment to realize what he had said. "I know you do not believe me, but it is so. Tell me, are you still certain you will never marry?"

I was lying on the beaten earth of the dojo where he had thrown me, having a polite conversation with a monk who had suddenly taken leave of his senses. Without warning, I was taken with an urge to giggle at the absurdity of it all.

"I am literally at your feet, Brother Tengen," I said cheerfully. "But I promise you, I will never be at any other man's feet. I have said that I am certain I will never marry. I have not changed my mind, nor will I. Why do you ask?"

He held his hand out silently and pulled me to my feet. This time, I did not resist. My crutch lay some distance away, where it had fallen. I could not reach it, and I was not going to ask Tengen to retrieve it for me. I balanced awkwardly, my clawed foot just touching the ground, and stared at him, tense as I waited for his next manifestation of madness.

He spoke bluntly. "Your parents are no longer young. They cannot live forever." He had said this before. It had hurt then, and it hurt now. "When that time comes, you will need to rely on your brothers, and I fear that they will not care for you as well as one might hope."

His words hurt, but they were nothing I had not thought of myself many times. I supposed when my parents left this world, I would be allowed to live with one or the other of my brothers, and if I did not cause a fuss and was not expensive, then they would tolerate my presence. My brothers might be lazy, but they were fond of money. If my plans to become a valued member of Father's staff came to fruition, surely they would accept me, if only as an unpaid clerk. And if I was wrong, and life as a dependent became intolerable for me, I would enter a monastery.

That thought did make me shudder. Confined within a community of women, many of whom would have entered the monastery not for religious reasons but because, like me, they had no other option. Condemned to listen to their endless trivial gossip all day, every day. Trying and failing to join one of their cliques. That would be a living death for me.

This vision of my future was so bleak I spoke harshly. "If I have no other alternative, then I will join a monastery. You did it. So can I."

Anger blazed in Tengen's face for a heartbeat. It was gone so quickly that I was not sure if I had imagined it or not. Still, my pulse throbbed a little quicker in my ears. I had to be careful. If he had truly run mad, even if I screamed, I would not be heard from the house, and I had seen no gardeners at work nearby.

"You are wrong," he said sharply. "Until death claims us, there is always an alternative if one chooses to look for it. You can read and write, Mi-san. You told me yourself that you are skilled with the abacus. You spent time in your father's place of business. You must have gained much knowledge about how such a business works. And still you believe your only future is as a dependent, despised by your brothers and bullied by their wives? Would life as a nun really suit you better?"

I wondered if he had read my mind, but I dismissed the idea as soon as it came to me. There was no need for clairvoyance. What other options were there for a woman alone? Especially for a woman who was deformed as I was.

He was staring at me intently, waiting for a reply. Since he had picked me up, he had stood a polite distance from me. I could see nothing unusual in the way he held his body, nor was there any fire of madness in his eyes. I was tired of both trying to placate him and talking of my future. I spoke angrily.

"Why did you throw me to the ground? Have you taken leave of your senses?"

"I told you. The time has come for you to move on in our lessons. You have become complacent, Mi-san. That will not do. Unless you wish to have your future dictated to you, you must be prepared to think and act for yourself. You may remember that some years ago, my temple was badly damaged by a very violent typhoon. A number of monks died in the devastation, and many more were injured."

I grunted impatiently. What had this abrupt change of subject to do with me? Tengen ignored me and carried on.

"The kannushi is a wise man. He noted the area of the temple that was least damaged and gave orders that when the temple was rebuilt, that part should contain a large room with walls and a roof of sturdy planks. In effect, a room within a room. It is the temple's storm room, where we all can go if the elements threaten danger.

"Do you understand why I am telling you this? At the moment, you are sitting firmly in your own storm room. You feel safe. Because of that, you are becoming lazy."

I gasped indignantly. There were many occasions when my leg did not want to exercise, yet I followed Tengen's instructions carefully. And now he was accusing me of being lazy?

"I needed to shake you out of your complacency. Speaking to you would have done no good. I had to shock you. Listen to me, Mi-san." His voice was suddenly urgent. "Whatever the future holds for you, it will be better for you if you can defend yourself. Even if you never need to do it, it is good that you know you can look after yourself if it becomes necessary. I intend to show you how to best any man who troubles you so that truly you need never be at a man's feet again."

I liked the sound of that greatly. Both my brothers still saw me as a vulnerable child. Occasionally, it amused them to snatch my crutch from me, refusing to return it until I forgot my dignity and begged them to give it back.

If they were reprimanded more severely than usual by Father, then they would invariably take their anger out on me. After a few too many cups of sake, verbal cruelty often degenerated into games of "pinch the little sister" or "tug at her hair until she has to beg to be left alone." I could almost see the amazed disbelief in their eyes if I could give them a taste of their own medicine. Was it really possible I could throw big, well-fed men such as my brothers to the floor as easily as Tengen had thrown me? I was delighted by the idea.

"Teach me," I said impulsively. I raised my head and met Tengen's eyes. I expected him to be smiling at my response, but oddly, his expression seemed to hint at hidden pain.

THIRTY-ONE

Fish shoal together
For protection. The hungry
Tuna is not fooled

Tengen told me over and over again that the mind is greater than the body. That the power of the mind can achieve anything.

It seemed nonsense to me, especially when Tengen tried to tell me I could overcome my disability with my mind as he threw me repeatedly and very easily. If it had not been for my stubborn streak, I would have given in and admitted that I could never hope to learn to defend myself. But I was determined that this new discipline would not defeat me, and I began to wonder if my stubbornness was another way of believing in myself, and that perhaps Tengen was right after all.

I was so buoyed up by the thought that I concentrated hard and began to anticipate Tengen's moves. I waited until he was off guard and then swiveled on my good leg and neatly landed a blow with my elbow in his ribs. It was not a hard blow, but it startled him, and with his attention distracted, I had just enough time to grab the front of his robe and then pivot, using his body as my anchor.

I let go of the robe as I felt his balance leave him and hopped back to watch the dust rise from the dojo floor with the impact of his body. Pure elation bloomed in my mind as my shadow fell on him and, for a moment, blotted out his familiar features.

"You always told me that the secret of bodily combat was using the strength of one's opponent against them," I panted. "Now, I understand what you mean." At that moment, I felt strong. If I could do this, I could do anything. Achieve anything.

Tengen got to his feet lithely. "I am delighted you finally believe something I have told you," he said drily. "You took me unawares, Mi-san. Next time, it will not be so very easy."

From that moment on, it seemed to me that there was a sense of urgency in all that Tengen taught me. He insisted that we resume our schoolroom lessons. I agreed reluctantly. I enjoyed the fresh air and physical contact of the dojo far more than sitting inside with a brush in my hand. When I argued, he agreed to divide our time between the schoolroom and the dojo.

I noticed that Tengen seemed to have become increasingly impatient with me. He pointed out the slightest error in my kanji and corrected my reading briskly. At the same time, the lessons in the dojo changed.

"I opened my chest to you, but you did not take advantage," Tengen scolded. "If you see the opportunity again, then ram your elbow as hard as you can here." He put his hand just above his flat stomach and patted it. "Don't hesitate. If your opponent sees what you are about to do, then he will have time to tighten his stomach muscles and your blow will glance off. You must strike like summer lightning —fast and unexpectedly."

"It would hurt you," I protested.

"Try it and see."

The next time I saw my chance, I took it. Tengen winced and sucked in a breath of pain.

"Better. Much better," he gasped.

On another occasion, he grabbed my shoulders and spun me around, keeping one arm around my throat. I could breathe easily enough, but I knew that if his forearm pressed just a little harder, I would be unconscious very quickly.

"And now, Mi-san? Pretend that we are no longer in the dojo. I am a stranger with evil intent who has taken you by surprise and there is nobody near to help you. Screaming would do no good except to leave you breathless. So, what are you going to do?"

I clawed at his arm. It was like fighting a tree trunk. Tengen grunted with amusement; he had expected that. So, I went as limp as a dead animal. I allowed my head to loll forward and gave a little gasp.

It worked. Instantly, Tengen was all concern. "Mi-san? Have I hurt you?" His grasp relaxed and I wriggled away from him. My hands grasped the front of his robe and I tried to throw him, but he recovered quickly and grasped my kimono in his turn. For a moment, we rocked to and fro, both knowing that neither had the advantage.

I was elated when Tengen gave in first and released his hold. I followed cautiously.

"Well done. I didn't teach you that, but it is a good strategy." He stepped back to indicate he would not follow through with another move. I watched him suspiciously.

"But if I was a man intent on doing you harm, I would not care if you had been hurt or not and would not let go. What would you do then?"

"I don't know," I admitted.

"If you were outside the house, you would be wearing either geta or zori. I suggest you always wear geta. The back tooth will be more effective."

"Effective for what?"

"I will show you. Turn around and I will put my arm around your neck again." I did as he instructed. "Now, you have pretended to faint and I have not let go. What now?"

I bent my head and tried to bite his arm, but my chin got in the way. I wriggled, but Tengen simply tightened his grip. His ribs were protected by my body, so I had no opportunity to strike him there. I could think of nothing else and admitted it.

"I don't know. I can't reach you."

"Balance on your left foot. It should be easy because I am taking your weight. Now ram your right foot as hard as you can into my instep, just where the foot meets the leg."

I did as he instructed. Even though I was bare-footed, I heard him grunt with pain. He released me at once.

"I understand why you said geta would be better than zori," I said thoughtfully. "The bar across the sole at the back of a geta would cause great pain if I stamped hard enough. But I am small and light. If you had held me off the ground, I would not have been able to reach your instep."

Tengen stared at me and a smile crossed his face slowly. He smiled so very rarely that I was surprised.

"You are correct. But there are ways to counter that. Your attacker will have one arm around your throat. That is only natural as it is a simple bandit attack. He will probably attempt to pinion your arms with his other arm, but even if he does, it will be your upper arms. Your hands and lower arms will be free. If you cannot kick—and kicking anywhere but on the instep will do nothing but exhaust you—then reach down and grab for his kintama."

I flushed with embarrassment at his words, but Tengen appeared not to notice.

"Grab as hard as you can and squeeze even harder. Unless you are very unfortunate and he is a eunuch, it will cause him unbearable pain. Do not let go until the man has let go of you and is bent double in pain. When that happens, make a fist and hit him with a straight arm, here." Tengen put his finger on his temple at a spot above his right eyebrow. I pursed my lips doubtfully.

"My hands are very small. Will I be able to hurt a grown man?"

Tengen put out his hand, palm up. I laid my hand obediently on his palm and grunted in surprise as he pushed back the sleeve of my kimono almost to shoulder level.

"You appear small, and delicate, Mi-san. But because of the exercises we have been doing and because your arms and shoulders support your entire body, your upper body is very strong indeed. If you straightened the whole of your arm and let loose like a flying arrow, putting your anger into the blow, when you strike in the place I have shown you, then it would be a remarkably strong man who did not fall before you."

Abruptly, I found it hard to catch a breath. Tengen was staring at me intently, and I could not read his expression. All my worries fled like dust before a brisk breeze as I blurted without thought, "And are you that strong man, Tengen?"

THIRTY-TWO

Grass shrivels and dies
When the field is harvested.
Rain will bring new shoots

I had been so certain that I knew what his reply would be that when he spoke, I shook my head, unwilling to believe what my ears had told me.

"You have surpassed anything I could have hoped for you, Mi-chan. You no longer have any need for me."

I fastened hungrily on his use of Mi-chan. It was the first time he had ever used the endearment. He was either lying to me or deceiving himself. He had to be. I remembered—oh, so very clearly—how he had reacted when he had touched my thigh. Accidentally? I had convinced myself that it had been an accident, but suddenly I was prey to doubt. His expression a moment again had been, I was certain, hungry. For me. And now he dared to say he was of no use to me? When I replied, my voice held a calm certainty I did not feel.

"You are wrong, Tengen. Or you are lying."

"I am a monk, Mi-chan."

The words sounded as if they had been wrenched from deep inside him. Suddenly, I knew how very dangerous the game I was playing was. I didn't care. It was already too late to step back, so I gambled everything on a few words.

"Then go, Brother Tengen. Now."

He held his hands out, fingers spread, as if he was physically warding me off. I did not move. Did not speak.

"I cannot." His whisper was a leaf blown on the wind. I said nothing. Tengen's decision had to be his own. "I have taught you everything that I thought might help you, but nothing at all about the longings that lie between a man and a woman. But I should not be the one to enlighten you about the ways of the world. The fortunate man who you take for your lover will do that. I should go."

Should, not will. Triumph made my head throb. "Then go," I said softly.

"I cannot."

"Then stay."

"I should not."

Impatience consumed me. My flesh felt like a living thing. I could feel my skin tingling even as my stomach felt liquid and heavy with longing. I knew of no cure for what consumed me—except for Tengen. Tengen the man, not Tengen the monk. Yet I knew I would not try and persuade him to stay here with me. That if I had to beg, then there would be no joy in whatever was to come after. It was an oddly mature thought for a young girl.

I folded to the ground as gracefully as I could, for once not sparing a thought for how bad my withered leg must look, sticking out from the skirts of my kimono. Tengen was swaying slightly, like a man who has drunk too much sake. Finally, he shook his head and sat down, facing me.

"I knew this day would come the moment I saw you," he said. "After that first lesson, I begged my kannushi to release me from my duties, to allow me to go back to teaching children."

"So, you came back because he instructed you to carry on," I said flatly. My disappointment was so deep I was drained of all other emotion. I stared at the beaten earth of the dojo and felt as if I had been beaten flat myself.

"No. The kannushi said it was my decision. That he would not make that decision for me. So, I came back to you. I could do nothing else. I could not stay away. But neither could I allow myself to tell you how I felt. I was a coward. I tried to seem cold toward you, to make it appear that I thought of you as a child, as nothing but my pupil. I was severe. I did not make any allowance for a single mistake. Did I make you hate me for it?"

Instead of answering his question, I said, "Anzu told me that you saw me as a wounded bird, something that needed to be cared for and protected. I thought she was mad. Was she?"

He exhaled sharply. "Anzu sees far more than I would ever have guessed. You didn't believe her?"

"No. I thought she was imagining it." I watched his face. Carefully. "Is that truly how you see me, Tengen? As an object of pity?"

"Would you ever allow anybody to pity you, Mi-chan?" There was warmth in his words, and I was tempted to smile as I shook my head. "Then you have answered your own question. When I first saw you, I was sorry that the paralysis of the morning had caused you so much harm. But after a while, I gave thanks for your illness."

His words were deeply hurtful, so I responded angrily. "That's more than I ever did."

Tengen raised his hands, palms outward, in a gesture that said clearly, *Wait,* and I understood that he was searching for words. The right words. Finally, he said hesitantly, "I'm sorry. I didn't mean I wanted you to be hurt in any way. I would never want to see you suffer. But if you hadn't been as you are—" Such a delicate way of phrasing it! "—then you would have been married to your betrothed and I would never have met you."

"Then you would never have missed me." I was still hurt and in no mood to make him feel better.

Tengen hung his head and spoke to the ground so softly that I had to strain to hear him.

"No. Had I never met you, I suppose I would have grown old and contented in the service of the Buddha. Never again would I have known the joy of loving a woman."

Before this moment, I had never so much as flirted with a man. And now Tengen—*Brother* Tengen—was telling me he loved me. And I had no answer for him. Things had changed between us so swiftly, my mind was whirling. This was what I had longed for. Waited for. Yet, I had given no thought at all to what would come if the moment arrived. I was struck dumb and looked at him, silent and helpless.

As long as I could remember, I had longed for somebody to love me. To tell me they loved me. And now that the words had been said, I had no idea how I was supposed to respond. It was all so unfair!

"That is very kind," I said lamely.

Tengen threw his head back and laughed. It was a rich sound, full of joy.

"Ah, Mi-chan. One day very soon you will be a grown woman. You will know how to answer a man when he says he loves you. I am glad you are not yet worldly enough to give a glib answer."

I wasn't sure if I had been insulted or complimented. I froze as Tengen reached out and stroked the side of my face with his fingertips. My cheek flamed under his touch. I forgot that I was terrified, that I had no idea what to do or say, and grabbed his hand, rubbing my face against it like an affectionate cat demanding to be stroked.

"I'm sorry," I said absurdly.

"You have nothing to be sorry about. And I will make sure that does not change." He took my fingers in his hand and kissed my fingertips. His lips were warm. Why, then, did I begin to shiver? I tried to tuck my withered leg beneath my skirts to hide it from his view.

"No, Mi-chan. It is part of you. Do not try to hide anything from me now."

Tengen had seen my leg many times before, but only when he was trying to massage life back into the deformed limb. I felt that he had looked at it with the neutral gaze of a physician. Now, that had changed, and I did not want him to see its true ugliness.

"I hate it," I blurted. "I have thought time and time again that I would be better off without it."

"You would not," Tengen said calmly. "Look at your leg, Mi-chan. Can you not see how much straighter it is now than when we started to treat it? Then, it was nothing but a scrap of flesh over bone. Now, it has muscles and is shapely. It is part of you, and so it cannot be anything but beautiful."

To my horror, he bent down and kissed the crook of my knee.

Had he kissed my other leg, I would have taken great

pleasure in it. As it was, my lips peeled back from my teeth in distaste.

"No," I whispered. "It is withered like a bit of old firewood. It is so ugly, I don't want to look at it myself."

"It is part of you. It could never be ugly."

Tengen ran his hand down my deformed leg and then began to rub it gently with his fingertips. With each stroke of his fingers, I felt warmth suffuse the limb. It was so pleasurable that I held my breath, wanting nothing to stop him from caressing me.

But he did. He took his hand away and slipped his arm around my shoulders. He sank to the ground and I went with him, willingly.

We were joined along the length of our bodies. Absurdly, I wished I was taller—even lying down, my head barely reached Tengen's shoulder and I could not see his face. I badly wanted to see his expression, to read the truth or the lie in it, but for once my courage failed me and I spoke into his shoulder.

"Am I truly beautiful to you?" I asked softly. I held my breath, knowing I would hear the lie in his voice if it was there.

"You are beautiful, not just to me but to anybody who has eyes to see." His fingers began to stroke my leg again. It was not at all as it had been when he massaged me. Then, his touch had been firm, as if he was pressing out creases in a robe. At this moment, I could barely feel the pressure of his fingers. His touch made my skin tingle. It was delightful.

"Have you heard of mizuage, Mi-chan? The traditional ceremony all maiko must go through before they can become geisha?"

I had, but I couldn't understand why Tengen was

talking about it now. No matter, I had no wish at all to distract him from touching me. It was wonderful. I was floating in an unruffled sea of pleasure. I made a noise of agreement, and he laughed softly, deep in his throat.

"Ah, but I doubt you will have heard what I am about to tell you. Before the mizuage ceremony can take place, the maiko's aunty will have chosen a dana for her. A sophisticated older man who is rich enough to pay for the pleasure of taking the maiko for the first time."

Tengen's hand was circling higher and higher on my thigh. If he hadn't been speaking to me so calmly, I would have been strung as tight as the strings on my biwa. As it was, I could at least pretend I understood what he was talking about.

"And what about the poor maiko? Does she have no choice but to have a stranger make love to her?" My voice trembled. I thought I must sound exactly like a maiko waiting for her first lover.

"She knows her dana, I promise you. She will have met him many times before that night." His voice was lightly teasing. I shivered. "And she will know her lover-to-be intimately. Beginning seven days before they are united, her dana will visit her in her room. He will bring a raw egg with him each time. He will break the egg and eat the yolk, but he will take the white of the egg and massage it into his lover's legs, starting here." Tengen's fingers made slow circles on my thigh, just above the knee. "Each day, her dana's massage will get a little higher, as will his lover's anticipation. By the last day, the maiko will welcome him into her embrace. And her dana will be so strong from eating so many egg yolks that he cannot fail to do her justice."

I gasped as his fingertips brushed lightly against my

inner thigh. This time, it was not accidental. He paused for a moment and then his fingers pattered back, light and gentle as a mouse. Only then did I realize that all the time he had been talking his hand had been moving higher and higher. I understood now why he was telling me about the mizuage ceremony. Had he not distracted me, I would have been wound so tightly I could never have welcomed his touch.

Tengen took his hand away and trickled his fingers up my stomach. It took him so long to undo my sash that I had to clench my hands into fists to stop from helping him. Had I not thought of the maiko enjoying her lingering courtship, I would have been unable to stop myself. Perhaps it was that thought, but for some reason it seemed important that I allowed him to take the initiative at this most delicate of moments.

My patience was rewarded. The intricate knot parted finally and Tengen pushed my robe to one side and lowered his head to my breast, teasing my nipples with his tongue.

I forgot about my deformed leg. Forgot that Tengen was a monk and that I had tempted him into wickedness. Forgot everything but my own need. I cried out loud and tugged at his robe, trying to peel it off his back. I needed to feel his flesh rubbing against me with nothing at all between us. A flash of insight stopped my fumbling fingers for a moment. Was that all it was? Or did a small part of me want to remove anything that reminded me that Tengen was not just a man, but also a monk?

Tengen drove all my fears away. He reared away from my body, clawing at his robes and throwing them aside as soon as they were loose. When he was naked, he lay against me, rubbing his body sinuously against my flesh.

It was more than I could stand. My body was screaming

for him. I had never felt anything like this. Had no idea such strange needs could exist. I clawed at him, dragging his lean body closer to me.

He slid against me and I felt his tree rubbing against my belly. I had no idea what I should do and froze in misery, whimpering with distress at my lack of knowledge.

Tengen rubbed his lips against my ear, nibbling my neck. He stroked my breasts, my belly, waiting patiently until I relaxed. Only then did he part my black moss with his fingers, the movement so light and gentle that I barely felt it. But I did feel his tree sliding a little way into me, and then pausing. I had no idea why. Had I displeased him in some way? I melted with relief when he whispered,

"Mi-chan? Now?"

"Yes. Oh, yes!"

I had no idea what I was agreeing to, what I was asking for. Instinct ground the words from me. I felt a flash of pain that was more pleasure than hurt and all my fears left me as my bodily needs took over and I knew that this was right. Right for me, and right for Tengen.

I wanted to shout out with pleasure, but even though my mouth stretched wide, nothing came from between my lips except a sigh. Tengen was beginning to move faster, his movements jerky. It was exhilarating, but I knew he was moving toward his climax. I sank my nails into his back as my fists spasmed. He gave a groan that sounded as if it had been wrenched from deep inside him.

I clenched my thigh muscles tightly and found that at the same time my private parts gripped with them. Absurdly, the thought came to me that all the exercises Tengen had made me endure had been well worthwhile. Tengen grunted with surprise as I began to rock back and forth, all the time holding on to him so fiercely that he had to move to my rhythm.

I felt the fire beginning to burn in my belly and spread until my whole body was teetering on the edge of something I had never dreamed existed. Then my yonaki claimed me and waves of pleasure shook me, making my toes curl and my mouth open wide in a silent scream. From far, far away, I heard Tengen groan deeply and knew he was sharing my pleasure in his own body.

When I finally came back to my senses, I found Tengen had pulled my robe closed and was holding me against him. I was not tired but deeply relaxed.

"Mi-chan?" He spoke softly, close to my ear. "Have I hurt you? Are you…happy?"

I thought he sounded worried, almost frightened. I could not understand that. We had wasted so much time, but after what had finally taken place between us, how was it possible that he could be anything but as joyous as I was?

"I am happy," I said simply and moved slightly away from him so I could see his face. There was a question I needed to be answered. And at this moment, I knew I would get an honest answer. "And you, Tengen? Have I made you happy?" I hesitated and then spoke quickly. "Do you have any regrets?"

THIRTY-THREE

The bird that flies high
Is only free until the
Hunter draws his bow

"No," Tengen said at once.

That pleased me, but already the delicious languor that enveloped my body was beginning to vanish and my mind began to function again. I asked cautiously, "Will you tell your kannushi what has happened?"

"I will speak to him."

I grimaced, expecting no less. It would cause him significant trouble, I knew. Also for me if the kannushi decided he should tell my father. I shuddered at the thought. Father was rich and money had a loud voice. Father would not bring charges against Tengen. That would bring the family name into disrepute. But he could ensure that Tengen simply disappeared. Who would miss a lowly monk?

And as for me? I had brought dishonor on to the family name. A monastery for me was certain.

"Will he be very angry?" I wanted to ask if Tengen thought his kannushi would tell Father what had happened, but I could not bring myself to ask. I was hurt when Tengen laughed softly.

"I said I would speak to him. I did not say I would tell him what has happened between us."

I considered his answer carefully and found it gave me no comfort. "I suppose you must tell him something of what has passed between us. And he will surely be displeased with you. Will he punish you? Forbid you from coming back here?"

"He will say the decision is mine alone, as he did before."

I guessed he had seen the worry in my expression as he stroked my hair gently and shook his head. Instantly, my happiness flew away from me. I did not want to hear what he was going to say, but Tengen held my head in his hands and forced me to look at him.

"Life is not always as straightforward as we would like it to be, Mi-chan. When I joined the monastery, one of the younger monks was a remarkably handsome man. He was pursued endlessly by women who would pretend to visit the temple to pay homage to the Buddha, but in reality only wanted to catch a glimpse of the young monk." I opened my mouth to protest that none of this had anything to do with us, but Tengen kissed me briefly and went on before I could speak. "Listen to me, Mi-chan. It is important that you understand. Some of the women became very daring. They even passed him messages, telling him that their husbands would be away from home on such-and-such a day. The poor young man was at his wit's end. He asked the kannushi what he should do, and he said the monk should do nothing at all."

This time, I was not to be silenced. I could not understand why he was telling me all this. Still less could I understand why the kannushi had refused to help the young monk.

"What sort of advice was that? The poor monk came to him for help and got none. Had your kannushi forgotten what it was like to be a young man?"

"You are wrong, Mi-chan. My kannushi is a very wise man. Wise enough to know that the young monk had to make his own mind up."

"I see." Although I didn't see at all. "So, what happened to the handsome young monk in the end? Did he tell the women to leave him alone?"

"He could see no way ahead. The women crowded his thoughts day and night. He could not honor the Buddha without hearing their voices, feeling their hands clutching at his robe. If he forgot his vows and lay with one of them, he knew the kannushi would forgive him, but he could not forgive himself. So, one day he went to the river. It was after the spring rains, so it was in full flood. He took his robes off and lay them neatly on the riverbank, together with his zori. Then he stepped into the river.

"When they found his body, his face was very tranquil. It appeared he had not struggled at all."

"That is dreadful." I felt sorry for the unknown monk and great anger at the unfeeling kannushi. "He did not respond to any of the women? Did not encourage them in any way?" Tengen shook his head. "Then he had no reason to feel guilty and certainly no reason to kill himself. What did your kannushi say? Was he proud of the poor man's terrible decision?"

"No. He said that the young monk had taken the easy way out. That he should have resisted the women and put all thoughts of the flesh away from him so that he could worship the Buddha with a clean heart. For as long as the temptation continued, he should have fought it."

"Your kannushi must be the most unfeeling man who has ever lived. If he had advised the young monk, he might still be alive today."

"No." Tengen shook his head. He wrapped his hands around mine and held them tightly. "He is a wise man. The decision was not his, it was the monk's. He will be the same with me."

"No." I shook my head, slowly at first and then—when Tengen remained silent—faster and faster until I was dizzy. "You will tell him how you feel about me and he will say it is up to your conscience what you must do. And you will choose the Buddha over me, I know you will."

"You are wrong."

For a heartbeat, I was relieved at his words. But then I saw the pain in his eyes and knew there was more, far more, to come. I was bewildered and hurt and cried out loudly.

"But you will still leave me, I can see it in your eyes. Why, Tengen? If you are not going to forget about me and dedicate the rest of your life to the Buddha, why? Is there somebody else in your life? Somebody you care for more than me?"

The word *love* would not pass my lips. Until a moment ago, I had had no real idea of what love was. Did I now? I was so unsure, my head reeled. It felt like it had when my brothers had played one of their favorite games, blindfolding me and then darting around me. I had to touch one of them before they could touch me. If I succeeded, then they would leave me alone. I spun from one direction to another, desperate to make contact, but it never happened. When they were tired of tormenting me, one brother would approach me from behind, put his hands on my shoulders and shove me hard. I was always caught by my other brother, who repeated the process. The game lasted as long as it amused them and left me reeling and dizzy. Just as I felt now.

All the joy I felt after our lovemaking fled in a wave of confusion. I sucked in a deep breath and commanded my thoughts to lie still. This was important. I watched Tengen's face and understood that he was wrestling with his own emotions.

"No. There is nobody in my life now except you. You have taught me it is not possible to live with the dead. I never thought I would say it, but I am truly grateful for that."

Abruptly, I was consumed with a jealousy so deep, it left me shaking. I demanded, "Who was she? Your wife? A lover? What happened to her?"

"She was my wife." He rubbed his face with his hands, almost as if he was wiping away memories. "Her name was Cho."

"Butterfly." I forced myself to add, "A beautiful name."

"She was a beautiful woman."

I waited in vain for Tengen to say, *But not as beautiful as you.* Had I really expected it?

"She died, Mi-chan. Her and my son with her."

My jealousy of the beautiful Cho fled at his terrible words. I felt his pain and spoke gently. "What happened to them?"

"I should have followed in my ancestors' footsteps and became a bonesetter." Tengen's voice held such pain I flinched for him. "If I had, neither Cho nor my poor Doi would have died." He turned to look at me then and I almost cried aloud at the sorrow in his eyes.

"I'm sure it wasn't your fault," I said comfortingly. "How could it be?" I believed my own words. How could a man as good as I knew Tengen to be have had any part in his family's deaths? Tears spilled from Tengen's eyes. He shook his head, the tears pattering like rain on the hard-beaten earth beneath us.

"It was my fault. It was down to my ambition and nothing else. I saw how little cash Father made as a bone-setter. Often, if the patient was very poor, he refused to take payment altogether, even though it meant that his own family went hungry as a result of his generosity. I was determined that that would never happen to my family. Father wept when I told him what I was going to do, but he couldn't change my mind.

"I was young and headstrong. I had always been inter-ested in martial arts and had worked hard to become an expert in the arts of jujutsu and kenjutsu."

I was startled. I had never seen Tengen wear a sword. Even less could I imagine him drawing one in anger.

"I left home determined to seek my fortune in any way I could. Fate was kind to me. At that time, there was great trouble between two rival daimyo families in our area. The dispute was an old one, about some land both claimed, but things had become very heated recently and both sides were recruiting as many fighting men as they could find. I was fortunate, I chose to work for the victor. Even more fortunately, I was lucky in battle. My daimyo was pleased with me and appointed me to a senior position among his guards. Suddenly, I had cash in my pocket and a position in the world."

"I suppose it was natural that you got married then," I said encouragingly. Suddenly, I felt I needed to know everything there was to know about Tengen, about my lover, whether I liked it or not.

"Marriage was the last thing on my mind." Tengen laughed shortly. "I had my independence. A position in the world. And for the first time in my whole life, I was not poor."

"But you married your Cho anyway," I said flatly.

"I think it would have been better to say that she married me." Tengen smiled at my astonished expression. "She was a highly-placed servant in the service of my daimyo's wife, and of a far higher caste than I was. I saw her often and it would have taken a stronger man than I was not to notice her. She was as tiny as you are, and just as beautiful. But she had none of your strength of mind, Mi-chan."

I was hurt. I did not want to be told about my inner strength. At that moment, I wanted Tengen to see me as fragile as his butterfly.

"But you fell in love with her," I persisted.

"I did. Eventually, I realized it was no coincidence that I saw her so often. I was flattered. She had so many suitors, she could have taken her pick of men much wealthier and of far higher caste than I was. Even if that had not been so, it was inevitable that I would fall in love with her. She was so sweet-natured and gentle."

I was surprised. Tengen was the only man I had ever heard admit to loving his wife. Men sometimes loved their concubines or a favorite yujo—a woman of pleasure—but never their wives. Wives were more like a necessary commodity. They were expected to bear male children, see that the house was clean and sweet for their husband's return, and make sure his favorite food was on the table. But love? No. To declare love for one's wife was extraordinary.

Now, I was as curious as I was jealous. How was it possible for a fighting man with a wife and a child to end up as a monk? Tengen was staring at the earth, his expression saying as clear as words that he was lost in the past.

I spoke very softly, fearing that he might decide he wanted to keep the rest of his history to himself. "You were happy with your Cho?"

"I thought I was. I thought the gods had smiled on me. I had a good position in life and a wife who loved me as much as I loved her. What more could a man ask? In no time, I was her slave. I treated her as if she was made of the most precious porcelain and might break at the slightest touch. I made sure she wanted for nothing. She had only to hint, and I went out and bought her whatever she wanted. She had new kimono for each season. Precious ornaments for her hair. Servants for the house so she didn't have to lift a finger. She loved the kabuki, so I took her often. I preferred the Nō theatre, but Cho said it bored her, so I tried to take an interest in kabuki. I did everything I could to make her happy. When our son was born, I thought I had truly found heaven on earth. I wanted nothing more."

I asked softly, "How did they die, Cho and your son?"

His response left me gasping with disbelief. "They were murdered. Beaten to death."

THIRTY-FOUR

Autumn mists beckon
The approaching winter so
Rain may quench the earth

Horrified as I was by Tengen's terrible words, everything fell into place for me. He had adored his wife and son. Their murder must have left him on the verge of madness. No doubt he had needed to get away from his home, where every glance roused memories of what had been. For such a tender-hearted man, it must have been a natural step to seek consolation in a monastery.

With the same certainty as the beads on an abacus reached the correct answer each time, I also understood why Tengen had insisted that it was necessary I learn to defend myself. Had he blamed himself for the tragedy, wondered over and over again, that if he had taught his wife at least the rudiments of jujutsu, she might have been able to defend herself and his son from their attacker? I felt sure he had, and because of that, he was now determined to do his best to ensure I could protect myself.

The idea pleased me greatly, but only for a moment as my thoughts went to Cho. I was half-horrified, half-fascinated by the tragedy. Love suicides—not just in the theatre, but in real life—were common. If a situation was hopeless in this life, then there was always the possibility that lovers might be reunited more favorably in a new incarnation. But this was no love pact. Rather, it was the sordid murder of a woman and a child.

"I am so sorry," I said awkwardly. "Is that why you became a monk?"

I wanted to put my arms around him and offer him the comfort of my body, but it would have felt wrong. I shifted slightly and a flicker of soreness reminded me of the pleasure I had just taken with this man. I winced with guilt.

"No," Tengen said. "I have only told you half the story. At first, I thought I was going to go mad. I had no enemies that I knew of. Or at least none that would do such a terrible thing to an innocent woman and child. There is a code amongst warriors, Mi-chan. We may hurt each other on the field of battle, kill if necessary, but no warrior would stoop so low as to take such cowardly revenge. I could think of no reason why anybody would want to kill Cho and Doi. I told my daimyo what had happened, and he in his turn reported it to the magistrates. He assured me that they would hunt down the attacker.

"I could no longer live in the house I had shared with my family. I moved back into the barracks with the rest of the men. At first, I was too full of grief to notice anything different. But after a while, it seemed to me that I was no longer quite as welcome as I had been before my marriage. I shrugged it off, thought my comrades were uncomfortable with my sorrow. I began to drink heavily. It did no good, but at least while the spell of the sake lasted, my memories of Cho and Doi were softened slightly.

"I think I may have become a hopeless drunkard if trouble hadn't flared between my daimyo and his rival again. I was delighted. I flung myself into the conflict and fought like a madman. I took stupid risks, not caring if I lived or died. In fact, I hoped I would die.

"But I did not. My daimyo was deeply pleased with me. His captain of the guard was getting old, he told me. He would welcome retirement soon, and I could take his place. I agreed. It didn't matter to me in the least.

"Even in my despair, I noticed something had changed in the attitudes of my comrades. Suddenly, I was accepted again. Although nothing could ever make up for Cho and Doi's deaths, it was comforting to have friends once more.

"Or so I thought. To celebrate our success in battle, one of the men suggested we commandeer a house of pleasure. We would have it all to ourselves and could take our pick of the yujo. He raised his eyebrows suggestively at me as he said it. I wasn't in the least interested, but I understood it was meant kindly, so I agreed.

"The house was a good one, and we were welcomed. We had cash in our pockets and swords by our sides. A couple of the men chose their yujo at once and vanished with them. The rest of us were not in such a hurry. We drank the house's excellent sake and lolled around swapping yarns.

"After more flasks of sake than I could count had been drunk, there were only a few of us left. The man who had suggested our escapade poked me in the ribs.

"'Nice to see you alive again, Tengen,' he slurred. 'I don't know about you, but I've had enough to drink. I think

I'll take my pleasures upstairs. I rather like the look of that one.' He grinned at a pretty yujo, who giggled and hid her face behind a fan. 'Still plenty left for you to choose from.' I was about to refuse when he dragged his attention from the girl and looked at me with the exaggeratedly serious expression of a man who is very drunk and knows it will take an effort to get his words in the right order. 'I owe you an apology, comrade. We all do.'

"For some reason, the sake that was clouding my brain evaporated suddenly. I shrugged and murmured cautiously, 'Not at all.'

"He clapped me on the shoulder and nodded wisely. The effect was spoiled when he burped loudly.

"'You're a good man. A good comrade. We were all wrong about you, and I'm pleased to admit it. Here's to better times to come.'

"He raised his sake cup to his lips and seemed astonished when he found it was empty. I had no idea what he was talking about, but I wanted to know. He was already making eyes at his yujo. If he went off with her now, I would never find out what he was talking about. I reached across and lifted a flask from its warming vessel and gave it a little shake. It was half-full.

"'She can wait for a while.' I filled his cup and said casually, 'Of course we're comrades. We fight together, don't we?'

"'S'right. Course we do. I can see that now. But when you married pretty little Cho, well…things were a bit different, weren't they? You weren't yourself anymore. Instead of being a fighter, a man you could trust to guard your back in a fight, you were mooning around her like an aunty determined to protect the prettiest maiko in the place!'

"I filled his sake bowl again and forced a grin. 'Was that what it looked like?'

"'To be honest with you, it did. You were more like a father with her than a husband. We were all amazed when you got her pregnant. We thought you hadn't even managed to work up to touching her, you were so frightened of hurting her. Doi was yours, I suppose? Not her lover's child?'

"I felt as if somebody had struck me hard in the stomach. I searched for words, but nothing would come out. I think my companion must have realized he had gone too far as he began speaking quickly.

"'Of course he was your son. The image of you, he was. Don't you worry. With our daimyo to keep them on the job, the magistrates will find that bastard who killed them. Should be easy enough. They know who he is. It's just a matter of catching up with him.'

"He nodded wisely and hauled himself to his feet, tottering over to his yujo. I watched him go. I was so shocked by his words I made no attempt to call him back, but sat staring into space, my mind reeling as if I was the one who had drunk far too much sake.

"A few girls were left. None of them would have been my first choice in any other circumstance, but as it was when one of them came across to me and began to rub her face against my cheek, I agreed readily when she suggested going upstairs. It seemed that if I refused, my comrades would begin to doubt me all over again, and I did not want that to happen.

"It didn't matter anyway. I couldn't do anything. The girl was very skilled, but I lay at her side like a log. All I could think of was my Cho with her lover. Had they both laughed at me, the idiot who worshipped his wife? Did he make love to her in ways I didn't? Ways she preferred? Finally, the yujo gave in and sat up, fiddling with her hair sulkily. I paid her anyway and went back downstairs.

"A number of my comrades had returned by then, and they greeted me with laughter and applause. I pretended to be injured by their reception, and they laughed all the louder."

"They could have been lying to you," I said desperately. But the remembered hurt was rolling from him like sea mist.

"They were not. They slapped me on the back and forced sake on me. That night, it might as well have been water for all the effect it had on me. I watched my comrades grow befuddled and stupid as they toasted me time and time again.

"'Cho was a pretty woman to be sure,' one of them slurred. 'But far more than any one man could handle.'

"I shrugged and muttered something about doing my best. That got another round of laughter.

"'Come on, admit it. You were too soft with her. As soon as you found out she'd taken a lover, you should have been firm with her. Taken a whip to her hide. Shown her who wore the sword in your family instead of mooning about like a love-sick calf. We all thought she'd eaten your kintama with her rice. We know better now, of course,' he added cheerfully.

"How I managed to sit there and take their jokes, I have no idea. Almost worse than anything was the fact that everybody—except me—appeared to know that Cho had taken a lover. Did my daimyo know as well? It was a bitter thought, but given the lack of progress from the magistrates, I thought that perhaps he did. What was the point in spending time and cash in pursuing the murderer of an unfaithful wife? These things happened. No point in making things worse by fussing over them.

"I was beyond anger by then. My mind was coldly rational, and my thoughts were as straight as arrows in flight.

"I would find out who Cho's lover had been. And I would find him. Beat him until he screamed for mercy in just the same way Cho must have pleaded with him. And just like him, I would show no mercy at all.

"I laughed with my comrades and encouraged them to talk about Cho's lover. Pretending it meant nothing to me was the most difficult thing I have ever done. I must have been convincing, as one of my friends leaned over and spoke confidentially to me.

"'I can understand you hesitating about coming between Cho and Taiho. I saw him wrestle when he was a young man. Even then, he was a very talented sumo wrestler, and with his height and weight, he could have made a real name for himself. But he didn't have the discipline to keep it up, and after he was reprimanded a few times by his master for missing practices, he took jobs from anybody who wanted someone to keep the peace in their establishment. He was a big man and got more solid as he got older. He never ran to fat like most sumo wrestlers do when they don't exercise.' I nodded casually as if none of this was news to me. 'He always had women chasing him. Treated them all like dirt, knocked them about a bit to keep them in line. And the worse he treated them, the more they came back. No accounting for women.'

"Bitter bile came into my mouth and I swallowed it before I could vomit. My butterfly, who I had always treated as if she were as delicate as a folded paper origami, had preferred a man who treated her like dirt to me? It was beyond my comprehension."

A chilly wind made me shiver. Tengen noticed immediately and rose to his feet.

"You are cold. My fault. I was so lost in my past I…I wasn't here for a moment. Let me help you."

He kneeled and pulled my kimono in place. The sash defeated him. He glanced at it and then handed it to me with a rueful smile before gathering his own robes together and slipping them on. I finished dressing rapidly. I wanted —no, I needed, to hear the end of his story and was anxious that he might not carry on.

"I'm fine. Not cold at all," I lied. "Tell me the rest."

"Perhaps we should go back to the house? If any of the servants find us, it will look odd that we are just sitting in the dojo, doing nothing."

"No," I said hurriedly. "There's no one about. If anybody comes this way, we'll hear their footsteps on the gravel path. Here." I picked up one of my brother's discarded wooden practice swords. "If anybody comes, you can pretend you are instructing me."

Nothing short of an earthquake could have moved me at that moment. Tengen looked so doubtful, I wondered if he was regretting sharing his terrible memories with me. My emotions were ragged. Already our lovemaking seemed unreal, as if my longing for it to happen had made it seem true, in my mind at least. And Tengen's story didn't help. It was so extraordinary, it felt more like something out of a kabuki drama than real life. I was bewildered and not a little frightened of the man who was now my lover. The man who was not the man I had thought him to be.

It seemed as if he had spent half a day telling me his history, but a glance at the sun assured me it had been no time at all. I sat up straight, forcing all my worries to one side. I knew it was ridiculous, but I was jealous of the unknown Cho, no matter that she was dead. Once, she had lived. Once, Tengen had loved her. Did he still? I needed to know. If I did not, the uncertainty would haunt my dreams forever.

"Tell me the rest," I said.

"I have never told anybody this much. There has never been any need before." Tengen looked at me curiously, as if he was as unsure about me as I was about him. I felt a surge of relief. I was very special to him. It had to be so.

"Tell me," I repeated.

THIRTY-FIVE

Each grain of sand is
Polished lovingly by the
Sea throughout each day

"You may not like what you hear," he said. "I do not want to run the risk of having you hate me, Mi-chan."

I was aware that I was stepping blindly into deep, dark waters. Did I want Tengen to care about me? I put the uncertainty from me. I would consider it later, when I knew all I needed to know and had time to think things through logically. When I was not still languid from our lovemaking.

"You will never know unless you tell me." How very calm I sounded! "Go on. Did you find this man?"

Tengen hesitated and then shrugged, as if he had reached a decision.

"I did. I began the next day. It seemed to me that there would be the same sort of close companionship between sumo wrestlers as there was between men who fought together, and that somebody at one of the training heya would know what had happened to Taiho after he fled from Edo. I went to wrestling bouts at several heya, making a point of buying the triumphant wrestler sake after the contests. I found the heya I was seeking on my third attempt.

"I said casually that I had made a lot of money betting on Taiho, and it seemed a shame that he no longer wrestled. The man-giant I was sitting with downed his sake at a gulp—the bowl looked like a thimble in his gigantic fingers—and nodded.

"'You're right there. I trained with Taiho in this very heya. He had all the makings of a yokozuna, a grand champion, but the discipline of sumo irked him.'

""'I want to be able to get up in the morning when I feel like it, not when I'm told," he used to say. "And I want to eat what I fancy, not sit down and be forced to eat chankonabe stew at every meal."

"'I told him he was a fool, that he should stick it out, but he wouldn't have it.'" My companion burped and covered his lips with a hand like a plate. "'Pardon me. One of the regulars told him he could use a good man to keep the customers in order at his brothel and offered to pay him twice what he was earning as a trainee in the heya. I told him that in a couple of years he could name his own fee as a wrestler, but he was having none of it. Taiho didn't stick it out there, either. He moved on after a while. Not a problem for him, of course, there's always somebody on the lookout for a good man who can throw his weight about.'

"My sumo wrestler giggled at his own wit. I smiled politely but was torn between elation and despair. I had found somebody who knew the man, but by the sound of it, they had lost contact years ago.

"'Funny you should say that,' I said. 'That's exactly why I was trying to track Taiho down while I was here in Edo. I have a nice, respectable sort of establishment myself in Kyoto. You know how it is, now and then one of the customers takes too much sake and makes a nuisance of himself. And sometimes one of the girls gets a bit above herself and needs a bit of discipline, if you get my meaning.'

"'Oh, Taiho's your man alright. Nobody would answer back to him, and he would never take any cheek from a woman, that's for sure.'

"'Shame he seems to have vanished. I heard he had had a bit of trouble recently. I thought he might be pleased to get out of Edo for a while, but it looks as if I've missed my chance.'

"I shrugged, standing as though I was about to take my leave."

"'Not so fast, my friend. I might be able to help you there.'

"My new friend looked sadly into his empty sake cup. I took the hint and signaled to the server to bring another flask as I sat down."

"'You know where I could find him?'

"The wrestler made an side-to-side gesture with the flat of his hand. 'I didn't say that. But I do know somebody who probably knows where he's gone. His woman, a yujo called Emi.'

"I was disappointed. I knew only too well who Taiho's woman had been, and the dead cannot speak to the living. I was angry and spoke bluntly.

"'I think you are wasting my time, my friend. I heard

Taiho had to flee from Edo after he murdered m—his woman and her son.'

"The words almost stuck in my throat. *My* wife. *My* son.

"'That's right, he did. But Taiho always had more than one woman on the go, although this particular yujo lasted much longer than the rest of them. Taiho complained he couldn't get rid of her, but I think he found her useful when he was between other women. If anybody knows where he is, it's her.'

"I held a silver ichibugin up between my thumb and finger and kept it there until he told me where I could find Emi.

"She would be easy enough to find. If his information was correct, she worked in one of the better brothels in Edo. I found my way there as soon as I left the wrestler, but I was disappointed. Emi was not there, I was told. She had worked there, but lately she had been surly and rude to clients, so she had been told to pack her bags. My trick with the silver coin worked just as well there, and I was given an address in another part of Edo, together with a discreet warning to leave my purse at home if I knew what was good for me.

"It was late and I was weary, so I decided to find Emi the next day. But fate is strange beyond the perception of man. My duties tied me to my master for a few days, and I could do nothing to search for Emi. I was woken up some days later by one of the servants, who grinned at me and said I had a visitor. I grunted and turned over. I was not expecting anybody, especially at such an hour. I had no interest in talking to a stranger.

"'Tell him to go away,' I muttered and rolled over.

I sensed the servant was hovering and was about to speak roughly to him when he said, 'It's not a he, it's a she. She said to tell you her name is Emi and that you would be pleased to see her.'"

I blinked at Tengen in amazement and asked, "How had she come to find you?"

"I don't know for sure, but I imagine my sumo wrestler got word to her. I was amazed she had come to me. I would have expected her to leave Edo when she heard someone was searching for her. I fully expected her to lie to me, so I was wary. I was also very surprised when I saw her.

"She was a yujo, so I had expected a woman raddled by her profession, a woman with a painted face and a hard heart. What I saw was a young woman, probably in her early twenties. She wore no makeup at all, and her clothes were subdued. She might have been an ordinary housewife, except that she was extraordinarily pretty.

"I welcomed her and offered her tea, which she declined. Before I could ask her anything, she plucked the questions from my mind and spoke bluntly.

"'You're Tengen. You're searching for my Taiho.'

"'That is so.' I was cautious, still suspicious as to why she had come to me.

"'I heard you're looking for him. I suppose somebody will tell you where to find him if you give them enough money. I know where he is, but before I tell you, you have to promise that you won't hurt him.'

"Grief blazed so hard in my body that the muscles in my jaw clenched and I could barely speak. I took a deep breath and managed to grind out, 'He murdered my wife and my son. A defenseless woman and a child. And you ask me not to hurt him?'

"'You don't know what she did to him, your precious wife!'

"My mouth dropped open in disbelief. Before I could find words, Emi carried on relentlessly.

"'He was my man before she came along. Oh, I know he had other women sometimes. A giant of a man like Taiho has the appetites of two men. But always he came back to me, until she smiled at him and hid behind her fan, pretending to be all sweet and innocent. She sucked him in. Made him fall in love with her. She took him away from me!'

"'Enough!' I snapped. 'You don't know what you're talking about. Either tell me where Taiho is or get out.'

"She was panting with emotion, staring at me with eyes that were almost mad. But she did not rise, and with an effort that was more than human, I reined in my temper and waited for her to speak.

"'I will tell you where he is. But only if you promise you won't hurt him when you find him. Promise, on the memory of your wife and son.'

"'Get out.'

"The words were wrenched from me. I could not believe that the gods could be so cruel. Here was my chance to find Taiho, but I could not take it. If—when—I found him, he would be a dead man. And I could no more give Emi the promise she wanted than fly to the moon.

"'You must promise,' she persisted.

"'He killed my family!' My voice rose to a howl. 'How can you ask me to leave him unpunished?'

"'And your wife killed me the day she took a fancy to him!'

"Emi's words were full of pain. We stared at each other

silently. I could not believe what she was saying. She could not understand my agony. She broke the silence first, speaking in a whisper so low, it was as if she was speaking to herself.

"'You'll find him eventually. I had hoped that you would give up, but now that I've met you, I know you'll keep going no matter how long it takes. And it doesn't matter what I tell you about your wife. I don't suppose you'll ever believe me.' She shook her head violently, as if shaking off her own thoughts. When she spoke, her voice was firm. 'Very well. I will tell you where he is. But first you must promise me on your honor that you will tell him who you are and allow him to face you in a fair fight.'

"In spite of the seriousness of our conversation, I almost laughed. Everybody said Taiho was a giant of a man. A man who possessed enormous strength. What chance would I have of beating him in a fair contest? Not that I cared. If I died trying to avenge my family, I would depart this world a happy man.

"Sorrow consumed me at the thought of my wife and son. I looked at Emi, but saw Cho. And at that moment, I knew that I would give Emi her promise, and that I would keep to it. To do anything else would have lowered me to Taiho's level. Unlike him, I was not a coward.

"'You have my word on it,' I said simply.

"Emi studied my face for a while and then nodded. 'You will find him in Sakai, a brothel called the Pink House.'

"She rose abruptly and turned to leave. I called her back. 'How do I know you aren't going to warn him?'

"She smiled. It lit up her face and, for a moment, I saw her as the lovely young woman she might have been if her fate had been different.

"'There's no need. You have given me your promise that you will meet Taiho fairly. If you do that, he will kill you. Once you're dead, he can come back here. To me.'

"She walked away then, leaving me wandering in so many emotions that I was lost to the world."

THIRTY-SIX

Ravens gather to
Celebrate death. Pray that it
Is not mine or yours

My thoughts were racing as pointlessly as kittens chasing their own tails. This man who had just made love to me, a man I thought I knew well, was suddenly a stranger to me.

In spite of that, for the first time, I understood the power that a woman can have over a man. Tengen's wife had betrayed him, yet still he loved her memory. Was it possible that I, deformed as I was, might be able to wield the same power?

I was certain that I was correct. This man loved me in his fashion, I understood that now. Did I also love him? The thought startled me, but I knew the answer at once. I *liked* him greatly. I had very much enjoyed our lovemaking. I felt deeply sorry for his loss. But love?

No. What I felt for Tengen was not love. I could not put into words the difference between what I felt for Tengen now and true love—love that could survive anything and would last down the years undiminished. But one thing I was sure of; when I truly did fall in love, I would recognize it without any doubt.

I saw that Tengen was looking at me intently and I felt selfish. He needed to finish telling me about his tragic past. It was important to him, and yet I had allowed my mind to wander to my own concerns. He had given me such great pleasure this day. The least I could do would be to allow him to tell me the rest of his tale. I was about to touch his face to offer comfort, but when I wondered if the gesture would be intrusive, so I allowed my hand to fall on his sleeve instead.

"You found Taiho." It was a statement, not a question.

Tengen nodded. He relaxed visibly, and I knew I had made the right decision by encouraging him to go on. It was not just curiosity on my behalf, I insisted to myself. He needed to share this terrible story to heal his pain.

"As it happened, my salary had just been paid. I had a lot of cash saved as well. Since I had moved back to the barracks, I had spent hardly anything. I packed a furoshiki with a change of robe and a comb and a razor—I wanted nothing at all that reminded me of my lost family—almost as soon as Emi had left and walked away without a word to anybody. I had my savings secure in my sash. I needed nothing more for my journey. I didn't even consider what would happen after I found Taiho. It was as if my mind refused to go beyond that moment. Was I anticipating death? I suppose I was, but it held no fear for me.

"I had never been to Sakai, but it seemed to me that the gods favored my journey. The weather stayed fine and I had no trouble on the way. Once I arrived in the city, I began to ask where I could find the Pink House. The first few men I asked seemed almost offended by the question and insisted they had never heard of it. I wondered if the place had a bad reputation, so I made sure that the next man I stopped was already roaring drunk. He swayed when he spoke and stank of sake.

"'The Pink House?' He almost shouted the words, he was so drunk. 'You want the Pink House? Well, funnily enough, so do I. You come with me and I'll take you there right enough. You can buy me a flask of sake in exchange.'

"He grabbed my arm and towed me with him. People stepped aside to let us pass and I was beginning to worry that we would be remembered when we arrived at what could have been any other large, prosperous ryokan. The only difference was the amount of noise coming through the open doorway."

"'This is it,' my companion bellowed. 'Now, you've never been here before, whereas I'm a regular and well-known. You stick with me and I'll see you taken care of.' He walked in as he spoke, and I followed.

"Although it was early evening, the Pink House was already full. The air swirled with smoke from numerous pipes. When I glanced around, I thought every table was full. My companion grasped my elbow and steered me toward a low table I had not noticed, just below the stairs. He almost pushed me to the tatami as he signaled urgently to a server for sake.

"I sipped my sake slowly. My companion downed his first cup and then poured himself more. As long as I was paying, he didn't care if I drank or not. I peered through the murk of tobacco smoke, quickly losing heart as I could see nobody who resembled the Taiho I had heard so much about. I was about to ask if my new friend knew of him when the steps above my head vibrated and a shower of dust landed on the table."

"'Taiho, in the name of all the gods! Why can't you tread softly once in a while?'

"A roar of laughter, rich and happy, answered my companion's question.

"'My friend, if you don't like dust, you shouldn't sit beneath the stairs. If it offends you so much, you have my permission to clean the place.'

"A murmur of amusement from the other clients greeted his words and my companion retreated behind a grumble of garbled complaints.

"I shrank back into the twilight cast by the stairs as I watched Taiho walk about the room as if he owned the place.

"He was a big man. Taller than I was, and far more heavily built. But more than that, it seemed that his personality was also immense. Everybody knew him, everybody greeted him. I watched him hungrily. He was not at all handsome. He was beginning to run to fat, and his hairline was receding. He must have been fifteen years older than me. Yet my lovely, delicate Cho had preferred his attentions to mine. I was bewildered, and deeply jealous.

"I sat there all evening, watching as the crowds began to thin in the early hours of morning. My companion had long since slipped into a drunken sleep. I began to wonder how long it would be before Taiho noticed him and came across to wake him up and throw him out. I waited until Taiho was occupied—he appeared to be sharing a joke with a group of men across the room—and then rose and slipped out quietly.

"I stood outside, breathing deeply, trying to appear like a man who was clearing his head for the walk home. Actually, I was trying to collect my thoughts. I had put all my effort into finding Taiho. It had never occurred to me to plan for what I was going to do when I found him."

"You had thought about how you were going to punish him, surely?" I interrupted. I stared at Tengen avidly, seeing not his priestly robes but the man beneath them. If I had noticed his saffron robes I would have dismissed them. Tengen was no longer a monk, he was a man as far as I was concerned.

His story had left me breathless. I felt sorrow for him, but more than that, I wanted to know how the tale ended. I regretted interrupting and waited quietly for his response, forbidding myself from fidgeting in case I distracted him.

"I had thought of nothing else. That was the problem." Tengen shook his head and closed his eyes. I held my breath, willing him to go on. "I suddenly realized that it was entirely possible that Taiho lived in the brothel. If he did, I would have to haunt the place during the day in hopes that he would come out at some point. It would cut my chances of getting him on his own in a safe, quiet place to almost nothing, but so be it. If that was what the gods willed, then I would wait.

"But still I lingered, standing in the shadows well away from the entrance. The last few customers drifted out. My companion was helped out by Taiho, who supported him through the shoji and then let him go without a second glance.

"The lamps in the house began to go out one by one, and my spirit was extinguished with them. As the last light died, I was about to leave—I had no idea where I would sleep. Perhaps I could rouse the owner of a ryokan and demand a futon for the night. I stood upright and stretched and then I heard the sound of the shoji sliding back.

"I have often heard the phrase about one's blood running cold and thought it nothing but nonsense. But at that moment, I knew it was not. I was cold, so very cold. I felt the hair on my arms stand erect as if I was walking under icy water.

"Taiho passed me, unnoticing. He was humming to himself, relaxed, as if he had no need to fear any man.

"I forced my rigid limbs to move. I felt like somebody who had been ill for a very long time and on standing for the first time finds it an almost impossible task. Just as you must have done, Mi-chan." Tengen smiled at me. I was elated by his understanding. "I kicked off my zori to ensure my footfalls were silent and followed Taiho down the street. He turned left at the bottom and then abruptly right into a narrow alleyway. In the dim moonlight, it looked to me as if this was a new street, where houses or perhaps business premises were still under construction.

"I could hear him, still humming contentedly to himself, as we walked on. I was prepared for a trap and was barely surprised when we reached a dead end. Taiho stopped, and so great was his self-confidence that he spoke to the stone wall in front of him without bothering to turn.

"'So, my friend, we seem to have come to the end of our walk together. What do you want?'"

"His voice was comfortable. It worried him not at all that he had been followed. I took a deep breath, and then another, to calm myself before I answered the man who had murdered my family in cold blood. You understand, I did not want to let my temper overflow and lose any slight advantage I might have over this monster.

"I said, 'My name is Tengen. You may know of me.'"

"I had startled him. There was enough light for me to see that he had stiffened. He turned to face me, his movements controlled and surprisingly graceful for such a big man.

"'Tengen. Yes, I know your name. How did you find me?'

"'That doesn't matter.' His casual tone inflamed me. "You murdered my wife and my son. Before I kill you, tell me why, Taiho.'

"My voice was steady. But when he spoke, he tore my composure to shreds with his words.

"'Why? Because I loved her. Far more than you ever did.' I gasped in outrage and put my hand on the hilt of my sword. Taiho lowered his head and swayed a little from side to side. He looked like a goaded bull who was about to charge. But he did not move. 'I loved her, I tell you, like I've never loved another woman. I wanted her to leave you and come away with me. To bring her son with her. I wanted us to live together as a family.'

"The agony in his voice rang true. His pain mirrored mine. Through the pounding of the blood in my ears, I managed to say, 'You're a liar. Cho was my wife. She would never leave me. Not for you, not for any other man. No matter what happened between the two of you, she loved me. If you truly loved her, how could you have killed her? And why my poor son? He was an innocent. Why him?'

"I was howling with grief. Taiho swayed and I tightened my grip on my sword, praying my moment had come. But he did not make any move toward me.

"'Your son?' There was such hurt in the words that I was suddenly chilled. 'When she found she was pregnant, Cho told me the child was mine. I was the happiest man on earth.' Taiho's voice was as bitter as my thoughts. 'From that moment on, I began to talk to her about leaving you. She said neither yes nor no, just laughed at me. When the boy was born, I tried again and again to persuade her. She began to avoid me. When I stopped by, her maid told me she was not in. When I insisted on seeing her, Cho was cold to me.'

Tengen paused and I knew his thoughts were back at that moment. Finally, he said, "I thought I was gripped by the palsy all at once. I could do nothing but shake my head. Our servants had known about Cho's affair? She had... entertained her lover in my house? On our futon? I felt sick. When I could find my voice, I said, 'That was why you killed her and my son? Because she rejected you?'

"'I killed her because I loved her.' Oddly for such a large man, Taiho's voice sounded high-pitched, almost squeaky. 'That last time, I went on my knees before her. I begged her to run away with me, to bring our son with her. She laughed at me. Told me that Doi was not my son, but yours. That there had never been any doubt of that. She said—' He stopped and swallowed as if he was tasting his words and found them bitter. 'She said that there had never been anything that mattered between us. That she got bored with you away from home so much and needed a little distraction. That I had never meant anything at all to her. That she loved you and nobody else. She...she told me to get out. That if I came back, she would report me to the militia for bothering her. Have me arrested. Said that with an important man like you for a husband, they would believe her without a doubt.

"'I hated her at that moment. Hated her as much as I had ever loved her.

"'So you killed her. Her and my poor son.'"

Tengen was staring into space, his face empty. I felt his agony but knew nothing of how to comfort him. Before I could think of anything to say, he went on.

"Taiho shook his head. He said, 'Your wife tortured me, hurt me like no man ever could. I wanted to do nothing but walk away from her. Walk away and try to forget her. But the bitch was having none of it. All at once she smiled sweetly at me and patted the tatami at the side of her invitingly.

"'"Oh, Taiho, if only you could see your face. You really believed me, didn't you?" Her voice was full of laughter. "Oh, my poor man. Surely you know when I'm just teasing. How tense you are. Come and sit with me for a while."

"'My senses were reeling, Tengen. I didn't know what to do. But your wife smiled at me and put her head down and looked at me from beneath her eyelashes.' I caught my breath. How well I knew that look! 'And I couldn't resist her. I went to her and she ran her fingers down my chest and told me what a big man I was, how she was proud to have me as her lover. Before I knew it, we were making love and it was wonderful and I thought everything was alright again.

"'When we both had our breath back, all I could think of was asking her again to get Doi and for both of them to come with me, somewhere far from Edo. Even if Doi wasn't my son, I was prepared to accept him and treat him as if he was mine. When I asked her, she looked at me as if I was something dirty that she had just noticed on the sole of her zori.

"'"You really don't understand, do you? Look around you." She waved her hand at the elegant room. "Do you really think I would trade all this for a life spent in poverty with you? You may be a good lover, Taiho, I'll give you that, but we can't spend all day and all night making love. What do we have in common that we could talk about? My husband has a good position at our daimyo's court. When he comes home, he tells me all the latest gossip, he entertains me with the newest intrigue. When the shogun next visits our daimyo, it is even possible that I might see him.

"'"I'm not a fool, Taiho. I chose my husband very carefully. My mistress spoke about him often, saying the daimyo liked him greatly and that her husband held him in high esteem. I knew before I married him that Tengen had a great future before him, that he would soon be a rich and respected man. And I was right. Now, apart from your tree of flesh—which I admit is very impressive—what can you offer me to compete with any of that? Oh, don't get me wrong. I'm more than happy to allow our affair to continue—you are most definitely an excellent lover—but it will be on my terms. I want you here when I feel like seeing you and it's safe, not when you want to drop in. And there's never going to be any more to it than that."

"'She turned away from me, your beautiful wife, and picked up a mirror and began to attend to her hair, smoothing it back in place. I couldn't take any more. I lashed out and the mirror flew from her hand. It broke on the floor and she glared at me.

"'"You've broken my lovely mirror," she snarled. "It was new, and very expensive. Get out! And keep away from me. Don't you dare ever come back here."

"'She turned away from me to pick up the shards of the mirror, making it as clear as possible that she was more concerned about her trinket than me. That was when I lost control. I picked her up with one hand and I shook her. When she screamed, it had the same effect on me as a cat that has cornered a rat. I was so full of fury and pain I couldn't stop hitting her. The only thing that mattered was that I made her feel my pain. She tried to scratch me, but I held her at arms' length and kept on punching her until she stopped screaming and just sobbed.

"'Your son came in then. He crawled on all fours toward us and wrapped his arms around my legs, as if he understood I was hurting his mother wanted me to stop. I didn't mean to hurt him, Tengen. Believe me. But I looked down at him and thought that he might have been *my* son, that he should have been *my* son and my anger overflowed and I slapped him to make him stop touching me. I must have hit him harder than I intended as he flew across the room and hit a chabudai table with such a thud it stopped the breath in my throat.

"'Cho was lying at my feet. I can't remember what I said to her. She was lying with her face toward the tatami. I turned her over and I knew straight away that she was dead. There was nothing I could do. I took the coward's way out, Tengen. I turned and walked away. Went back to my home and gathered all the money I had. One of my friends—' He hesitated and I knew that the friend was Emi. '—stopped me in the street and asked me what the matter was. I wasn't thinking at all by then. I blurted out what I had done and said I was leaving Edo for good. I remembered then that I had a distant cousin who lived in Sakai who owned a prosperous brothel. I would go there, ask him to take me on to keep the customers under control. I asked her not to betray me. She said she would never do that. Like a fool I believed her. I should have known better than to trust another woman.'"

Tengen wet his lips with his tongue as if they were dry. He sounded puzzled when he spoke again.

"For some reason, I felt the need to defend Emi and said, 'She told me where I would find you in exchange for my word that I would only meet you in a fair fight. She knew I would find you eventually and that you would defeat me.'

"He stared at me and finally nodded.

"'Then I owe Emi an apology. I suppose I knew all along it would come to this. You had to be somebody special to keep a woman like Cho. Come then, Tengen, let's finish this.'"

The still sea shivers
At the touch of the full moon.
Strong tides will follow

"He drew his sword as he spoke. I thought his voice sounded casual, almost bored, as if he was so sure of himself he had no need to worry. I flamed at his attitude and then forced myself to think coolly. If I attacked in blind fury, Taiho's confidence would undoubtedly be rewarded. I would lose and follow Cho and Doi into the next incarnation.

"I watched Taiho warily, stepping back to give my sword arm room to swing. We were in a confined space with barely room to circle. But for a big man, he was surprisingly lithe in his movements.

"'Thinking better of fighting me already?' Taiho sneered. 'Probably the sensible thing to do. Why don't you run back to Edo and play at soldiers, protecting your daimyo?'

"I realized just in time that he was provoking me deliberately, trying to force me into a rash move. I glanced from side to side, as if I was uneasy, and half-lowered my sword.

"Taiho was quick. He darted forward and if I had not been prepared for his attack, I would have been skewered on his sword. But I was no longer there. I had stepped aside and his killing blow whistled harmlessly past me.

"'My, but you actually know how to fight!' He sounded amused. 'But I still think I know one or two tricks you don't, daimyo's man.'

"I guessed Taiho was a man who had learned to fight in the gutters of Edo. He would have no finesse, but would rely on speed and brute force. Whereas I had learned to use a sword from a master. Better still, I had fought as a mercenary and knew as many unsavory tricks as Taiho.

"I taunted him, wanting to provoke his temper. An angry man makes mistakes.

"'If that's what you think, stop playing and start fighting. Or are you only brave when facing helpless women and babies?'

"Taiho bared his teeth. It was like looking into the mouth of a hungry wolf crouching to spring. He thrust forward so quickly he was nearly a blur. I barely had time to step aside and catch him with a glancing blow before he turned. I heard him gasp and then saw the gash in his robe. It was too dark to tell if he was bleeding. I hoped he was.

"He turned rapidly, facing me silently. We dodged from side to side, and then Taiho stumbled on a bamboo scaffolding pole that he had not seen. He was inviting me to take advantage, so I did not. He recovered his balance so quickly, I knew it had been a feint.

"His eyes were everywhere, assessing his chances and

calculating my weaknesses. I stepped back to give myself more room and held my sword in front of me, raised in the classic killing stance. Enough. I would play with Taiho no longer. This was my moment. Kill or be killed. I had no preference for either as long as the thing was ended.

"He laughed, throwing his head back, exposing his throat. I could have taken the chance and severed his head then, but I remembered my promise to Emi and waited until he was looking at me again.

"Taiho took a step toward me, his own sword held low. His eyes were fixed on my face. When he was so close I could almost touch him with the tip of my sword, his deliberate progress turned into a rush.

"He was so big, I felt the air ripple past me as if a sudden wind had sprung up. I lowered my sword abruptly and watched Taiho's astonished face as his feet tripped on the same bamboo pole he had pretended to trip on earlier. I did not move and he impaled himself on my sword. Still, he did not give up. He wrenched himself away and stood, his sword arm at his side, looking down in disbelief at his belly.

"From somewhere, he found the strength to run at me again. I knew the blow he had taken would be fatal sooner or later. I told myself I was acting out of mercy as I raised my sword high above my head and brought it down cleanly on his neck.

"Taiho's head rolled on the ground at my feet. It bounced once and then came to rest, his eyes wide open and staring at me."

Tengen paused and I looked at his face. I expected to see remembered triumph, possibly even pleasure, but there was nothing but terrible regret.

"What else could you have done?" I asked. I was bewildered. How was it possible for him to feel sorrow for this thug? "He murdered your wife and son. You even kept your promise to Emi and faced him in fair fight. You did everything that was right and honorable."

"Did I?" Tengen's voice was bleak. "I've thought about that moment every day since it happened and I still don't know. He murdered my wife, yes. But she was also his lover, and I think he really did love her. When she laughed at him so cruelly, I believe she destroyed something in him, turned him to madness. And I believed him when he said he had no intention of killing my poor son." He raised his eyes and stared at me. "Did I really keep my promise to Emi?"

I had no idea why that should matter to him so much, but I answered quickly anyway. "Of course you did. If you hadn't killed him, then he would have killed you."

"I don't believe it. Taiho was a huge, strong man. He knew how to use a sword. I thought at the time—and I still think it now—that he allowed me to kill him. It was his way of committing suicide, and he was considerate enough to allow me to take my revenge on him at the same time. I think he died happy in the knowledge that he had atoned for his evil deeds in life."

That sounded like nonsense to me, but I did not say so. If it made Tengen happy to think it, who was I to destroy his conscience?

"That is all in the past, Tengen. No amount of wondering can change anything." I paused, searching for the right words. "But what about the future? What are you going to do now?"

I really meant, What about us? The thought knotted my

stomach and I waited painfully for Tengen to speak, wondering all the time if he understood how I felt.

"As I told you, I must seek an audience with my kannushi."

I sucked in a sharp breath, on the verge of saying no. I was relieved I had not spoken when Tengen went on.

"I will not tell him what happened between us today. That would relieve my conscience, but it could make a lot of trouble for you. I would never want to see you hurt because of me, Mi-chan."

He smiled at me fondly and I sent up a silent prayer of thanks to the heavens.

"So, what will you tell him?" I asked tightly.

"I shall tell him that I have developed strong feelings for you. And because of that I can no longer go on teaching you. It is no more than the truth. Not the whole truth, but it is what matters."

I nodded, but inside I was confused. Surely, this was exactly what I had hoped to hear. We could not continue as lovers. Eventually, somebody would notice. Ours was a close household. Father would hear of it, and then what? I shuddered to think of the consequences. Tengen was being sensible, so why did I feel let down by his response?

I asked, "And if he says, as he did with the young monk who committed suicide, that you should simply resist temptation? What then?"

"It doesn't matter. My mind is made up. My place is no longer in the monastery. I understand now that I was only ever hiding from myself there. I have told no one but you about Cho and Doi and Taiho. Not even my kannushi. When I asked to join his monastery, he must have guessed that I'd had some sort of tragedy in my life, but he never asked me to speak of it. Now that I have finally spoken about what happened, I feel…I feel cleansed. I cannot undo what happened, nor will I ever forget it. But perhaps in time there might be a day when I do not think of it second after second. Wonder how much of it was my fault. If I could have behaved differently."

Tengen dropped his head into his hands and his shoulders shook. He was crying, and I was shocked. I had never seen a man cry before and had no idea how to deal with it.

I took refuge in pretending I had not seen his tears and asked as calmly as I could manage, "And when you have spoken to your kannushi, what then?"

Tengen took a breath so deep I heard his lungs fill. "I shall leave the monastery at once. I will walk away and start my life again." He raised his head and looked at me searchingly. "I will miss you so very much, Mi-chan."

I waited for declarations of love. For him to thank me for freeing him from his past. I almost still expected him to ask me to go with him. Even though I knew I would have refused, I found myself disappointed when he did not. Wryly, I thought of one of Father's favorite proverbs: The person who chases two hares at the same time will catch neither.

Truly, I was that person. Tengen had nothing but the robes he stood up in. I had to resist the urge to giggle as I wondered if the kannushi would take even those from him, leaving him as naked as the day he was born. Whatever happened, Tengen would be poor in a way I could not begin to comprehend. I could not see myself giving up all I had to follow Tengen in his uncertain new life. But at the same time, I couldn't help hoping that he needed me so much that he would ask me to go with him.

I hid my confusion and said cautiously, "Thank you." Tengen clearly expected more, so I added, "I will miss you as well."

With the tears still shining on his cheeks, he threw back his head and laughed, the sound almost raucous on the still air.

"Dear Mi-chan, of all the many qualities I know you to possess, I think it is your honesty that I treasure above all. Tell me, if I asked you to leave your family and follow me to a bleak future, would you throw all you have away and agree?"

I could not lie. "No."

"Then it is just as well I have no intention of asking you. I believe that you have a very great future ahead of you." Tengen leaned toward me, suddenly serious. "Whether you decide to take a husband or not is up to you, and that in itself is unheard of for a girl such as you from a good family. If you ever do choose to marry, then your husband will be a fortunate man. Wherever I go after today, I will listen for your name. I will hear it, I'm sure, and I will always be proud that I saw you take your first steps into the future."

He stood and offered me his hand. I suddenly felt awkward, not because I needed his help to stand, but because I had no idea how to say goodbye to a lover. In the end, I said, "Take care of yourself, Tengen. Don't let any other woman break your heart."

"That I will not. Two are surely enough for any one man." He was smiling, and I couldn't decide if he was serious.

"Thank you," I said finally, "for all you have taught me. And for today."

He let go of my hand and stepped away. The distance between us was suddenly as deep as the sea.

"There is one more thing. I have a very special leaving gift for you." I gazed around bewildered as Tengen was empty-handed. "I am certain that your leg is far, far stronger than it was. Keep doing the exercises we have done together, every day, and it will get stronger still."

Was that his idea of a gift? It was certainly not mine. "I will do that, of course. But you spoke of a gift...?"

"A very great gift. No matter how hard you exercise that leg, it will never be as straight as the other. I doubt you will ever get that foot to sit flat on the ground." I grimaced; why tell me what I already knew? "But there is a way you can walk again. Not as well as you did before you caught paralysis of the morning, but far better than you can now. I could not tell you about it before, as my advice would have been useless until you had sufficient strength in that leg. And I don't doubt that you would have been determined to try it at once and would have been bitterly disappointed when it did no good."

I didn't believe him. I was sure that he was simply trying to distract me from his leaving, and the thought made me angry and sullen at the same time.

"Well? If more exercise will not help me, what will?"

"A new shoe."

I thought he was making fun of me. A new shoe? That was his precious leaving gift?

"And that will do what anything else cannot?" I said incredulously. "I am to buy not even a pair of shoes, but just one?"

"Yes." He was smiling, but his expression was tender rather than amused. I put my disbelief aside unwillingly. "Just the one shoe, but not one that you can buy at any merchant. Does your father employ craftsmen for his estate?"

I thought sourly that Father had no need of a shoemaker and said so. "Of course he does, but if we need shoes, we buy them."

"Of course, and you don't need a shoemaker for what I have in mind. You need a skilled carpenter, a man you can put your trust in."

It sounded nonsense to me. Certainly, Father used a carpenter, I had seen him about the estate often, but I had never spoken to the man. I supposed he must have made my original crutch for me, but Anzu had taken care of that. Then I remembered our blacksmith, a man who had always been kind to me. But what good was a blacksmith when it came to making a shoe for me rather than my pony? But I was feeling confused and stubborn at the same time, so I answered Tengen's question literally.

"There is one craftsman that I would trust, but he is not a carpenter."

"No matter. It would embarrass you to explain what you want to somebody you don't know. Talk to this man you trust. Show him your foot and explain to him that you need a very special shoe made. One that fits your sole exactly and is also just high enough to ensure that your left leg is the same length as the right whenever you wear the special shoe. I have no doubt that all your father's tradesmen know each other very well. Your blacksmith can explain to the carpenter what you need."

My breath left my body with a gasp. So simple! And, now that Tengen had explained it, so very obvious. Why had I not thought of this myself long ago? Then I thought of Tengen saying it would have done no good until my withered leg had been made strong again and I understood how deep my despair would have been when the shoe was useless to me.

"It will make me able to walk as I used to?" I asked breathlessly.

"It will help," Tengen corrected. "You must persist with all the exercises I have taught you. If you stop, your muscles will become weak again and your new shoe will be useless. Even wearing the shoe, your leg will drag, but it will make walking far easier for you."

"Thank you," I said it sincerely, but at the same time my mind was working furiously. "I will no longer need my crutch?"

Tengen waggled his hand from side to side. "I think you will always need a walking stick to give you support and help with your balance. But that is surely a great deal better than your crutch. I know how you hate it," he added kindly.

He thought he was letting me down gently, I could see that. But for me, it was not enough. I could see that the built-up shoe would help me, but what was the point of half-measures? An idea began to unfold in my mind, and I was so deep in my thoughts that I was startled when Tengen got to his feet.

"You are leaving? Now?" I asked.

"I think it would be better if we said our farewells here, where we are alone, rather than back at the house. Of course, if you would prefer that I went back with you...?" His voice trailed off in invitation.

I had no need to consider it. If Tengen went back with me, the memories of our time together in the house would be overwhelming. It would make his final leaving very difficult for both of us.

"No," I said. "If you must go, then let it be at this moment."

I held my hand out so he could help me to my feet. I hoped fervently that Tengen would understand how much trust lay in the gesture.

"Goodbye, Mi-chan." Tengen was so much taller than I was, he had to stoop to kiss me very gently on my lips. It was the briefest of pressures, but only Anzu had ever kissed me before and I found it delightful.

"Goodbye, Tengen-chan."

Our parting was so awkward, I was relieved when he turned and walked away without another word. I waited until he had turned down a bend in the path before I stooped awkwardly and picked up my crutch. Perhaps it was the certain knowledge that I would not need to rely on it for much longer, but I found I didn't hate it at all.

I walked carefully. Our house was a long way away, and if I fell, I had nobody to help me. At once, I missed Tengen and the confidence I always felt when he was at my side. I would miss him. And having newly discovered the joys of love, I would regret almost as much his touch, the feel of him against my flesh. Even the recollection of it made my skin prickle and my belly churn.

Enough! Tengen was gone. He would not return to my life. Once shattered, the mirror can no longer reflect. There was no point in wishing and wondering.

Instead, I forced my thoughts toward my wonderful new shoe. The blacksmith would know the carpenter. I imagined they would work together often, perhaps to make a new saddle or a piece of furniture. I would explain to the blacksmith what I needed, and he would instruct the carpenter. Tengen had been quite right, I had no apprehension about discussing my peculiar needs with the blacksmith, a man I had known for many years, but the idea of talking to a stranger about my deformity filled me with horror.

In spite of Tengen's warning, I could not accept that I would still need a walking stick. It would be far better than the crutch, but it would still be obvious to the world that I was a cripple.

Curiously, the image of a saddle would not leave my mind. I could see it clearly, the glowing leather tacked neatly onto a wooden frame, the straps holding metal stirrups for the rider to insert their feet...there! At last, my troubled thoughts were clear. I did not need a walking stick.

I needed a stirrup. A slender, discreet stirrup made to fit the contours of my new shoe. Attached to it would be strips of fine leather, like reins, that would end in a loop just big enough to fit my small hand. The stirrup would fit beneath my shoe. The reins could be virtually hidden in my skirts. I would conceal the reins' loop discreetly in my left hand and use it to pull on the reins to make the stirrup force my useless left foot to lift and move. With practice, I was certain I could walk in an almost natural fashion.

It would work. I would make it work.

I remembered Tengen telling me that if I could see something in my mind, then it would happen. That it could not fail to happen.

"Thank you, Tengen," I said out loud. "Thank you for everything you have given to me."

The dusty tracks had left clear imprints of Tengen's feet. I walked alongside them, deliberately comparing his straight footfalls with my crooked gait. Not for long, I told myself. Soon, I would walk so well nobody would notice my deformity.

Tomorrow, I would visit my old acquaintance the blacksmith. Explain my plans to him. Surely it would not take him—and the carpenter—long to make my shoe and stirrup and reins.

It would be my birthday present to myself. For once, the thought of my birthday gave me joy.

THIRTY-EIGHT

Do not be deceived.
An early mist may conceal
The most perfect day

I slept uneasily that night. Every time I dipped into sleep, I awoke immediately, tormented by doubts that had never crossed my mind yesterday. What if Father took it into his head to ask me how my studies were progressing? He had never mentioned it to me before, and I had not been surprised. He had many other things to concern him than my efforts to learn to read and write.

But...what if he was receiving regular reports from Tengen's kannushi? What would that honest, holy man tell him now? From what Tengen had said of him, I imagined the answer would be straightforward. He would tell Father that Tengen had gone from the temple and why. I shuddered at the thought. Surely, even if Father believed I was entirely innocent in the matter, he would be angry. He would demand to know why I had not told him that

Tengen had gone. I was a terrible liar; he would see through me at once.

I would tell him Tengen was no longer teaching me. Perhaps I would simply say that Tengen said he could teach me no more. But not until I was sure I could speak without blushing and stumbling over my words.

And what of Tengen, my absent lover? Already he was fading to a bittersweet memory. He had gone from my life. I would never forget him, but—with the blithe unconcern of youth—I was already looking forward, not back.

The morning sun was bright and with it I shook off my fears of the night. There was no point in worrying about what might be. Tengen had promised he would tell his kannushi that I had no idea of his feelings for me, that I had been no more than an attentive pupil. Father would have no reason to doubt such a distinguished man, even less reason to doubt his dutiful daughter.

Even so, I found my breathing was a little easier when I heard Father's horse clip-clop its way to Edo. For the first time since I had awoken from my illness, I did not wish for him to take me with him.

The house became busy as soon as he left. Servants cleared away the remains of breakfast, cleaned the rooms, and put away discarded clothing. Still, I waited, listening to the rhythm of the household making its steady way toward noon.

I took a bath—I had long since mastered the delicate art of climbing in and out of the tub myself. Anzu usually soaped and rinsed me before the tub. This morning I asked one of the other maids. Anzu knew me too well. I feared she would sense my excitement and ask questions.

Finally, I decided the time had come. If I lingered any longer, I would lose my nerve and my chance would be lost.

The cash box was so heavy, it almost slipped from my grasp.

I opened it very carefully. If it slipped, then the contents would go all over the tatami and it would take precious time to collect all the coins up.

I was seeing shadows where they were none. I took a deep, cleansing breath—one of Tengen's belly breaths—and let it out with a hiss. Nothing would go wrong. I would not allow it to. I pried open the cash box carefully and gasped as I saw the contents.

Coins were heaped in carelessly, mainly silver, but also a number of gold coins. A single bronze mon lurked in the corner, almost as if it knew it had no place alongside such illustrious company. I had expected orderly piles of coins. This was far better. Father would never notice that a couple of coins were missing.

Now that the moment had come to choose my prize, I was uncertain. Would two silver ichibugin be enough? Would it be better to take a gold koban? As there were not many kobans, I would have to shake the box to hide the fact that one was missing, but that might draw Father's attention to the fact that somebody had been inside his box. I was annoyed by the unforeseen complications.

Although I had calculated sums far greater than the contents of the box on the abacus, that had been...different. Those were mere figures, to be passed to a clerk who would make a precise record of the amount. They were not real money in the way that this was.

I was astonished by the difference.

A slight sound distracted me. I relaxed after a moment. It was nothing but the habitual wind that always arose in the late morning at this time of year. Father had chosen the site of our house well. The summer heat would soon become oppressive and the breeze would be welcome.

My concentration had been disturbed and I decided abruptly that two large silver ichibugin should suffice and closed the lid of the cash box with a decisive click. I had put it back in its home in the chest when a thought came to me and I paused, working my reasoning through.

The box contained a mix of coins. Mainly large and small silver ichibugin, but also gold koban, and the single, low denomination bronze mon. I found that intriguing.

Father was a rich man. Had he wanted, he could surely have stocked his cash box entirely with gold. But he had not chosen to do so. Why was that? I stared at the two silver coins in my palm, rubbing them idly with my fingers.

When the answer finally came to me, it was obvious. If Father had offered a merchant a gold koban for a small purchase, then the merchant would have been confused. It was likely that he would have been unable to make change for the gold coin, and rather than lose a good customer, he would have allowed Father to leave his shop without paying. Good for Father, but very bad indeed for the merchant.

Contrarily, if Father wanted to make a major purchase —to commission new furniture for the house, or perhaps purchase a fine horse or oxen for the farm—then if he offered a silver ichibuban it would be taken as an insult by the vendor, who would think that Father was trying to belittle the transaction. It was unlikely that a deal could be made, and both parties would lose face.

And even the humble mon had its place in the scheme of life. If Father was traveling and was thirsty, then it would buy his fill of water from some village well. Why bother with gold or silver when bronze was all that was needed?

I slid my coins into my obi thoughtfully. It seemed that I had achieved far more than I had set out to. Not only did I have my cash, but I had learned a precious lesson. The true value of money. Not the value of money spun in the brisk beads of an abacus, but real money, weighted in the coins in my hands.

I found the idea tremendously exciting. Truly, I was my father's daughter!

THIRTY-NINE

My palms are dry. When
I rub them together, they
Sound like autumn leaves

T he blacksmith refused to meet my gaze.

He kept his eyes fixed on the ground at his feet so firmly, I began to wonder if he had developed some ailment of his neck that meant he was unable to lift his head properly. He mumbled when he spoke as well, and after a short while my excitement began to get the better of my manners.

"Well? Can you do it or not? Speak up, blacksmith."

"Mi-san, I am sure that between me and the carpenter, we can do as you ask. But..."

He tailed off helplessly. He was clearly worried, and if he was worried, then so was I. I had made my plans so carefully. How was it possible that I was about to fail? If the blacksmith could not help me, then I had no one else to turn to. He had shoed my ponies for me ever since I had learned to ride, and that had been almost as soon as I could walk. He had always had a kind word for me, and I had come to think of him almost as a friend.

Apart from that, I had welcomed his visits to the estate as a pleasing break from the daily routine. His presence was always announced by the sound of his cart, drawn by a heavy horse. It was a different sound entirely to the other tradesmen. Both cart and horse were big and sturdy, like the blacksmith himself.

Although there was space set aside for him in the stables, he always brought his own tools and anvil. He heaved the hefty lump of iron off the back of the cart as if it was nothing. I had tried to lift it once and found it as impossible as moving the cart and horse together.

I was allowed to watch the blacksmith at work. I loved everything about it. The transformation of iron as it was shaped into everything from new pans for the kitchen to horseshoes. The heat of the fire and the constant danger of stray sparks. Even the stink of the iron when it was dunked in cold water to cool it pleased me. On one visit, the blacksmith did me a very great favor.

I had a large, painful stye on my left eye. Every time I blinked, it rubbed and felt as if I had been stung by a bee. Nobody else noticed it but the blacksmith.

"My goodness, Mi-san. That eye looks very sore. Perhaps you should come a little closer to the anvil so that you can see properly."

Cautiously, I moved a little closer. The blacksmith smiled at me and pointed to the anvil.

"You will be interested in this," he assured me. "I am making a new rack for the kitchen to hang herbs on to dry them properly. It is very fancy work, and I must be very careful. Do you think you will be able to tell me when you think each hook is the same size as the other ones?"

"Of course," I said promptly. Forgetting my fears, I put my head as close to the anvil as I dared. Every time the hammer struck the red-hot iron, I blinked hard.

It took a long time before the blacksmith was satisfied with his work. He thanked me very nicely for helping him, and I was pleased. When I went back to the house, I was even more pleased. My horrible stye had burst with all the blinking I had done in the heat of the forge and was hardly painful at all anymore.

I had no idea at the time that the blacksmith had encouraged me to watch him closely deliberately, knowing that it would help me get rid of the stye. But I knew that now, and I was hurt that he should suddenly show me such a closed face when all my plans for the future depended on him. Because of the hurt, I spoke brusquely.

"If you can do it, then what is the problem? I have enough money to pay you both if that's what you're worried about."

"No, Mi-san," he said humbly. "It's not a question of money. Not at all. It's just that you shouldn't be here. It's not right that you should come to me on your own. I take my instructions from the estate manager, who in his turn is told what is needed by your honorable father."

He tailed off helplessly. I understood. I should have thought of this. Of course, the blacksmith—as did all the tradesmen employed by the estate—took his orders from the estate manager. The blacksmith must have been bewildered by me turning up on my own with such a strange request. Clearly, he was worried about the consequences of going behind the estate manager's back. Undoubtedly, he depended on the work he did for us, and now he was torn between offending me and fear that he would lose his livelihood if he angered the estate manager. What a complicated place the world was!

I thought carefully, and when my thoughts were in order, I spoke gently.

"I understand. But please don't worry. It is my birthday very soon, and Father has told me that I can choose whatever I wish for a present. You see, the things I have asked you and the carpenter to make for me will be my birthday present and I want to surprise Father with them. He will be so delighted when he sees how well I can walk again, I assure you he will not be angry with you for taking instructions from me."

The blacksmith was frowning, but I could see he was thinking over my words carefully.

"In fact, I'm sure Father will be very pleased that you have helped me. Now that I've explained all that to you properly, you can talk to the carpenter. When my shoe is ready, you can bring my birthday present with you the next time you visit the house."

I held my breath. I could almost see the blacksmith's slow train of thought reflected in his expression. Finally, he smiled and nodded.

"Now that you have explained, Mi-san, of course I will be happy to make my part of your birthday gift, and I will talk to the carpenter about the shoe at once. I could make one for you, but it would be forged out of iron and it would never do to have you clattering about sounding like a pony." He chuckled at his own wit. I laughed with him and he grinned at me with a smile in which many teeth were missing.

"That would be excellent. Shall I dismount for you so you can take the measurements?"

"Oh, no need for that. I've adjusted your stirrups so many times over the years that I can easily see the difference there is now between the length of your legs." I managed not to wince at his innocent words. "But to make the shoe fit your needs, I must see the foot."

I thrust my leg out of the skirts of my kimono and the blacksmith took my foot in his hand very gently. How tiny it looked in his massive fingers! He held it for no more than a moment and then tucked my leg back into my skirts almost tenderly.

"I see the problem." He sounded so business-like, we might have been discussing the need for a new shoe for my pony. I was grateful for his tone. "I am sure that between us, the carpenter and I can sort something out that will help you greatly. But…"

"What? What is it?" I was anxious and sounded abrupt. I softened my response with a smile.

"I am so sorry, Mi-san, but I need to take a cast of your foot." He laughed nervously. "I am used to shoeing horses, and I am very good at that, but I cannot tell the carpenter exactly what you need. I have to show him the shape of your foot so he can make a shoe that will fit it perfectly."

I had not thought of that. I nodded and the blacksmith went off at a run, returning a few moments later with a shallow, wooden bucket. He held it up with his head bowed. I wondered why he would not look at me. I found out when I looked curiously in the bucket.

It was filled with a firm, stinking mixture of rotted straw and horse dung. The surface was level, as though it had been patted down. I glanced at the blacksmith's lowered head and he raised the bucket slightly. I flinched. I was supposed to push my bare foot into a bucket of fresh horse manure?

"There's nothing else that would do to take a cast? Sand, perhaps?" I said hopefully.

"I am sorry, Mi-san. I have nothing else. This will do. If you could just push your foot into it as far as your ankle?"

I shook off my repugnance. What did a moment's disgust matter when weighed in the balance of my whole future? Before I could change my mind, I thrust my foot so firmly in the mush the blacksmith nearly dropped the bucket. I wriggled it until the dung rose up grudgingly around the sides of my foot.

"Will that do?" I asked.

The blacksmith risked a look inside the bucket and then pulled it away gently. My foot left the mess with a slight sucking sound. The blacksmith pulled a worn tenugui from his sash and used it to wipe me clean so carefully, it was clear he was worried he might hurt me.

I was humbled that this simple man, a man whose status was even less than a house servant, was so concerned for my welfare. Embarrassed by my emotion, I dug in my obi for my coins. Alas, my searching fingers could find only one ichibugin. I held it out to him anyway.

"Will this be enough for the cost of the work for both you and the carpenter?" I thought I had insulted him with my meanness when he stood back, his arms clamped firmly at his sides and his face stone. I was wrong.

"That is far too much, Mi-san. Ten mon will pay for the materials. For our time as well. An ichibuban will be generous payment for both of us."

My voice was very small as I said, "I have nothing less than the ichibugin with me today. May I pay you when you bring the things to the house for me?"

"Of course. I will be at your father's house three days from now, as usual. I'm certain I can do my part of the work before then. I will speak to the carpenter later today and ask him to have the shoe ready for me by then."

It was my birthday in three days, and this birthday would be different.

FORTY

The perfumed garden
Is subtle. It entices
The bee with its scent

My friend the blacksmith greeted me cheerfully, asking if my pony's hooves were causing problems. I was grateful for his discretion and waited quietly while he lifted each hoof in turn, prodding them with a sharp tool, and finally nodding wisely.

"No, they are good. Nothing needed this time, Mi-san." He stood closer to stroke my pony's neck. My mount hid him from view, and I snatched quickly at the roughly wrapped parcel he pressed against me. I pushed the coin into his hand at the same moment.

"Thank you so much, blacksmith." My voice sounded overly bright and loud to me, but nobody seemed to notice, and I rode away with my heart beating at a faster gallop than my well-fed pony had ever managed.

The stables were some way from the house. As usual, I left my pony with the same servant who had brought my mount over for me earlier. He would walk her back to the stables for me. Normally, I thought nothing of the small service, but this morning I thanked the servant and he blinked at me in surprise. My bedroom had already been cleaned and left tidy—not that I had made much mess— and I flopped onto the comfort of the tatami, turning my package over and over in my hands.

Now that the moment had arrived, I was reluctant to even look inside the thick, paper wrapping. If it hadn't been my birthday, I would have torn the package open eagerly, on fire to see if the tradesmen had got it right. If, finally, I might become more like everybody else around me. Ah, if only! But it was my birthday, and I could not help pausing, worrying that fate might once again destroy any pleasure I might take on this day.

I shook the parcel, hearing a muted jingle from inside it. Finally, I told myself that I was being ridiculous. Right or wrong, hesitating would make no difference.

I picked the thick binding that bound my parcel apart. The paper was so coarse it did not fall away, and suddenly anxious to see what treasures it contained, I thrust my hand inside and tugged out the contents.

At once, I knew I had been right, and my spirits rose until I felt like singing out loud. The shoe was unlike anything I had ever seen before. The sole had been shaped to fit the contours of my deformed foot exactly, and the surface was waxed so that there was no danger of a stray splinter hurting my foot. It was far thicker than a normal geta at the heel and sloped down to the toes. It was quite simply perfect. I could see that at a glance.

My stirrup was exactly as I had seen it in my mind. Slender leather thongs were attached to a silvery support in the shape of an arch. At the other end, the thongs ended in a loop, nicely calculated to fit my small hand. Everything was so *right,* tears of pleasure and gratitude gathered in my eyes.

I leaned forward and slipped the shoe onto my bare left foot. It fit every contour perfectly and immediately felt comfortable. I eased the stirrup over the shoe carefully and felt it click into a groove in the sole of the shoe. So much kindness had gone into crafting my shoe that the tears came back and threatened to overwhelm me.

It would work. I was certain of it. I took a deep breath and wrapped the leather loop around my palm. This would be my crutch from this moment forward. I would hide the leather reins as well as I could in the skirts of my kimono and use them to lift the stirrup beneath my shoe. Now that both my legs were the same length, I was sure it would take no effort at all to help myself walk.

Eager to make sure I was right, I put my right hand flat on the tatami and pushed myself up, taking my weight on my right leg and standing cautiously.

At once, my balance waivered and I had to thrash my arms for balance. I was bitterly disappointed. I could not believe my plans had failed so soon. I felt the tatami tickle my bare right foot and tears of relief blurred my vision. The special shoe had been made to wear with a normal geta on my right foot, and naturally I had kicked both shoes off when I entered the house, so now my legs were still of unequal length. I turned, intending to find another shoe in my chest. So great was my hurry, I swayed and almost fell.

Although I knew I was alone, I heard Tengen's voice so clearly that I turned my head, expecting to find him standing next to me.

The frog in the well has no knowledge of the sea. You are no longer that frog. Take a moment to balance yourself in body and mind and the whole world will be open to you. All will be well, I promise you.

I nodded, as if Tengen was really beside me, and tightened my leather reins, going on tiptoe on my right foot as I walked to the chest.

My journey had begun. My future was mine once more. I rejoiced in the knowledge.

You will not fail. You will not allow yourself to fail.

Tengen's voice was no longer close. His whispered words seemed to come from far away. I spoke equally softly, knowing that he would hear me.

"Thank you, Tengen. Thank you for everything that you have given me."

I was sure I could hear his laughter and rejoiced for all he had given to me, and all that I had given to him, and I knew at that moment that we both had a new future to look forward to.

Would Tengen really hear my name spoken with reverence in the years to come? I hoped so.

I wriggled my toes in my new shoe and changed my mind. I didn't *hope* so. I *knew* it would be so.

THE TREE OF PERSEVERANCE

books2read.com/u/mdqxMl

In the shadow of a poignant Japanese proverb advocating self-reliance—*Rely on your own walking stick rather than people*—Mi's life takes an unforeseen and harrowing turn. Overcoming the paralysis of the morning left her with a deformed leg, rendering the proverb a cruel reality. As if guided by an inexorable hand of fate, those she holds closest to her heart, one by one, betray her trust, leaving Mi to navigate a world of isolation and despair.

Caught in the suffocating grip of a loveless marriage to a foreign doctor who aided her in regaining her mobility, Mi's existence mirrors that of a caged animal—trapped and yearning for freedom. The echoes of her past love and the dreams of a future once cherished are silenced by the heavy chains of her present reality.

In this riveting tale of betrayal, resilience, and intrigue, Mi's journey is a testament to the enduring power of the human spirit. Join her as she navigates a treacherous landscape, where the line between friend and foe blurs, and the path to freedom is fraught with danger. Discover how one woman's unwavering determination and self-reliance can ultimately lead to her redemption and the unearthing of truths hidden in the darkest corners of society.

ABOUT THE AUTHOR

 With a literary journey spanning more than a dozen captivating novels set in historical Japan and a collection of evocative haikus, India Millar has embarked on a diverse career. Her professional odyssey commenced amidst the machinery of British Gas's heavy industry, eventually culminating within the hallowed halls of the British Library, where the tapestry of knowledge and storytelling merged seamlessly.

Now, India finds herself in the idyllic embrace of early retirement on the enchanting Costa Blanca. As she continues to explore the realms of history and poetry, India remains deeply grateful for the winding path that has led her to this peaceful and creative haven. Each word written, each page turned, is a testament to the enduring passion for storytelling that continues to shape her life's narrative.

Website: www.indiamillar.co.uk

ABOUT THE PUBLISHER